I0541263

The Fabergé Conspiracy

Douglas King

E-PRIDE Books • Beaumont, Texas

For Jerome, who has long tolerated this obsession.

Prologue

Nicholai Alexandrovich Romanov, the second Tsar Nicholas, autocrat of Imperial Russia, paused in his pacing before the vaulting, ice-glazed window over-looking the courtyard below. He stood, clenching and unclenching his hands behind his back, watching the heavy snow fall about the grounds of his palace at Tsarskoye Selo. A roaring fire crackled in the cavernous hearth behind him, but the heat it generated did little against the chilled air. The Russian winter had set in and the Palace was, by all appearances, now snowed in. The Tsar's courier had not yet arrived, but this was not because of the snow. While the snow fall would certainly delay the advance of the Red Army, it would not deter agents of the Tsar. Still, considering the rumors of late that were terrorizing his household, Tsar Nicholas had been preparing for the worst for some time.

He turned back to face the fidgety little man, perched wide-eyed on a straight back chair angled before the Tsar's immaculate desk. Swiss bankers never seemed to relax and His Imperial Majesty despised having to deal with them personally. The Tsar's gaze cut through the man to the double doorway at the opposite end of the regally appointed study—a room into which all of ten peasant hovels could have fit. Tsar Nicholas crossed to his desk and stood drumming his fingers impatiently on the mirror-polished rosewood.

Helmut Reisinger watched the monarch's pacing with a growing sense of unease. The prospect of actually meeting this, the last of the continent's absolute ruling monarchs, had at first seemed intriguing. That was, of course, before the uprisings in Moscow had gotten out of hand. The Bolsheviks were advancing their revolt throughout the Russias faster than anyone had predicted. Reisinger had not been worried when he arrived at St. Petersburg some three days before. Soldiers of the White Russian Army seemed to be everywhere and well armed to protect their Tsar. That was, of course, before the other day's massive defections from the Tsar's troops to the revolutionaries.

Reisinger fondled the handle of his valise and closed his eyes, trying not to think about the fate of anyone caught in the middle of what could be an extremely bloody coup. He prayed for the courier to arrive so that he could complete this final transaction. His job depended on it, and now it seemed, so did a great deal more.

Tsar Nicholas glanced down at the ledger sheets lying open on his desk, reflecting the substantial quantities of gold and silver bullion he had recently moved out of the country. The side of his mouth drew up as if in a snarl. If he and his family were forced to flee, he would be amply prepared. The Bolsheviks would be left with nothing to finance their unholy revolution, and he, by divine right, would have all he needed to finance their downfall from the safety of foreign soil.

Pearls of sweat clung to Reisinger's brow as the moments passed in tense silence. The Tsar's nervous agitation only served to increase the banker's anxiety. He calculated he could be on a train far ahead of the clutches of the Red Army if he could only conclude matters in the next hour. He was torn between leaving then and risking the Tsar's wrath, or staying to satisfy his curiosity concerning this last transaction. He was charged with transporting something of great value for His Imperial Majesty, which meant something truly extraordinary.

The double doors rattled with the clatter of feet on the marbled hall beyond. Reisinger sat up expectantly as the doors flung open. Armed soldiers of the White Army stood in a ring outside the doorway around the obviously frightened courier.

Tsar Nicholas motioned with an impatient wave for the cringing minion to be brought into the room. "Leave Us!" he commanded, hurling the majestic plural pronoun at the accompanying soldiers like a spear.

The ragged, uniformed men shut the door quickly and trotted noisily down the hall back to their respective posts.

"Over here, man, quickly!" Tsar Nicholas hammered the desk with his fist.

The courier stumbled to the desk as quickly as he could while trying not to jostle the contents of the square, leather hatbox-like case he balanced away from his body by its handle. He set the box gingerly in the center of the desk and stepped back at attention.

His Imperial Majesty ran his long, manicured fingers over the outside of the case with intense pleasure. He released the catches on both sides and the front, chuckling to himself and smiling openly. With some presumption, Herr Reisinger moved closer around the desk, his curiosity getting the better of him.

Tsar Nicholas started, as if suddenly aware of the others' presence for the first time. He turned on the courier. "Out!"

The courier bowed low and turned smartly, relieved to make his exit along with the soldier-bodyguards.

"So, Herr Reisinger, this is your precious cargo." The Tsar smiled cannily at the banker's obvious interest. "You have the list of my numbered accounts?"

Reisinger pulled a small, sealed brown envelope from his coat pocket. "Here, Your Majesty. The complete listing."

"Excellent." The Tsar smiled with a patronizing glint. He raised the lid on the box, allowing the light from the window to strike the contents a little at a time.

Reisinger peered into the box and caught his breath. "Exquisite," he breathed.

The Tsar raised the hand-sized gold and bejeweled egg from its nest within the travel case and held it up to the light. It sparkled with an ethereal delicacy as the light played between the confectioner's filigree of platinum striping the pearlescent polished gold beneath, not to mention the sapphires and diamonds which encrusted the creation all about.

When the Tsar had finished admiring his new possession he placed it carefully on the desk and reached to pull at a chain about his neck. A small gold object dangled from the chain. Its oddly jagged shape reminded Reisinger of something else he could not place. The Tsar only smiled and inserted the object into a small slit on the side of the egg.

"A key!" Reisinger whispered.

"Of a sort," the Tsar replied, manipulating the key too fast for Reisinger to notice. The egg opened easily on its hidden hinges and Reisinger looked for its contents. Empty.

Tsar Nicholas reached for the envelope in the banker's hand, retrieved a small, almost transparent slip of paper from it, folded it neatly, and inserted it into the egg's belly. "This is now the most valuable work of art in the world, Herr Reisinger . . . in the history of the world."

"Your Imperial Majesty, if you'll pardon me," Reisinger began, clearing his throat. "Is this wise? Should anyone come into possession of this item and its contents they would have instant access to all your numbered accounts. Proper security precautions would suggest—"

"Do you think I'm a fool, Reisinger?" the Tsar interrupted.

The banker backed away, regretting his presumption.

"We have, of course, taken precautions for just such a possibility," continued the Tsar contemptuously. "We have over thirty numbered accounts in Swiss banks. Do you think We can memorize them all?"

"Of course not, Majesty," stuttered Reisinger.

"Of course not," the Tsar echoed, mocking. "The key, once inserted, triggers a timing mechanism ingeniously worked into the egg's design by our esteemed jeweler. Within a precious few seconds the key must be turned one way, slid to the side in another direction and then turned again. If the egg is not opened in the set time, or any turn of the key made in the wrong direction, the egg will explode in an acid fire that will obliterate both its contents and the fool who tampers with it."

"A remarkable creation, Your Majesty. My humble apologies," Reisinger whispered.

"Indeed." The Tsar removed the key and closed the egg. He placed it carefully back into its snug hole of velvet within the travel case and snapped the latches into place. "The numbered account into which this item is placed is the only number I or any member of my family need to memorize."

"Ingenious," Reisinger remarked with a nod. He added with a laugh, "The Golden Egg of legend."

Tsar Nicholas raised an unamused eyebrow. Reisinger's expression changed immediately to one of meek seriousness.

"You have a train waiting for you, Herr Reisinger. Go quickly, and take care of Our new bauble."

Reisinger nodded obediently and pulled a slip of paper from his valise. "One final formality, if it please Your Majesty," he said, filling in the appropriate blanks and signing the receipt. He handed it over for the Tsar's approval before reaching for the travel case.

"All seems to be in order, Herr Reisinger," said the Tsar, nodding to a point over the banker's right shoulder.

Reisinger turned and started as two Russian giants lumbered up behind him. In his preoccupation with the egg, he had not noticed either of them enter the room. They stopped on either side of the banker and bowed stiffly to the Tsar.

"In the interest of your safety and the safety of your cargo, my agents will accompany you to your destination, Herr Reisinger."

Reisinger bowed nervously. "Your Imperial Majesty." He backed quickly for the door flanked by the intimidating presence of the Tsar's agents.

"Godspeed, Herr Reisinger," the Tsar called after him, toying with the oddly-shaped key he had replaced about his neck.

Chapter 1

"Jesus Christ, Robert! We wanted an historical overview not a reprise of *War and Peace*." Madelyn Arnold dropped the heavy manuscript on her desk for emphasis.

"Madelyn, you asked for research on a rather broad subject," responded Robert Tate. He ran an agitated hand through his dark brown hair. "You can't overview the history of former Soviet satellite states in a paragraph. Give me a break, for heaven's sake."

Madelyn looked at the epitome of tall, dark, and handsome standing in front of her desk, glaring down his patrician nose at her. "It's a thorough job," she said, sighing deeply, "I'll give you that, Robert . . .a little too thorough." She was almost fifty and he was almost forty. That would not have stood in her way if she thought she had a chance in hell with him. "You should know what the guys at the news desk are like by now."

Robert scowled up at the ceiling. Yes, he knew all too well. "I have condensed thirty-seven volumes of eastern bloc history into a little over three hundred pages. It won't kill them to go through it. If anything it will improve their perception—"

"It *will* kill them to go through it and it *will* kill me to have to listen to all their bitching about it," Madelyn said, tapping the manuscript with the point of one gleaming, polished fingernail.

"Why don't we just send out for a comic book on the subject?" Robert suggested sarcastically.

Madelyn only sighed again. "Just edit it down some more, okay, Robert . . . like about two-thirds?"

Robert grabbed up the manuscript. "Whatever you say, Madelyn," he said with an annoyed sniff. "*Ave imperator, morituri te salutant.*"

"Right," Madelyn replied, bewildered. "That's what I'm talking about. You speak Latin, while the news guys . . . well they barely speak English. Say things so that ordinary mortals can understand them."

"Fine," Robert said through clenched teeth. "Maybe you'll understand this way." He snapped his heels together and jerked his hand up in a mocking, Nazi salute, then stormed out of her office.

Madelyn watched him leave, admiring the cut of his trousers across his posterior. What a pity to waste such a body on too much brains, she thought.

Robert Tate IV, Ph.D., marched across the sprawling, open sixth floor of the McNaughton News Corporation, to his cubicle office. He slumped down in his chair and glared at the computer screen before him, venting his silent anger at the inanimate machine humming softly on his desk.

"She didn't like it?" purred a voice from the cubicle behind him.

Robert turned quickly. "What?"

"She didn't like it?"

"What else is new, Rhonda?" Robert said to the shapely brunette peering at him over the partition.

"I can't believe it. It was a wonderful piece of work."

Robert puffed up a little at the compliment. "I thought so."

"You're just too good to be working here, Robert." Rhonda leaned into his cubicle, positioning her ample cleavage into his line of sight. "You should be teaching history at the university... writing books, or something."

"Or something," Robert agreed. He squirmed uncomfortably in his chair, sensing the all too familiar come-on. "Well, I'd best get to it." He turned back to the computer.

"Would you like me to get you some coffee or something, Robert? Or should I call you Dr. Tate?" Rhonda asked with a flutter of eyelashes.

"No thanks," Robert said without turning around. "I mean, no thanks for the coffee, and Robert is fine." He had learned early on in the job not to encourage her.

"Well, holler if you need something. I'll be close by," Rhonda purred.

Robert didn't answer. Instead he scrolled through his manuscript on the computer trying to figure out just what he could cut without distorting a very delicate historical perspective. He did agree with the brunette about one thing. He was too qualified for the job. Still, the position was less demanding than teaching and the pay a little better. And he *hated* teaching.

He hit a key on the computer, deleting several paragraphs in the process, and sat frowning at the altered document. If it weren't for the upkeep on the house his mother had left to him, he would consider chucking the whole machine out the window and walking. A four-story, Manhattan, brownstone townhouse was an expensive piece of real estate to own and maintain. Why hadn't his mother left him a chunk of the family cash as well before fleeing the Big Apple and the family stead back to her Bostonian roots, just to die in her favorite hotel room?

What the hell. It was a job within his field and greatest love—historical analysis. It allowed him to read and study at great length even though the troglodytes two floors up couldn't appreciate the academic wealth of his analysis. It was an easy, often enjoyable, frequently frustrating living. Concentrating on the fact that he desperately needed money to repair his house's roof, he deleted another slice of the manuscript.

"Here's another one, Doc," came the second interruption from the pathway outside his cubicle.

"What is it this time, Rick?" Robert asked in a bored monotone.

"Hell if I know, Doc. Something about an egg getting swiped from the Ruskies."

"An egg, did you say?"

"Read it and figure it out." The copy boy thrust the sheaf of teletype into the cubicle at Robert.

Robert snatched the papers and snapped his foot around, faking a good-natured kick at the boy who dodged backwards out of the cubicle.

"Too slow, Doc," laughed the boy continuing on his rounds. "You shouldn't of eaten that last donut."

Robert stretched back in his chair and skimmed the news copy quickly. "Jesus!" he said with renewed annoyance. He spun out of his chair and back across the line of cubicles towards the glassed-in office in the center. He entered the office without knocking and threw the type down on the desk. "What am I supposed to do with this, Madelyn? I'm not an expert on jewelry. What's the deal?"

Madelyn looked up from the office schedule she had been working on. "Read the damn thing, for God's sake, Robert. It's an *objet d'art* from the turn of the last century. We'd like a little background."

"It was an imperial plaything, Madelyn. Hardly of much historical importance. Don't you have an art expert or the like to handle this?"

"Mort wants this worked into the analysis you're presently editing . . . you are editing it I hope . . . as a sidebar."

"Come on, Madelyn, I don't have time for this."

"Make time for it," replied his boss with tight-lipped finality. "Noah over in Fine Arts can give you a hand with it if necessary."

"Noah?"

"Noah Taylor. God, Robert! You've worked for McNaughton for three years. Don't you know anyone here yet?"

"Are you talking about that . . . that yak-milk drinking, yoga-new-age, weird kid? The one with the," Robert gestured above his head, "hair?"

"He is not weird, Robert," said Madelyn, trying not to laugh.

"He looks and dresses like a teenage Abercrombie & Fitch model."

"Artsy types are a little different, I agree, Robert, but he knows his field and is a graduate of the Illinois Institute of Art for God's sake. Talk to him." She shoved the stack of papers toward him. "Now get out. I'm busy. I also work here, you know."

Robert grabbed the stack of papers and headed for the cubicles at the other end of the room. He cocked an ear for a moment, listening for the familiar drone of

sitar, Tibetan bowl and ocean waves that comprised the
meditation music—or what Robert like to refer to as
medication music—and the acrid, oppressive incense that
made the back corner of the research floor a place he
avoided like a Pentecostal church—what Robert referred
to as the Art and Fashion Ghetto. Sure enough, Robert
easily zeroed in on a cubicle dwarfed by an enormous
potted palm.

"Mr. Taylor?" he called out hesitantly, frowning at
the strings of glass beads that draped the cubicle's
entrance.

"Come on in," came the cheery reply from within.

Robert pushed the tinkling beads aside and entered
the cubicle. He stopped short and grabbed for the side of
the cubicle to keep his balance, and avoid stepping on
the figure stretched out in the center of the floor.

"What the hell!" He suppressed a gasp.

"I'll just be a moment," the slender male figure said,
writing furiously into a steno pad held above his face.
"You'll have to excuse me but this is the only way I can
get any work done. Those chairs are so bad for the back."

"I'm sorry," Robert stuttered. "But I thought . . ."

The pale, young man sprawled out on the floor wore
a pair of skin-tight jeans bound at the hips with a silver,
seashell buckled belt, two shirts, the inner layer of muted
eggplant and gold and the outer layer a bright red, the
collars pulled out over the collar of a white and matching
eggplant checked blazer dappled with various silver pins
and broaches. His hair was black and thick with loose
curls just over the top of his ears—and then there were
the earrings, multiple silver earrings—definitely some
kind of a gypsy, Robert nodded, forgetting what he was
doing at the moment.

"Are you listening? I said can I help you?" the young
man asked again.

Robert blinked his eyes, suddenly aware of the sound of the boy's voice. "I'm sorry. Yes. I was a little taken aback to find you on the floor. Are you all right?"

"Of course I'm all right. I just like to work this way." Noah smiled and pulled himself up to his knees to hold out a hand. "I'm Noah Taylor, and you're . . . you're the history professor aren't you?"

"Dr. Tate . . . Robert Tate . . . I do historical research . . . my office is on the other side of this floor."

"Oh, yes. I've seen you about. Funny how we haven't met before now."

"Probably my fault," Robert confessed. "I tend to stay at my desk most of the time."

"What brings you all the way over to this side of the office this morning?" The gypsy teased with a smile.

"I have an item I'd like your opinion on. Madelyn said you would be the person to ask."

Noah patted the floor beside him. "Have a seat and show me what you've got."

Robert eyed the floor uncomfortably. "I . . . couldn't we find a chair?"

"Never use them. Who can think in a chair?"

"Really." Robert lowered himself to the floor slowly. "This looks a bit odd to passers-by, don't you think?" The boy seemed way too young to have a job, much less a degree.

"Who cares? It's none of their business." Noah reached for the paper in Robert's hand with a flourish of silver rings. "The Abdication Egg," he said excitedly, scanning the teletype. "What a foolish thing to steal. Impossible to fence."

"You're familiar with the object, then," said Robert, sounding a little more hopeful.

"Oh, yes. The Imperial Russian Easter eggs are quite famous and quite extraordinary. This was the last known example of the House of Fabergé's contribution to Tsarist extravagance."

"I'm working on an historical perspective for the news desk," Robert confided, "some documentary they're working on concerning the recent resurgence in nationalism among the former satellite countries of the defunct Soviet Eastern Bloc."

"Whoa, Bobby. I'd hate to have to read that book," said Noah with a laugh.

Robert looked at him, unamused. "I admit it's probably not as significant as how high hemlines were in 1920, but some people are interested in the subject," no one called him Bobby—not anymore anyway, "and the name is Robert."

"Touchy, aren't we, Bobby?" Noah poked at his shoulder with a slender, manicured finger.

"This is not going to work," Robert said, starting to rise.

Noah pulled him down. "Now don't go off mad. I'm only playing with you. Besides, what's all that got to do with the Abdication Egg?"

"That is the question," Robert replied, trying to regain a comfortable position on the floor. "The desk wants some background for a sidebar on the incident."

"Do they think the theft has some sort of political significance?"

"I wouldn't have thought so until you said it would be impossible to fence," said Robert thoughtfully. "Perhaps the theft was instigated by a private collector or someone wanting to melt it down and sell the gold and jewels."

"I doubt that," Noah said. "Someone wanting to sell gold and jewels doesn't risk a theft in communist Russia from a state museum."

"They're not really that communist anymore."

"Whatever." Noah batted his long, black lashes. "Security at Moscow's Armoury Museum is very high and visits restricted to foreign visitors."

"Still, a private collector . . ."

"There were other Fabergé eggs in the museum of greater value than this one, Bobby. Other precious art works as well. And besides, as a work of art, the egg is worth a hell of a lot more than the materials it's constructed of."

"What's the significance, then, of this particular Imperial Egg? And please . . . it's Robert."

"You've got me there. All I know is what it is, who made it, and where it was."

"Great." Robert started to rise again. "Now what?"

"We go to the source, like all good news reporters," Noah offered, jumping to his feet before Robert could get up.

"What source . . . and we are not news reporters. We are researchers," Robert corrected.

"Oh, get a life, Bobby." Noah stretched his arms out and rotated his head, absolutely unconcerned as to how odd his behavior might seem.

"This is work," Robert said, ignoring the young man's persistent use of the diminutive. Annoying as he was, the young man made Robert think of Dorian Gray. No one was that beautiful without making a pact with the Devil. Robert smoothed at his trousers. "Now what source are you talking about?"

"There's an elderly gentleman . . . born into an exiled White Russian family. He works at Bartley Jewelers on Fifty-Second Street. His father was a workmaster—a master jeweler in the Fabergé workshops at the time of the Russian Revolution. I spoke to him briefly when the Imperial Egg collection from the New Orleans Museum of Art was shown at the Metropolitan."

"He must be over a hundred if he was born around the time of the Revolution."

"Really?" Noah smoothed out his jeans. "Looks over two hundred."

"You'll call him up again?"

"No. He hates telephones. We'll go and see him. It's time for us to leave this stuffy office and do a little leg work."

"Really, Mr. Taylor—"

"Noah."

"Really, Noah, I have too much work to do here, to go off—"

"Work which you'll never get finished unless you get this information. The only way we're going to get it is to go there and interview the man."

"Can't you do it?" Robert almost begged.

"Hey. It's your piece, remember? Now, I'll make the introductions if you're interested, but . . ."

"All right! All right," Robert said, giving up. "Let's go. The sooner the better to get this over with."

"Great. Let me get my bag," said Noah cheerily. "Any excuse to get out of this place," he said, hoisting up a tooled, leather messenger bag. "We can grab a bite to eat, too, while we're out."

"Fine," said Robert wearily. "But I don't know any restaurants where you sit on the floor."

Chapter 2

Robert felt particularly self-conscious strolling down the sidewalk on Fifty-Second Street with the exotic creature he had just met. Especially with the boy's penchant for looping his arm through Robert's while they walked. Robert kept pulling his arm away, but Noah would not be deterred.

Robert stopped. "Is it possible for you not to do that?" he asked looking down at the young man.

"Not do what?" Noah asked naively. "You don't like my humming?"

"No, not . . ." Robert sighed. "Holding onto me like . . . like . . ."

"Oh, don't be silly." Noah waved a silvered hand. "This is New York. Men walk arm-in-arm across Europe everyday without the hang-ups this country whines about. Look about. No one is paying us any attention."

"That may be but—"

"I am not going to apologize for being a very physical person," Noah said, taking Robert's arm again and pulling him along. "I have to get to know the people I'm working with. I'm more tactile than verbal."

"And delusional," Robert said under his breath, rolling his eyes. No matter what the boy said, this approach to walking and talking was certainly not New York. And he had been talking nonstop since they left the McNaughton Building about anything and everything that seemed to pop into his head. Still, it wasn't a completely unpleasant experience.

"Bobby, you're not listening to me again."

Robert stammered something innocuous and quickly shifted his gaze back down the sidewalk.

"Would it make you uncomfortable," Noah asked, teasing again, "if I ogled some of the passing women with big tits while we walked?"

"If you what?" Robert asked, stumbling.

Noah's laughter sounded like a coloratura roulade. "Don't worry," he said. "I'll try to keep my eyes on where we're going." He pulled Robert along good naturedly. "I'll guide you by the arm. Just try to keep a little of your attention on what I'm saying to you."

Robert decided silence was the best way to deal with the situation. Which was fine since Noah picked up where he had left off and continued to talk all the way to the front of the Bartley Jewelry Company. It was not an imposing front like Tiffany's and had no display windows to speak of, only a brass plaque on the door. He reached absent-mindedly to open the door for Noah.

"Such a gentlemen," Noah cooed.

"Just go in," Robert said, heaving a sigh.

Noah breezed through the door laughing again, a hearty sort of sound that crescendoed into the building. Robert felt his ears burn with embarrassment but the boy seemed not at all concerned that someone might hear him. Huge slabs of walnut paneling towered over the parquet floors and glass display cases. The only light in the room seemed to emanate from the cases. The faceted gemstones and polished gold the cases contained gave the illusion of amplifying the light's intensity. Noah went straight for the cases, gasping like a small child in a candy store. Robert walked along behind him trying not to be embarrassed by the little shrieks of delight he would make at this or that unapproachably priced item.

"May I take out something in particular to show you?" came a voice out of nowhere.

Robert started, jerking his head around to the display cases on the other side of the room. A door had quietly opened in the paneling behind the case, and a middle-aged man, balding, and approaching obesity, stood diffidently behind the cases, smiling aloofly.

"Yes!" Noah almost shouted. "How much is this silver ring?" He pointed down into the case, bouncing on the balls of his feet.

"Business, Noah, please," Robert moaned, pulling his younger companion by the arm over to the side.

"Oh, all right," Noah said disappointed. "Hello." He crossed over to the salesman, holding out his hand. "I'm Noah Taylor and this is my colleague, Bobby Tate."

"Robert Tate," Robert corrected, throwing a glare at the boy before holding out his hand also.

"We're from McNaughton News," Noah continued, without missing a beat.

"How may I help you?" asked the man, a little more aloof.

"We're working on a story about the theft of the Abdication Egg from the Armoury Museum in Moscow and wondered if we could speak with your master jeweler, Mr. Kozlovsky. He helped me last year when the New Orleans collection came to the Metropolitan."

The man's bulk swelled ominously. "Vasily is very busy at this time on some new constructions that have a deadline."

"I'm sure he is and we're very sorry to have to disturb him," interrupted Robert quickly. "Any time he can give us would be appreciated, and we would, of course, be sure to mention Bartley's in the article."

The salesman's interest bolstered at that, and he eyed the two thoughtfully. "Very well," he said finally. "Come this way." He turned his back to them and walked through the door in the paneling. "But do try to keep it short. Vasily is very old and frail . . . the only master craftsman of his period and experience left."

"Of course," Noah sympathized. "We'll keep it as brief as possible."

The man led them down a stark white hallway past various workroom and offices. The atmosphere was quiet except for the occasional hammer on metal or the whir of a diamond lathe. At last they were led into a large open room lit by low hanging, back-shaded, naked light bulbs. Sitting hunched over at a heavy scalloped work bench, a lone, white-headed figure labored meticulously over the small gleaming object perched on the leather pad before him. He took no notice of the intruders at first and it wasn't until the salesman approached and tapped him on the shoulder that he looked up from his labor, blinking his eyes through thick wire-framed glasses.

"Pardon the interruption, Vasily, but these people would like a moment with you," said the salesman, patting the old gentleman on the shoulder.

Kozlovsky pulled off his apron and laid it over the object on his workbench. He stared for a moment at the visitors, trying in vain to achieve some sort of recognition. "Yes?" was all he said in a high-pitched, child-like voice.

"Mr. Kozlovsky," Noah began, stepping forward. "Remember me? I'm Noah Taylor. We spoke last year when the Imperial Egg collection from New Orleans came to the Metropolitan." His voice rose hopefully.

Kozlovsky strained through his spectacles at the beautiful boy.

Noah moved forward holding out his hand. "It's so good to see you again."

Kozlovsky's eye caught a glimpse of the large amethyst cabochon Noah wore on his right hand. Suddenly his eyes brightened with recognition. "Yes, my dear boy," the old man said in a voice thickly accented. "I remember you now . . . you and this beautiful old ring." He lifted Noah's hand closer to his face and deftly slipped a jeweler's glass over his glasses and admired the ring close up. "Exquisite," he piped reverently.

Noah smiled back at Robert. "This is a friend of mine, Mr. Kozlovsky, Bobby Tate."

"Robert Tate," Robert said emphatically as he stepped forward nodding. "A pleasure. We're working on a story about the theft of the Abdication Egg and hoped you would help us with some background."

"Abdication Egg? What is that?" asked Kozlovsky shaking his head, obviously puzzled.

Robert looked at Noah, raising his hands imploringly.

"Of course," Noah said, unaffected, "the name is only an historical reference, not the item's true designation." He raised a sarcastic eyebrow in Robert's direction. "You'll have to excuse my friend, Mr. Kozlovsky. He knows nothing of fine art."

"Nothing?" the old man said in a voice approaching horror. "Such a pity." He fondled a small platinum case at the edge of his workbench. "Being near such treasures has given me a long and full life."

"Mr. Taylor is right about my ignorance on the subject, Mr. Kozlovsky," tried Robert, looking for some way into the workmaster's good graces. "But I am a student of history and would like to learn as much about your work as I can."

Kozlovsky seemed to warm at this invitation to nostalgia. "I have worked with these precious metals a long time, my boy. Surely you would find it boring for an old man to ramble on about the past."

"Not at all," Robert said truthfully. "The past is a particular passion of mine."

"Very well," Kozlovsky said, pushing his tools to the back. He slipped slowly off the stool. "Let's have some tea." He motioned to the two of them with a crooked finger. "We can talk more comfortably back here."

They followed him to a small sitting room at the back of the workshop. A single bed and wardrobe stood against the stark brick wall. Robert began to wonder if the old man's whole world existed in that room.

"Please be comfortable," said the old jeweler graciously, spooning tea leaves into a porcelain pot. "I always have hot water ready for tea." He cackled to himself at some private joke.

"Please don't go to any trouble," Noah said. He sat down on an overstuffed divan next to Robert and pulled a small notebook from his bag.

"It's no trouble." Kozlovsky poured a kettle of steaming water into the pot. "Allow me to enjoy your company. I have so few visitors here."

"We know you must be very busy," Robert offered. "We don't want to keep you from getting your work out on time."

"On time?" Kozlovsky coughed and laughed again. "I see Maurice has been talking deadlines again." He poured each of them a cup of tea, shakily. "I pay no attention to such insults. I am an artist and I finish things when I finish." He sipped his tea noisily. "Now. What can an old immigrant tell two such fine looking young people."

"It's about this theft," Robert said getting straight to the point. "We would like a little background on the particular Imperial Egg that was stolen from the Armoury Museum in Moscow yesterday."

"An Imperial Egg, you say?" The old man hummed softly to himself. "Truly inspired works. Master Carl was unsurpassed in the genius of his ideas and my father a true artist at rendering them."

"This particular egg, Vasily," Noah said, growing all at once familiar, "was one of the last, if not the last, Imperial Egg commissioned. It was captured at the time of the Revolution on a train out of St. Petersburg, believed headed for Switzerland. This was just days before the last Tsar's forced abdication."

Kozlovsky nodded with interest. "There were a couple of such pieces commissioned by the Tsar at the end. All were somewhat disappointing to Master Carl. Because of the war there was a shortage of precious materials. One actually had to be made of steel, like a bullet." His nose wrinkled as if responding to a bad taste. "And one was even fashioned out of wood."

"Yes," said Noah. "Those would have been the two last known examples. But wasn't Mr. Fabergé given one final commission? The one captured on the train in March of 1917 was an especially fine example. It was a little larger than the previous ones, of pearl-white enameled gold with diamond rosettes on a crisscrossing filigree. It contained a peculiar locking mechanism that has been left untouched to this day. It bore the jeweler's mark *H. W.*"

A smile broke across the old man's weathered face. "The special present for the Tsesarevich."

"Not for the Empress?" asked Noah, somewhat surprised.

"No, no. As I recall it was to be a special gift for the Heir on his fourteenth birthday."

"Most unusual," Noah commented. He scribbled a note on his pad. "A gift for the Tsarevich."

"Tsesarevich," corrected Kozlovsky.

"Tse . . ." Noah wrinkled his nose.

"Tsarevich is any son of the Tsar," said Robert, trying to hurry things along. "The Tsar's presumptive heir is the Tsesarevich."

Noah looked up at him smugly. "Thank you, Professor Tate."

Robert ignored him. "How was it that this egg came to be made of precious metals and gemstones when there was a shortage?"

"It was unusual," agreed Kozlovsky, nodding. "A shipment of gold coin and jewelry sent by the Tsar for the gift's construction. Workmaster Henrick Wigstrom —the H.W. is his mark—along with Master Carl himself, took personal charge of the entire project."

"Did you participate?" Noah asked.

"Oh my, no, I'm not that old dear boy, though I may look it," said the master jeweler with a chuckle. "The designs and the work itself were very secret. My father said the other workers were told that such extravagance during wartime would not likely sit well with the already complaining masses."

"So your father was not a part of the actual construction?"

"My dear, I was barely a newborn at the time, myself, so I don't really know the specifics. This was an Imperial commission, and I assure you, one that my father most certainly would have had a part in. My father taught me everything about the shop's major output."

"Even if you were just a baby," Robert said somewhat surprised, "that would mean you're . . ."

"Antique," said the jeweler with a slight smile.

"What was the egg designed to contain?" Noah interjected.

"Some little treasure for the Tsesarevich, I'm sure," responded Kozlovsky with a toothless grin.

"What do you mean?" Robert asked.

"All the Imperial Easter Eggs were made to contain some special little extra for their intended," Noah told him, setting down his notebook for the cup of tea. "Some contained photographs of the Tsar, his wife, or their children, and others contained spectacular creations such as gold miniatures of baskets of flowers . . . one even had a small gold coach inside."

"I see," Robert said. "And this one has not been opened."

"As I recall that's true." Kozlovsky added another spoonful of sugar to his tea. "No one could figure out the locking mechanism so x-rays were made showing the egg to be empty. By the time any real attention was being paid to the egg, Master Carl and Workmaster Wigstrom had already left the country. Many of us left with them . . . left everything behind to get out." Kozlovsky's voice lowered angrily. "My father said it was just too hard to imagine a future for jewelers among such rabble." He spat over his shoulder in disgust.

"I didn't see any examples of Easter Eggs in the showroom," Robert observed. "Were any made since your exile?"

"No, no, no." Kozlovsky shook his head emphatically. "That art belonged to Master Carl."

"Why would someone steal this particular egg?" Noah was scribbling in his notebook again.

"The gold? The diamonds, maybe?" The old man shrugged his shoulders.

"Why not one of the other, more valuable eggs that were with it in the museum?" Noah persisted.

"Now you're asking me to think like a thief," Kozlovsky protested. "Who knows what reasons such evil men have?" He crossed himself piously in the Orthodox manner.

"Thank you for your time," Robert said rising. "You have been more than helpful, Mr. Kozlovsky. We should be getting back now." He shook the old man's hand.

"Yes, thank you for seeing me again," Noah said, stuffing his notebook back into his bag.

"I always enjoy a little respite from my work," Kozlovsky said, rising slowly and starting for the door. "Especially when the company is so young and interested in this old man's passions." He winked back over his shoulder at Noah.

Robert walked alongside the old gentlemen toward the door, not noticing that Noah was making his way over to the work tables. Noah reached for the apron covering what Kozlovsky had been working on, trying to ignore the feelings of guilt at being so snoopy. Still, he wouldn't forgive himself if he didn't satisfy his curiosity with one little peek. He raised the apron just enough and stared in surprise at the gleaming oval of gold and loose precious stones laying underneath. Noah dropped the apron instantly, glancing back at the door to be sure his snooping had gone unnoticed.

Kozlovsky was just opening the door and Noah hurried to catch up with Robert who was looking at him with undisguised annoyance.

"Come again if I can be of further help," Kozlovsky said, looking back at them.

"We'll do that," Robert assured him. He grabbed Noah by the arm and tried to pull him along.

Noah resisted. "Mr. Kozlovsky, I thought you said you have never made one of the eggs."

"That's right, young man. I've always felt they were a special item, associated only with Master Carl and the Imperial Family. I could not profane that memory with my own poor skills." Kozlovsky lowered his head humbly. "The Royal Family are Saints of the Church."

"You underestimate yourself, Mr. Kozlovsky," Noah said. "I've seen your work and it's as fine as even the best examples of the House of Fabergé."

"My work?" Kozlovsky glanced back at his work table with an almost panicked expression.

"Yes," added Noah, thinking quickly. "Those miniatures in the display cases out front are exquisite."

Kozlovsky's expression relaxed. "Oh those." He smiled modestly. "Mere trinkets."

"Nonsense. They're are high art." Noah patted the old man's shoulder. "Thank you again for letting us stop in." Now it was his turn to grab Robert's arm and pull him through the door.

Robert stumbled beside Noah trying to pull free as the door was shut behind them. "What the hell was all that about?" he snapped, finally pulling free of Noah's grip.

"Don't ask yet," Noah whispered, half-running down the hall to the showroom.

Robert dashed after him. "Stop acting like a damn Mrs. Marple. It was just an interview."

Noah was through the door into the showroom before Robert could catch him. "Thank you so much for letting us speak to Mr. Kozlovsky," he said, cornering the salesman behind the display cases and shaking his hand vigorously.

"Certainly," the startled man said.

"And while I've got you here, there's this charming little medallion over in the case here." Noah lead him around to it. "I just love it."

The salesman took it from the case and set it out with a flourish onto a piece of velvet for Noah to inspect. "You have an excellent eye, young man. It is an original creation. Quite unique."

Noah picked it up and turned it over in his hand. "It is a beauty. Imported?"

The salesman shook his head. "Made here in our own shop by the old gentleman you just spoke to."

"Mr. Kozlovsky?"

"Indeed." The salesman turned the piece over in Noah's hand. "Here is his signature stamp."

"Noah!" Robert tapped his foot impatiently behind his companion.

"In a moment, Bobby. I must have this." He pulled a credit card from his wallet and handed it to the salesman who was already filling out the sales receipt. "One more thing which I forgot to ask Mr. Kozlovsky but which I'm sure you can answer for me," he said quickly to the salesman, waving behind him for Robert to stay back.

Robert leaned against one of the glass cases, shaking his head in aggravation.

"Has your shop produced any objects similar to the Imperial Eggs recently?" Noah asked, accepting his card back from the salesman.

The salesman raised an eyebrow. "We have many beautiful things."

"But any eggs?"

The salesman sighed. "Such an item is not part of our regular stock. Our jeweler has constructed such things in the past but only by special arrangement with the customer . . . a very costly arrangement." He eyed Noah haughtily as if to say such things were beyond the young man's means.

"How exciting," Noah said, leading him on. "A jewelry store that, even today, carries on the traditions of the old House of Fabergé. I would love to see an example."

"I'm sorry but we have none to show," the salesman said, somewhat disappointed. "As I said, they are commissioned objects." He handed Noah a small sack containing his purchase.

"Perhaps if you could give us the name of one of the patrons who purchased one."

The salesman stepped back imperiously. "Impossible. Our sales records are quite confidential."

"Just this once," Noah implored. "It would mean so much for our story. Just one name."

"Absolutely not. And there is only one such buyer. I have no intention of offending them in the least."

"Only one." Noah smiled conciliatorily. "I quite understand. Thank you for your help." He made one more quick scan of the showcase contents and then headed for the door to the street, waving Robert on as well.

Robert nodded apologetically to the salesman and started after Noah, who was already out the door. The boy had succesfully strained Robert's patience beyond the breaking point and he bore down on Noah angrily.

"Hurry, Robert." Noah stopped outside the door, waiting for him to catch up. "Can you believe that?"

"Can I believe what?" Robert sputtered angrily. "You were rude, nosey, obnoxious and a general pain in the ass."

"No, not that," Noah said, dismissing Robert's complaining with a wave of his hand. "I mean that song and dance about the egg."

"What . . ."

"Weren't you listening?" Noah admonished. "Kozlovsky said he never made eggs. The salesman said just the opposite."

"So what, Noah? For God's sake. What's the big deal?"

"Are you deaf?" Noah waved a silver-encrusted finger at Robert, almost shouting at him on the sidewalk. "I happened to look on Kozlovsky's table in the workroom at what he was making. It was as perfect an example of an Imperial Easter Egg as you could ever want to see. It was in pieces, but . . ." He nodded knowingly.

Robert rolled his eyes skyward. "It is really none of your business what he's working on."

"But why lie about it?"

"Why discuss confidential business with a nosy busybody like you?"

Noah shook his head in exasperation. "Don't you think it at all strange that someone is still commissioning these almost priceless eggs and that Kozlovsky would lie about making them?"

"Not really, Noah. It's none of our business. We came for background on the Abdication Egg, and we got it. That's what interests me."

"You're impossible!"

"Actually, I'm hungry," he groaned.

Noah brightened visibly. "Oh, I forgot. So am I." He started off down the sidewalk. "Follow me. I know just the spot."

"I probably won't like it," Robert grumbled.

Chapter 3

"Ha! What did I tell you?" Noah ripped the sheaf of paper off the fax machine.

"What are you ranting about now?" Robert tried to suppress another belch. Hotdogs and sauerkraut. He had been sure Noah was going to be one of those bean sprouts and alfalfa nuts.

"I know there's a connection." Noah waved the paper in his face. "See? Russian officials have begun an unprecedented manhunt for the thieves."

"So?"

"No one would buy the Abdication Egg except one hell of a serious collector who could stand living with no hope of ever showing it off."

"You call this a connection?" said Robert, starting for the door of the glassed-in computer room. "You're in another world."

Noah chased after him, tripping over the pages of copy falling from his hands. "Don't try and tell me you don't see it." He grabbed for Robert's sleeve. "Read this.

We have an anonymous, elusive collector who, even today, has these eggs made at a cost you and I could never make in our combined lifetimes."

"All speculation." Even though Robert cocked his head to the side, his gaze still managed to strafe down the bridge of his nose at the boy. "I'm still waiting for your so-called connection."

Noah sighed. "Our man could be their man. Don't you see it, Bobby? Think what a story this would make."

"Yes. Art researcher committed for extreme paranoid schizophrenia."

Noah laughed. "I'm serious."

Robert stood mute, letting the silence speak for him.

Noah pursed his lips. "Sticks and stones, Bobby. Call me crazy if you want but it *is* a possibility."

"One of about a hundred. Look, Mr. Taylor, you've had your fun in the sun this afternoon. You got to snoop around a little and play reporter." He snatched the wire copy from the younger man's hand. "Now I've got work to do." He spun on his heels and retreated toward his office cubicle.

"Don't you ever come out for air?" Noah called after him.

"What?" He turned back for a moment.

Noah smirked at him. "Well, I mean, it must be awful *stuffy* in your closet."

Robert narrowed his eyes at the boy.

Noah brightened suddenly. "I'll bet Madelyn would agree with me." He flew off in the direction of the department manager's office.

Robert sat down at his computer and called up his analysis on the former Soviet satellite states to try and prune a little more away. He stared at the words on the screen, rocking in his chair, unable to concentrate on anything but the exasperating kid he had just rid himself of. It almost angered him more that he couldn't get the gypsy boy-toy out of his head.

He wadded up a sheet of paper from his doodling pad and threw it with a vengeance at the trash can beside his desk. Madelyn was sure to put the boy in his place. Robert smiled to himself in triumph. Now there was a woman who couldn't stand wasted time. He pecked absentmindedly at the keyboard, trying to block off another paragraph for deletion.

"Oh Bobby?"

Robert started at the voice, turning to find Noah at his door, looking smug.

"What now?" Robert let his impatience show.

"Madelyn would like to see you in her office," Noah announced. He reminded Robert of a child just back from tattling. "Now, if you don't mind."

"Are you still going on about this?" Robert pushed back in his chair and stood facing the shorter man-boy. "What kind of nonsense have you been feeding Madelyn?"

"I only told her what I told you," Noah said sweetly. "I'm sure she just wants the benefit of your *age* and *experience* on the question."

Robert pushed past the boy, growling.

"Now don't go getting yourself in a tizzy," Noah said, following close at the older man's heels. "After all, we're gonna be working together and . . ."

"Not before Lenin flies out of his tomb singing *Sweet Jesus* am I gonna work with you," Robert said, increasing the length of his stride toward Madelyn's office.

Noah somehow managed to keep up with him, giggling in a way that annoyed him even more.

"What kind of crap have you let this artsy-tartsy, con artist feed you," Robert said, storming through the door into the over-sized cubicle.

"Robert, dear. I didn't expect to see you so soon. Usually you keep me waiting." Madelyn looked over the rims of her reading glasses at him. "I think the two of you work well together. Noah's already managed to make you more punctual."

"Madelyn, you've got to be kidding." Robert said, pacing in front of her desk. "This is going just a bit overboard."

"Now, Robert." Madelyn clicked her long, artificial nails together and smiled broadly from behind her desk. "I think Noah is right. This would make a super sidebar . . . a special interest piece the other news services would love to pick up. And, if it turns out there is some connection to the theft, it'll be icing on the cake. Either way, I think the story will help sell the whole package.

"Who would be interested in expensive trinkets like Imperial Easter Eggs?" Robert persisted.

"Just about everybody," Noah answered.

Robert glared at him.

"Don't be so sullen, Bobby." Noah shook him by the arm. "The networks will buy the piece in a minute."

Robert focused his reason on Madelyn. "Surely I have more important things to work on than fluff like this. If Mr. Taylor wishes to pursue it, fine. It's right up his alley, but please spare me. I've still got to edit the Soviet Bloc overview."

"Carson can handle that for you, Robert." Madelyn tried to look sympathetic.

"Carson!"

"You've done the writing. Now any good editor can trim the fat for you."

Robert groaned.

"It'll be fun, Bobby. You'll see," Noah insisted.

"We've already run into a wall with this story," Robert countered. "The store will not release any names.

I am not a reporter and neither is this . . . this kid!" He waved a menacing arm at Noah. "I don't see where we can take this any further."

"You have a P.I. license, Robert. Use it," Madelyn said. "I want this story researched. That is your job, isn't it?"

"A P.I. license?" Noah bounced with excitement. "You're a private investigator?"

"Oh for crying out loud, Madelyn!" Robert's voice rose an octave. "The company saddled me with that just so I could access the police computers for that organized crime story last year."

"It's still good isn't it?"

"I suppose, but—"

"This is perfect," Noah interrupted. "We can run a check on Kozlovsky first."

"Run a check?" Robert moaned. He turned back to his boss in desperation. "You'll have to find someone else, Madelyn."

"What makes you think that, Robert, dear?"

"Madelyn, I don't want to do this."

"But, Dr. Tate." Madelyn smiled icily. "This is what I pay you for."

Robert stood tapping his hand on the front of her desk helplessly.

"Come on, Bobby. We've got to get busy." Noah pulled at Robert's sleeve. "Don't worry, Madelyn. This story's gonna be great. We'll crack this case in no time."

"Crack this case?" Robert fought back a scream.

Noah was out of the office before Robert could grab the gypsy and shake some sense into him. He cast one more scowl at Madelyn and started after Noah.

Robert caught up with him, breathless. "What are you doing to me?" he asked, leaning against the door of Noah's cubicle, panting.

Noah grabbed a small tape recorder from his desk and stuffed it in his bag before looking up at Robert innocently. "Don't you see, Bobby? We're finally going to get out of this claustrophobic office for a while and do some real investigative reporting. Think where it could lead."

"I don't want to think where it could lead. I don't want to get out of this stuffy office. I like this stuffy office. If I wanted to go outside I'd be a construction worker, not a writer."

Noah laughed. "You can be so silly sometimes."

"I'm perfectly serious. I work alone. I don't want to work with a partner, least of all you."

Noah feigned a hurt look. "This is not a kind way to a start off a collaboration." He smiled up at Robert. "Especially one in which you have no choice."

Robert drew his hand up as if to strangle Noah, but the younger man's beauty held him at bay. It would be like strangling a Botticelli painting. "If you want to go out traipsing all over the city making a fool of yourself, go right ahead," Robert said, throwing his arms down in defeat. "But you'll be doing it without me." He turned to leave.

"Oh, Bobby, don't be such an old fart!" Noah grabbed Robert's coat sleeve, pulling him off balance. "You're the one with the P.I. license. I'll just be along to take notes."

Robert shook loose. "What kind of an idiot do you take me for?"

"I mean it." Noah laughed his light, sparkly laugh. "You can ask the questions. Come on. It'll be fun. Think of it. A jeweler, formerly with the Fabergé workshops in Imperial Russia, still making priceless Easter Eggs for some mysterious client . . . a fabulously wealthy client, judging by the price of precious metals and gems these days."

"You must literally support the cocaine dealers in this city," grumbled Robert, shaking his head.

Noah cocked his crown of curls to one side. "I can imagine without any chemical assistance, thank you very much." He found Robert staring at him. Blood rushed to his face. "Now let's go," he said, suppressing a grin.

"Where?"

"Out on the trail of this mystery."

Robert threw his hand in the air. "And where do you intend to begin?"

Noah's brow furrowed in thought. "We should probably stake out Bartley Jewelers. You know. Watch who comes and goes. Go through their garbage . . ."

"Good God, boy! Get a grip on yourself." Robert leaned in to Noah, nose to nose. The boy's scent was intoxicating. "The store will be closing soon and so will I. It's almost dark," he said, glaring into Noah's eyes expecting the boy to back away.

"Perfect." Noah didn't budge. He raised his face to Robert's. "Maybe we can get inside after everyone's gone and have a look around."

Robert felt the boy's breath against his cheek. "I knew it! Now you want to get us arrested."

"Oh, don't be silly." Noah gave Robert a push toward the door. "I smell a story."

"How can you smell anything behind all that cologne?"

"You noticed. Do you like it?"

"I have no opinion on it."

"What do you have an opinion on?"

"You're insane!"

Noah slipped up beside Robert and slipped his arm into the older man's. "As long as you like me. Now let's go."

"I want to be home by supper," he insisted.

"Supper?" Noah pushed him into the elevator. "I know just the place."

"Oh, God," he muttered, pressing a fist against the burning below his heart.

Chapter 4

Robert shifted nervously on his feet. The street lights on each end provided only a faint, yellowish illumination which he hoped would help keep his presence invisible. The noise coming from the large, gray dumpster beside him was nerve-wracking.

"Jesus Christ, Noah! What the hell are you doing?" Robert couldn't make out the muffled reply. "Well, keep the noise down. I'm surprised we're not already surrounded by a SWAT team."

A head sporting a black Castro hat poked out of the dumpster lid. "Chill out, Bobby. No one's going to see us. And, if they do, we'll just pretend we're street people, or something, looking for food."

"I'm standing here in a six hundred dollar overcoat holding your damn *purse*, which by the way, weighs a ton, while you scrounge around in there with half of Tiffany's silver stock hanging out of your ears. Somehow

I don't think we'll be convincing." He kicked the edge of the dumpster. "Get a move on. This is stupid."

Noah pulled himself up to the edge of the dumpster and hung glaring down at Robert. "Instead of the constant criticism, you could come up with an idea yourself that's better." He struggled to pull himself out. "Give me a hand, will you?"

Robert slung Noah's messenger bag over his shoulder and reached to give the boy a hand, trying not to let his coat brush against the oily side of the dumpster.

"Come on, Bobby. You'll have to do better than that."

"You're the one who wanted to rummage through this filthy thing, not me."

"Come on, Bobby!"

"Okay, okay." Robert looked down both ends of the alley nervously. "Try to find something to stand on. You need to be a little higher to get your leg over the side."

"I am standing on something."

"Try to find something more, a box or something."

"There isn't anything else."

"Well, what the hell are you standing on now?"

"I don't even want to think about it."

Robert felt the boy's smooth hand shiver slightly. "Just a second," he said, releasing Noah. "There are some crates over here to the back." He circled the dumpster and pulled the spindly crates to the front. He climbed up on them carefully, testing their shaky support until he was a head over the edge of the dumpster.

Noah smiled across at him. "Hi."

Robert blinked, trying to shake the obsession he was developing for staring at the younger man. "Just give me your hand and get out of this damn thing." He grabbed Noah under the arms and pulled as Noah struggled to pull a leg over the edge.

"Oh, wait. My belt's caught on something."

"Damn it, boy!" Robert puffed, red faced. "If you knew you were going to be doing something like this you should have dressed appropriately."

Noah laughed, ignoring him. "Belt's free. Now pull!"

Robert cupped his hands under Noah's armpits, and pulled the boy against his chest. He heaved mightily, trying to draw in a little air from beside Noah's ear where, much to his embarrassment, his face was buried. A lithe leg breached the summit. Noah jumped off his other foot and tried to swing his full weight up and over the edge of the dumpster. A loud, firecracker-crack sounded the surrender of the rickety crates under Robert's feet. He tumbled back onto the dirty, alley floor. The sheer weight of his body pulled Noah free of the dumpster and down on top of him. Robert opened his eyes to find Noah sitting astride him in a cloud of acrid dust.

The younger man bounced excitedly on his stomach. "Whoo! This is so cool!"

"Cool . . . cool?" Robert struggled to sit up, pushing Noah backwards. "You are certifiable, did you know that?" He pushed the boy off onto the ground. "I'm lying in a pile of God-knows-what with a lunatic runway model jumping on my rib cage."

"Sounds like you're pretty insane yourself," Noah said, jumping nimbly to his feet and brushing off his jeans. "Model? You mean it?"

Robert lay back in the dust and moaned.

"Oh, come on, Bobby. Get up. We've got work to do."

"And I thought, for sure, you had extracted all the secrets we needed from the trash."

"It was a good idea." Noah looked up at the dumpster, hands on hips. "Nothing there, though. Interesting."

"Interesting?" Robert struggled to his feet.

"No business papers at all," Noah replied in all seriousness. "Very suspicious."

"Good God," Robert said, unbelieving. "Now you're suspicious, not because of what you found in the trash, but because of what you didn't find."

"Well, you must admit it's rather odd. Not one single receipt, torn envelope, shipping label, anything."

"The question is not why isn't there something there for you to find, but why should there be?" Robert grabbed Noah by the shoulders and spun him around. "All right, Mr. Taylor. I have had it. It's late. I'm filthy, tired, and pissed off. And I am going home."

Noah grabbed for Robert's sleeve. "There's a story here, Bobby. I can feel it."

"Probably indigestion from those damn burritos."

"We've got to get to the bottom of this."

"We," Robert said with cold emphasis, "don't have to do a goddamn thing. I'm out of here." He started toward the street, shaking the dust from his coat.

"Why I thought you had any guts, I'll never know," Noah shouted after him. "I would have done better to bring the copy boy along. He probably wouldn't have been afraid to roll up his sleeves and do a little work rather than hiding in a dinky office cubicle all day."

Robert stopped abruptly and turned to face Noah. "Don't pull that macho-ego-insult crap on me, kid. It doesn't suit you, and I don't have to prove anything to anyone." He could not help but laugh at the sight of Noah standing, cap and clothing awry, under the harsh, yellow glare of the overhead security light. "Perhaps you would do better with the copy boy. Someone your professional equal." He turned to leave.

"Just one minute, buddy!" Noah bore down on him. "No one talks to me like that." He grabbed the belt of Robert's overcoat and jerked him backwards. "Especially not a stuffed-shirt, self-possessed, closeted do-nothing like you."

Robert looked down into the gypsy's blazing eyes, surprised. A flash in the corner of his eye stimulated his reflex to duck just in time. Noah's right arm breezed past his jaw in a perfectly executed roundhouse punch. Robert's speed surprised Noah as well. He caught the boy's punch before it completed the follow through and clamped it together with Noah's other fist which was preparing a combination to his solar plexus.

"Let go of me!" Noah cried, struggling against him.

"I'll let go of you when I think it's safe to," Robert replied, keeping an eye out for the possibility of a knee to the groin.

Noah glared up at him. "Do you enjoy bashing gays?"

"Only those who try to bash me," Robert countered.

Noah looked away haughtily. "I don't know what you're talking about."

"Bullshit," Robert said with a laugh. "Where did a twink like you learn how to punch like that?"

"I was the only little gay boy among four brothers," Noah said, casting an ominous glance to Robert's crotch. "And I'd let go if I were you. I know how to kick as well."

Robert released his hold on the boy and stepped back with his hands raised in the universal sign of surrender.

Noah rubbed his wrists, eyeing Robert's retreat with interest. "May I have my bag back? It doesn't go with your coat."

Robert remembered the heavy messenger bag still hanging from his shoulder. "Christ," he said angrily, pulling it off his shoulder as if it were a snake.

Noah took it from him with a sly smirk. "Can we get back to work now?"

"Doing what?"

"Checking this place out," Noah said, flinging a hand toward the jewelry store.

Robert sighed resignedly. "Come on," he said, shaking his head. He started to the back of the alley.

"What?" Noah followed him suspiciously. "What are we going to do?"

Robert looked at the boy with bored condescension. "We're going to check out the jewelry store. That's what you want to do, isn't it?"

"Yeah," Noah said, tentatively. "How?"

"Just stick close and keep quiet." Robert stood in front of the service entrance studying the exposed brick wall above.

"What are you looking for?" Noah asked.

"Shhhh!"

Noah followed Robert's gaze to the phone junction box bolted to the side of the building.

"Do you have your cell phone?" Robert asked.

"What?"

"Your cell phone. Do you have your cell phone?"

"Yes, but . . ."

"Get it out and call the number of Bartley Jewelers."

"Wha . . ."

"Just do it," Robert commanded. "And let it ring about ten times before hanging up."

Noah looked at him as if not comprehending.

"Hurry."

Noah obeyed without further argument.

Robert quickly opened the phone box and studied the parallel row of small brass screws to which junctioned the myriad phone lines for the many businesses in the large brownstone. "Is it ringing?" he asked.

Noah nodded and shrugged.

Robert wet two fingers with his tongue and then slowly ran them over the pairs of screws in the box. Midway down he was rewarded with a stinging shock from two of the screws. He pulled a dime out of his pocket and turned each of the screws to disconnect their respective wires.

Noah dropped his cell phone back into his bag. "What are you doing, Bobby?"

Robert shushed him. "Don't be so loud."

"Okay," Noah said like a petulant child. "What are you doing?" he whispered, mockingly.

"I've disconnected the phone lines to the jewelry store."

"Why?" Noah looked at him with new fascination.

"To disconnect the silent burglar alarm."

"How did you know which lines to disconnect?"

"When you dialed the number the incoming call produces an electric current at the line junction. It gives you a small shock when you touch a wet finger to the right set of wires."

"But why . . ."

"Jesus Christ, Noah. Enough with the questions." Robert headed back to the store's service entrance.

Noah followed him excitedly. "What now?" he whispered.

"It's too high up to disconnect."

"What?"

Robert pointed to another wire rising out of the top of the doorway to the top of the building and to a large, old-fashioned, burglar alarm bell. "We'll have to cut it."

He searched his pockets. "Do you have any scissors or something?"

Noah rummaged in his bag frantically. "Oh, wait . . . here." He produced a pair of toenail clippers. "Will these do?"

Robert snatched the clippers from him and strained on tiptoes to snip the alarm wire over the door. "All right," he said, returning the clippers to Noah. "Keep a watch on both ends of the alley."

Noah kept silent. His gaze darting from one end of the alley to the other while at the same time trying to keep an eye on what Robert was doing.

Robert knelt before the small, numbered keypunch pad above the doorknob. "A coded, electric lock."

"What now?" Noah breathed.

"You wouldn't, just on the off chance, have a compact . . . powder . . . brush?"

Noah dug in his bag again and quickly pulled out a small plastic box of gold metallic powder with a small, fine-haired brush.

Robert shook his head at the items. "Really?"

"I like a little sparkle around my eyes when I go out at night," Noah said defensively. "A lot of guys wear some at the clubs."

"Do they?" Robert took the brush and powder from Noah's hands. "It's been years since I've seen a drag show."

"Ha, ha." Noah crossed his arms. "It's probably been years since you've done *anything*."

"Don't be a little shit."

"A little explanation would make me less nervous," Noah said with a shaky smile.

Robert dusted the numbered buttons with the powder. "The numbers that are used should have skin oil residue from the fingers. More of the powder should stick to those numbers."

Noah nodded, watching him closely.

Robert shook the brush clean and then carefully removed the loose powder from the small white keys. "Four, three, seven, six," he said finally.

"But in what order?" Noah asked.

"There's the question." Robert studied the keys. People will usually program their codes in a sequence that is easy to remember."

"So."

"So more than likely the numbers will key in order."

"What if you're wrong?"

"Then we'll try the sequence in a different order. This at least narrows down the possible combinations."

"Won't it set off the alarm if you hit a wrong number?" Noah eyed the alleyway nervously.

"Probably not."

"Probably?"

"These commercial systems usually allow for operator error. They're not meant to be high security devices. Secondly—it's a lock, not an alarm, which I've already disarmed." He punched in the numbers. "Three, four, six, seven."

Noah heard a slight clicking sound. "Well?"

"We're in."

"Holy shit!" Noah gasped.

Robert turned the knob and opened the door easily. "Come on. Let's get in out of the spotlight."

Noah ducked in the doorway ahead of him, shifting nervously in the dark as Robert shut the door behind them.

"Well, Mr. Capone," Noah whispered, "what's our next move?"

"Don't be such a drama queen," Robert admonished. "Let's find the office."

They inched their way along the hallway toward a dim light peeking through a glass pane in a door ahead of them.

Noah's shoulder hit an object on the wall making a muffled thud as he moved along behind Robert. "Ouch," he groaned in a high pitched whine, trying not to be too loud.

"Careful," Robert snapped.

"I didn't do it on purpose," Noah sputtered from behind, rubbing his shoulder.

Robert stopped in front of the door and leaned close to it, listening. Noah pressed close to his back trying to hear with him.

Satisfied, Robert turned the knob and inched the door open, peeking through the crack as an added safeguard. "All clear," he assured, opening the door the rest of the way.

They entered the dark, adjoining hall with more confidence.

"Let's forget about reporting and become jewel thieves," Noah said with a nervous laugh.

"It is a statistical fact," said Robert, contemplating the various doors opening from the hallway, "that most all career criminals are eventually caught."

"Well, that's a comforting thought in our present position."

Robert cast an amused glance back at the boy. "Losing your nerve, Mr. Hot-Shot-Reporter?"

"Not a chance, Bobby." Noah smirked back.

Robert stopped abruptly, turning. "My name is Rob—"

"Shhhh!" Noah put a hand to his mouth.

A faint tapping sound echoed from the other end of the hall behind them.

Noah looked up at Robert questioningly. "This is the hall we came down earlier."

"That's Kozlovsky's workroom."

"What's he doing here this late, for God's sake?"

"From the look of things this afternoon, I'd say he probably lives in that room."

"Oh great. Now what?"

"We find the office," Robert said, nodding down the hall.

"But Kozlovsky?"

"Is too busy and making too much noise to notice two expert sleuths like us."

A smile broke over Noah's face. "Exactly." He moved ahead of Robert. "This way."

Robert sighed and shook his head. "Yes, Dr. Watson."

"Now who's being a drama queen," Noah quipped. "I'd say this would be the office." He stopped in front of one of the doors.

"That's what the sign says," Robert growled. He tried the door. "Locked."

"Need a hairpin?" Noah asked.

"Don't be a smartass," Robert replied, kneeling to study the lock. He looked back up at Noah. "And what in God's green earth do you have a hairpin for?"

"Joking!"

Robert suppressed a smile, reached in his back pocket for his wallet and extracted a credit card.

"Not that old trick," Noah teased.

"Whatever works." Robert slid the card into the door jam, releasing the bolt easily.

"God, you're good," Noah said admiringly. "Where did you learn—"

"Let's get on with this," Robert cut in, swinging the door open. He fumbled for the light switch. "Here." The overhead, fluorescent fixture flickered on. "You take the desk, I'll check the file cabinets," he commanded, hurrying across the room.

"Right, boss!" Noah said with a curt salute.

Robert ignored him and turned back to the file drawer he had pulled out.

Noah browsed through the desk top's contents. There was nothing of interest—a little junk mail, purchase orders for gold, silver, and uncut gemstones. He opened the center drawers and found nothing but assorted pens, pencils. "Anything yet in the files?" he called over his shoulder.

"Standard business fare," Robert replied in an I-told-you-so voice.

Noah spied a posting tray on a small credenza to his side. "Maybe our rich friend pays for his eggs in installments," he said with a chuckle and began flipping through the account cards.

"This could take forever and we still might not find anything," Robert grumbled. "The more time we take here, the greater the risk of our being caught."

As if in response, a door slammed somewhere close by causing Noah to jump. Robert signaled for silence. He leapt across the room to get the light switch. Noah fled to Robert's side and they both hugged the door listening to the footsteps shuffling out in the hallway. Instinctively, Robert threw an arm around his smaller companion. Several shadows moved past the opaque glass window of the small office heading in the direction of Kozlovsky's workroom. Another door slammed shut followed by a long silence.

"Are they gone," Noah whispered tremulously, grabbing for the hand Robert rested on the boy's shoulder.

Without answering him, Robert slowly opened the office door a crack and peered out into the hall. Satisfied that all was clear, he said, "That was close." He pulled his arm back.

"That *was* close." Noah put his hands to his head and took a deep breath.

"This is an awfully damn, busy place," Robert continued, "considering the hour. What the hell's going on around here?" He inched out into the hall. "Wait here. I'm going to see if I can hear." He looked at Noah's eyes, wide with fear or excitement, he couldn't tell which. "I won't be long. Turn on the desk lamp and keep looking."

"But what if someone else comes?" Noah asked, chewing on a fingernail.

"I think they'll be more concerned about me standing out in the hall, than a light on in here." Robert moved quickly down the corridor toward the door to Kozlovsky's workroom. He glanced briefly back at the office and gave a satisfied nod as a dim light was turned on. He inched closer to the door and could hear voices from the room. He tried listening through the door but the voices were too muffled to understand.

Letting his curiosity get the better of him, he turned the doorknob with painful slowness and eased the door open a slit. The men stood out of view behind the door, but Robert could now make out what was being said.

"You have been paid well for this, Vasily," a British accent said evenly.

"It has been a difficult piece," replied Kozlovsky. "You have not given me much time."

"If your work does not meet with approval, your excuses will mean nothing," said another voice with, what Robert surmised, was an East European accent.

"The other mechanisms you wanted were unfamiliar to me," Kozlovsky complained in a whine. "I'm a jeweler, not an engineer."

"Nonsense, Vasily," said the Englishman. "Your father worked on the original and you have the original designs. Your genius is too well recognized in higher circles for you to be so modest."

"I believe we should now discuss the matter of payment," Kozlovsky said more confidently.

"But, of course, my dear man," said the Englishman. "Your reward has been all arranged. Pay the Tsarist jeweler, Anton."

Robert heard a momentary gasp and then the spat of what, to his amazement, sounded like a pistol with silencer. Two more loud spats sounded and then a muffled thud as something hit the floor. Robert could not ease the door shut fast enough. He all but raced down the hall to the office where Noah continued his search.

Robert burst in on Noah giving the younger man a start. "Turn off the lamp!" he commanded in a desperate whisper.

Noah complied instantly. Simultaneously the door at the end of the hall slammed again and footsteps sounded beyond the office door. Robert crouched by the door watching the shadows pass by the window. Noah stood frozen in the darkness, afraid even to breathe. Another door shut and Robert collapsed to a sitting position against the wall.

Noah stared at him wide-eyed. The expression on Robert's face increased the younger man's sense of panic despite the fact that they were now, apparently, safe and undetected.

"Bobby?" Noah waited for an answer. "Damn it! Bobby, what's the deal," he continued in an instinctive whisper.

Robert looked up at Noah, his own face a mask of confusion. "I think Kozlovsky's just been murdered."

"Wha . . . ?" Noah jerked a hand to his mouth, almost knocking over the desk lamp.

"We've got to get out of here."

Noah recovered quickly. "You must be imagining things."

"I heard the shots."

"What shots? I didn't hear anything."

"They were silenced."

"Silenced?"

"Yes, damn it, silenced! You know . . . a silencer?" He pulled himself up from the floor shakily.

"I don't believe you." Noah rushed to his side. "How do you know what a silencer sounds like?"

"I know." Robert looked at the boy hard, knowing.

Noah frowned up at him. Before Robert could stop him, Noah pushed past him and threw open the office door. Robert reached after him, but Noah was already halfway down the hall.

"Noah!"

Noah looked back at him, determined, and raised a hand to rap lightly on Kozlovsky's door. No answer. Robert headed down the hall after him, but too late. Noah swung open the door to Kozlovsky's workroom and stepped inside. Robert reached Noah's side, but not before he had digested the scene.

Kozlovsky, or what appeared to be Kozlovsky, lay on his side by his work table. A flood of red spread out across his chest from a single, mangled black center. His head was upturned with another entrance wound on the forehead. The floor around his head was a morass of tissue, blood and bone fragments. The little finger of his right hand still twitched slightly as if signaling to the shocked observers.

"Oh, God!" was all Noah could manage.

"Come on." Robert physically dragged Noah out through the door and leaned him back against the wall. "Take a few deep breaths," he advised.

Noah took in a few shallow gasps. "Why?" He sputtered, gesturing weakly toward the workroom.

"I'm not sure." Robert held Noah's shoulders tightly until he was sure the boy would be all right. "Wait here. I want to check out a few things."

Noah leaned back against the wall without argument while Robert reentered the workroom.

Robert glanced about the cluttered table tops not quite sure what he was looking for. He stepped cautiously over the body, careful not to touch . . . or step in anything, and scanned the contents of the work bench. Tools and metallic shavings littered the surface. A large book lay open on the far end with another, smaller notebook lying on top of it.

Robert squeezed around the cramped space. He lifted the small notebook for a better view of the other. The large volume was of the coffee table kind, a photographic essay on various Fabergé collections. It was opened to a full-page, color photograph of one of the Imperial Easter Eggs. Robert glanced at the title. "The Abdication Egg."

He flipped through the smaller notebook which seemed to contain quick sketches and various exploded views of oval objects. "More damn eggs," he muttered to himself, trying to get back to the door without stepping on anything.

Noah was still propped up against the wall. He turned his head sharply upon Robert's approach, instantly relieved to see him. "Well?"

Robert shrugged. "Nothing much." He thrust the notebook at the gypsy boy. "What can you make of this?"

Noah forced the scene he had just witnessed from his mind. He grabbed for the notebook, his interest renewed. "Working sketches for assembling an egg," he said excitedly. "He *has* been making them." His eyebrows knit into a frown.

"What is it?" Robert asked.

"This sketch looks familiar." Noah studied the page from different angles. "This crest drawn in the center. I'd swear it's the seal of the Russian Imperial Family. That's odd."

"Why?" asked Robert, pulling Noah around so he could see the sketch.

"I'd almost swear that these were sketches of the Abdication Egg. It was the only one to present the Imperial Crest in this way."

"I found this notebook on a large color photo of the Abdication Egg," Robert said matter-of-fact.

"I'll be damned," Noah responded.

"Obviously Kozlovsky lied about not having any direct knowledge of the Abdication Egg. These would appear to be the actual working drawings."

"Not possible," Noah replied with a canny grin.

"What do you mean?"

"These sketches are recent. No way were these made seventy years ago." He held up the book. "Look how new the pages are. No yellowing. Nope," he said, shaking his head. "I think old Koz was working on a copy."

Robert puzzled over the notebook for a moment. "Well, we can debate all this later. We need to get out of here."

"Shouldn't we call the police or something?" Noah asked.

"Anonymously, and from somewhere else," Robert replied dragging the boy down the hall. "We're here illegally too, remember?"

"Oh God!" gasped Noah, beginning to outrun Robert.

Chapter 5

"God, that was exciting. What a trip!" Noah let out a whoop before collapsing back onto the overstuffed sofa.

"Make yourself at home," Robert said, giving Noah an exasperated look. "Try not to soil the furniture." He left the room but not before noting, with dismay, Noah's shoes propped up on the sofa arm.

Noah surveyed the room with a critical eye. The outside of the townhouse, crunched up between a row of others was not particularly eye-catching. Its four stories had been the most impressive feature. The interiors, however, were breath-taking. The fourteen foot ceiling gave the room a palatial feel and the hardwood floor was flawlessly polished. The antiques and their knick-knacks sprinkled expertly about the room were free of dust and the Persian throw rugs had every fringe in place.

The whole spectacle was quite a step apart from Noah's usual experience with the apartments of older men which were usually full of chrome, glass, and meaningless attempts at abstract expressionism. Robert's house was like a room in the Smithsonian. A stained glass lamp shade, framed in a window, looked astonishingly like a Tiffany original, and Noah jumped up from the sofa to inspect it more closely.

"Did you also pick up the china pieces and look for price tags?" Robert asked with a smirk, reentering the room.

"That's what I like about you Bobby," Noah admonished, satisfied that the piece was indeed authentic. "There's not a snobbish bone in your body."

Robert ignored him. "Making that call from a payphone was the only thing we did right. We can only hope we didn't leave anything behind to incriminate ourselves."

"Have you seen my bag?" Noah asked innocently.

"What?"

Noah thought the older man might faint. "Don't be such a prune," he said with a quick laugh. "I'm only teasing."

Robert released a long exasperated sigh. "I need a drink."

"I'd like one too," Noah said, watching with interest as Robert lifted the lid on a dark, walnut chest out of which rose a formidable collection of spirits.

"You sure you're old enough?"

"Oh, I'm old enough," Noah said suggestively.

Robert ignored him and checked through his collection.

"You drink all that stuff?" Noah asked in amazement, recalling his own meager supply of vodka augmented by a pint of Jamaican rum on holidays.

Robert poured a finger of single malt scotch. "How long do you plan on staying here? 'Cause I just might."

Noah waved away his sarcasm with a flick of the wrist and went to inventory the cabinet's selection. "Oooo! I want a little of this," he said with delight.

Robert watched the younger man extract an old, expensive cognac and reach for a tumbler. "No, no, no, no, no!" he said grabbing it from Noah. "Not in that." He pulled a small snifter from the chest. "If you're going to drink my best cognac, at least do it right."

"You're so knowledgeable, Bobby," Noah said with a saccharine smile. "Later maybe you'll show me your collection of beer cans." He accepted the snifter noting its miserly portion. "Sure you can spare this much?"

Robert merely sniffed at him and took a hefty swig from his own drink.

"I have to say this house is quite a treasure trove, Bobby. I'm going to have to speak to Madelyn about a raise. If not that, then you're gonna have to let me in on a few of the drug deals."

"Oh, ha!" Robert said. "I'll have you know this house has been in my family for generations. It was left to me by my mother."

"I'd hate to be the one to pay the electric bills," Noah said, eyeing the high ceilings.

"There's a small trust for upkeep but it takes everything I make to keep it going."

"I can imagine. How about a tour?"

"Later. Let's settle on what to tell Madelyn in the morning . . . this morning," he said, noting the clock on the mantle.

"Okay . . . now . . . what have we got?" Noah asked, warmed by the cognac. "Kozlovsky's dead. Murdered. He was working on a copy of the Abdication Egg. The men who murdered him came to pick up something and pay him for it. You said one of the men referred to him as the Tsar's jeweler. The real Abdication Egg has been stolen. I'd say we have a connection."

"Oh, come on, Noah. That's too big a leap."

"What else could it be, I ask you? There's a definite connection. Damn. I knew there was a story here."

"Don't go off half-cocked again. Before we write any stories we need little more than this guesswork."

"Let's have a look at that notebook again." Noah headed for the coffee table where he had left it. Before he could set his drink down on the wax shine of the inlaid table, Robert had slipped a coaster napkin down ahead of him. Noah gave him a sarcastic nod of thanks. He thumbed through the notebook carefully, studying the drawings, looking for some clue. "These are all exteriors of the egg," he said. "There doesn't seem to be anything about the surprise it was to hold."

"What was the original Abdication Egg supposed to contain?" Robert asked with a yawn.

"I'm not sure," Noah answered, puzzled. "I'll have to look that up."

A folded piece of paper slipped from the notebook's pages to the floor.

"Now what have we here?" Noah reached for it. He opened it carefully and held it to the side for Robert to see. "Greek to me."

"Russian," Robert commented thoughtfully.

"Of course. What is this design at the bottom, I wonder?" Noah pulled the slip of paper closer for a better view. "The Imperial Seal of the Royal House of Russia." He thrust the paper back at Robert. "Look. Those runes below the seal would be the name of the particular Royal using the seal. That doesn't make sense. There aren't any more true Russian Royals around to write notes . . . only expatriate. If only you could speak Russian."

"I can."

"What?"

"Well, I can't really speak it well but I can read it a little."

Noah smiled sheepishly. "I think we'd better have your security clearance rechecked."

"Very funny."

"What does it say?"

"As best I can make out it's a thank you note. Very simply stated and then this signature."

"The name, what's the name?" Noah implored.

"Nicholai. Yes, I would say that was Nicholai. Familiar?"

Noah's brow furrowed. He shook his head. "None of the surviving Romanovs have that name. This doesn't make sense."

"As I recall, the last Tsar was a Nicholai," Robert pointed out.

"Yes, but of course, the entire Imperial Family was assassinated during the Russian Revolution, and even if they weren't, they'd all be dead ... or well over a hundred. It's impossible. None of the surviving family ever uses Nicholai for their children since the man was declared a saint or something."

"What about that lady in Texas," Robert said with some amusement. "You know. The one who claimed to be the Grand Duchess Anastasia."

"Nothing was ever proven, though," Noah replied more thoughtful than amused. "It was never disproved either." He sipped at his cognac.

"Now don't go off on another tangent," Robert warned.

Noah smiled. "It does add an interesting slant though, doesn't it?"

"Now don't get started."

"No, really, it does. Imagine if the royal children actually survived the assassination." Noah grew more excited. "What if the entire assassination plot was a complete hoax?"

"Oh, good God." Robert headed back for the liquor cabinet. "If we're going to rewrite history why don't we also have the Titanic return from its ill-fated voyage to Boston Harbor tomorrow alive and well? Old as hell, but alive and well."

"I was just theorizing," Noah grumbled. "How can you have your level of education and no imagination?"

"There is a difference between informed creativity and lunacy."

"Yeah? Like what?"

"Can we stick to the subject of that damn egg, or perhaps even Kozlovsky's murder?" Robert poured another two fingers of scotch.

"I'm sleepy." Noah yawned.

Robert glared across the room at him. "I swear you're a manic depressive. One minute I can't shut you up, and the next you're ready to keel over asleep."

Noah kicked off his sneakers and stretched out on the sofa. "Wake me about five-ish, okay? I want to stop by my apartment to shower and change before time for work."

Robert could not believe his eyes. "You intend to sleep here tonight?"

"Well it seems awfully silly to try and get a taxi this late, don't you think?"

For a moment Robert couldn't answer. "Well, I . . ." he stuttered. "We wouldn't want the people at the office to get the wrong idea."

"The wrong ide . . ." Noah almost spilled the remainder of his drink. He sat up abruptly. "Really, Bobby. I think everyone here is over twenty-one." He pursed his lips. "Are you perhaps thinking that something might happen tonight to . . . compromise my reputation?"

"Don't be ridiculous," Robert stuttered. "Of course not."

"Oh."

"I just think we should consider office politics and gossip," Robert added quickly.

"Ah." Noah laughed teasingly. "You and Madelyn have something going then?"

Robert almost spit his drink. "Christ!" He wiped the dribble from his chin. "I'm going to bed."

"You are so uptight!" Noah said, setting the snifter down on the intricately carved coffee table.

"Not on the furniture!" Robert downed his scotch and snatched the offending glass and returned it to the liquor cabinet.

"It's a table, Bobby," Noah snickered.

"A table." Robert looked down at the boy. "Would you use a Monet as a dart board?"

"Oh, all right." Noah stood. "It must be difficult living in a museum. I hope there's at least one room in this house you can relax in."

"I do just fine, thank you," Robert said, backing up from the boy. "I just don't take my possessions for granted."

"This place must get very lonely." Noah moved closer. "I mean, you're not bad looking."

"Oh, thanks."

"I'm serious." Noah grabbed hold of Robert's coat lapels. "But you dress way older than you are. Just because you live with a bunch of antiques doesn't mean you have to dress like one."

"This is a Savile Row suit I had tailor-made," Robert protested. "I'll have you know—"

"Exactly," Noah said giving the lapels a jerk. "I thought it looked like something the Queen would wear on Sundays."

Robert tried not to laugh. "It's for work," he replied. "I happen to have a perfectly age and gender-appropriate wardrobe."

"Whatever." Noah looked up into Robert's eyes, shyly. "I'll bet you wear nothing but white, all-cotton boxers."

"What?"

"Dr. Taylor?"

"What are you on about now," Robert asked, trying to wrestle the boy's hands off his jacket.

"Come out, come out, wherever you are." Noah pressed up close to Robert. "Why are you afraid of me?"

"I am not afraid of you." Robert shook his head at the boy. "I'm a completely different generation from you. You play games. I don't."

"What's wrong with play?" Noah rested his forehead on Robert's chin. "I happen to like your generation."

"Life's too short for games," Robert said, pushing the boy away. "We need to get some rest." His face darkened strangely.

Noah looked at Robert, surprised. "What do you mean life's too..." His eyes opened wide. "You talk like someone who's . . . did you lose someone?"

Robert shook his head and stalked from the room to the stairwell. "You might be more comfortable in the guest room on the third floor," he called back to Noah sharply. "The fourth floor is off limits." He fled up the stairs.

Noah sat down on the sofa stunned and a little confused. After a moment, he grabbed up his shoes and, humming softly, padded across the floor into the foyer. He yawned, trying to decide which he wanted to do more, sleep or explore about the house—especially the fourth floor. Another yawn took hold and made up his mind for him.

He climbed the stairs lazily, letting his imagination go. He could easily picture himself living in such a house, breezing down the magnificent curved staircase, fitted Armani tux, cashmere overcoat. The owner of the house wasn't too bad either. Older—what's age got to do with anything—but not at all open. He sighed softly, pausing a moment on the first landing to admire a signed Bonnard hanging elegantly in its gilded frame. He glanced back to imagine himself being swept out the leaded glass entryway to a waiting limousine. Quite a leap indeed for someone from his background.

Startled, Noah dropped his shoes. The face staring up at him a few steps below smiled menacingly through a slit in the black cowl. A moment of panic froze Noah on the landing, giving the black clad figure time to leap the remaining steps to him. Recovering, Noah struck out with his foot, catching the intruder in the shin. The man grunted in surprise and went down on one knee but not before grabbing both Noah's legs in a vise-like grip and hoisting the slender boy up and over his shoulder. Noah cried out, digging his fists into the man's sides. The hulking man turned and toted Noah down the stairs like a sack of potatoes seemingly unconcerned with his screams and pummeling. Another man appeared in the foyer and signaled to the other to carry the struggling package back into the study. Noah grabbed at the door sills frantically, but the man managed to pull him on through and tossed him roughly onto the sofa.

"Robert!" Noah yelled at the top of his lungs. "Let go of me you son-of-a—"

The man clamped a hand over Noah's mouth and produced an angry looking stiletto which he flashed meaningfully in front of the frightened young man's eyes. Noah went limp, almost paralyzed with fear. His eyes darted to the door where the other man was standing off to the side, a heavy black pistol with silencer pointed at the open doorway.

"Noah!"

Noah could hear Robert stumbling quickly down the stairs. He burst into the study, trying to keep his bath robe tied about him. "What the hell's . . ." He stopped short, aware of the pistol aimed at the side of his head. He looked over at Noah, trying to interpret the bobbing of the boy's eyebrows over his saucer-wide eyes.

The man with the gun motioned Robert over to the sofa. The one with the knife released his hold on Noah and stepped back, retracting the blade into its handle.

Noah sat up slowly. He grabbed hold of Robert's arms. "What took you so long?" he asked weakly, trying for a smile.

"Silence!" commanded the man with the gun.

"Who the hell are you? What do you want?" Robert threw a protective arm around Noah and pulled him closer. "If it's money you're not going to find much."

"There's a pretty good painting at the top of the stairs. Why don't you take that." Noah said, trying to be helpful.

Robert's jaw dropped and he gave his young house guest a withering look. Noah merely shrugged his shoulders helplessly.

"You will both be quiet," the man with the gun said. He pulled a chair over in front of them.

The man with the knife eased around the sofa behind them. The one with the gun made himself comfortable, resting the pistol on his knee, still pointed at Noah and Robert.

"We are not thieves," the man with the gun said with a chilling smile amplified by the surrounding black cloth. "We wish merely to ask a few questions. You will only be . . . hurt . . . if you fail to be cooperative." He paused a moment, looking about the room admiringly.

"Ask your questions and go," Robert growled. He slipped his hand into the pocket of his robe. "What is this about?"

"We'll ask the questions, Dr. Tate."

"Who are you?" Robert demanded. His hand tightened about the cold steel in his pocket.

The man only smiled. "A . . . colleague of ours, Vasily Kozlovsky," he paused, watching their faces, "Was murdered tonight."

Noah and Robert looked at each other.

"You were the ones." Robert returned the man's cold stare.

"I beg your pardon, Dr. Tate?" The man with the gun sat forward.

"You killed Kozlovsky." Robert tightened his grip on the small pistol nestled in his robe pocket.

"Don't be absurd, Doctor. On the contrary, you and this young man were seen leaving Bartley's tonight. Kozlovsky was found dead shortly after *your* departure."

"You didn't kill him?" Noah found his voice.

The man smirked, sitting back in the chair. "The question, Mr. Taylor, is, did you and your friend? And why?"

"This is ridiculous," Robert protested. "Of course we didn't kill him."

"What were you doing in Bartley's so late then, Dr. Tate?"

Noah spoke quickly. "We're reporters. We were merely checking a few facts for a story we've been working on."

"A story?" The man seemed amused. "And how did you gain entrance to the store?"

Robert squeezed Noah's shoulder. "The back door was open," he lied. "We went in to see if anyone was there. Kozlovsky was dead."

"Really, Dr. Tate." The man raised his gun ominously. "Let's be honest here, Doctor. You broke into the store, quite expertly I might add. You were watched, Doctor."

"Is that so?" Robert shot back, growing angry. "While your spies were watching us did they fail to see the others who came in through the front?"

The man's eyes narrowed.

"There were at least two, one with an eastern European accent, the other British, though not completely." Robert looked at the man contemptuously. "Those are your murderers."

The man thought a moment. "Then, Dr. Tate, how is it that you and your young . . . friend were not also murdered?"

Robert shut his eyes at the innuendo. "For Christ's sake! We hid of course. As you've already pointed out, we were on the premises illegally."

"Describe these men."

"I didn't see them. I only heard a little of their conversation with Kozlovsky."

"What did you hear?"

"I was too far away—something about a payment. Then they shot him."

The man studied the two of them, evaluating. "You've been most helpful, Dr. Tate." He stood. "And so now we must say goodbye." He tightened the silencer on his weapon.

"You said we wouldn't be harmed if we cooperated," Noah cried, pressing closer to Robert.

"I'm afraid this is necessary, young man. We were alerted the moment you began asking questions. Your . . . little investigation must stop here."

Robert fired blindly through the pocket of his robe before the man could level his own pistol. The small bullet struck hard into the biceps of the man's shooting arm. He grunted loudly dropping the heavy pistol to the floor and grabbing for his arm. The man behind dove over the sofa grappling with Robert for the small gun in his pocket.

"Get the other gun!" Robert cried out to Noah.

Noah threw himself onto the floor and grabbed the gun in front of him before the wounded man could react. He scooted across the polished floor to a safe distance and then tried to aim the heavy pistol. "Everybody freeze!" he commanded with much more confidence than he felt. The gun wobbled precariously in his hands. "I'll shoot!" He pulled the trigger with some difficulty and the gun spat several rounds automatically, aiming itself at points about the room.

No bullet found a human resting place but a large Wedgewood platter displayed on a table by the window splintered into dust as one of the high-powered missiles found it dead center.

"Come!" shouted the wounded man to the other.

The other man broke free from Robert and headed out the door with his wounded accomplice. Robert struggled to pull his own small pistol from his pocket, but the two men had fled out the front door into the night.

"Damn!" shouted Robert.

"They're gone," Noah sputtered, still aiming the shaking pistol.

Robert rushed to the table by the window and knelt beside the shattered platter. "Damn it to hell!" He picked at the broken pieces. "This was a Fairyland Lustre plate—almost a hundred years old." He looked like he might cry.

"What about me?" Noah moaned.

"You can't be more than twenty-five," he shot back, cradling the larger pieces in his hands.

Noah willed himself not to pull the trigger again.

Chapter 6

Marya held the heavy padded purse like a new born baby. She watched the countryside fly past through the window beside her. Marya hated trains. But there had been no immediate way to slip the object through airport metal detectors. She would have preferred even to drive a car, but that was too individual—too exposed. Not to mention that most automobiles were being stopped and searched. Things would be easier once she had cleared the bloc of small countries in which the Russians still held some influence.

She patted the bag reassuringly, feeling the hard, rounded object within. She marveled at its significance, wondering what made it so important that so many had been asked to endanger themselves to secure its freedom. Marya tilted her chin up to the window, reveling in the pride she felt at having been trusted with this task.

Those sitting about her in the crowded compartment took only a summary notice of the shapely, dark-haired creature poised by the window. No one spoke to anyone else. That was the way of things. It would be a long time before the old habits of distrust were overcome. Everyone nursed their totes and parcels of what was still considered contraband—necessary items purchased from former black marketeers who still managed a thriving business in the continuing shortages. It was still the way of life. New officials replaced old officials with the same empty promises. And nothing else changed.

A rippling shudder rode the length of the train, unsettling Marya in her seat. She glanced out the window aware of the train's slowing. Familiar landmarks signaled the western Czech border and her heart beat a little faster in anticipation. It wouldn't be long now.

The train had almost come to a stop and people had begun to get out of their seats and mill about the compartment, gathering their belongings and preparing to disembark. Marya remained in her corner by the window, aloof from the rising commotion. She went over in her mind again what she was supposed to do. The man who was to meet her was unfamiliar and she strained to recall every detail of the photo she had been shown as well as the bits of behavioral idiosyncrasies she had been briefed to watch for.

Despite its slowing, the train jolted to a final stop, eliciting a patter of cliché insults from the various passengers about bureaucratic ineptitude and the failure of Socialism or the evil of the new capitalism. Marya rose from her seat and placed herself inconspicuously in the line of people filing out of the compartment. She reached into the pocket of her heavy woolen parka for her papers which someone was always on hand to inspect.

Marya stepped from the train, pausing a moment to get her bearings. A brisk north wind cut through the line of people prompting the tying of scarves and buttoning of coats. There would be another border check. Things had gone smoothly a few miles back at Cheb on the eastern Czechoslovakian border and she anticipated an even easier time at Shirnding Check Point just fifty feet ahead. She was in the West now. The risk of being challenged was considerably diminished.

Marya moved along in the line maintaining her facade of the bored, experienced traveler. The tension in her gut had slackened some since the train had breached one of the many gaping holes now torn in the once impenetrable Iron Curtain. She could feel the full weight of the object in her bag and shifted its weight from arm to arm during the long trek from train to check point.

At last the older couple ahead of her was passed through with their load of bundles. Marya, shouldering her bag, moved up to the stern-faced guard and presented her papers. He stood silently in the small window studying her papers, looking from picture to her and back again. Marya opened her coat revealing a well-proportioned figure exploding from a beige, silk blouse and smiled at him with timid coyness. The guard's eyebrows rose conveying a baser meaning, and he returned her smile cockily along with her papers.

MOary took them and strolled away from the checkpoint, aware that he was leaning slightly out the window to better appreciate her retreat. She threw him another shy look and smile, then shifted her heavy bag from shoulder to hand and hurried out onto the street. Her task now was to find Dieter, her contact. He would drive her the rest of the way of her journey. She gazed through the crowd of milling people looking for possible candidates.

"*Fräulein?*"

Marya turned to the gravelly, tenor voice. The man was shorter than she, thick and stocky, wearing a worn suit. What little hair he had was graying, and the fingertips of the hand he raised in greeting were stained yellow with nicotine.

"*Da?*" Marya answered flatly in Russian.

He switched immediately to English. "You had a long trip?" He seemed amused by the necessary coded exchange.

"No," Marya replied in kind, "my trip was short."

"You have brought much with you?"

"Only what was necessary."

They sized each other up for a moment.

"You are Dieter?" Marya asked, showing her impatience.

"*Ja.* And you would be the lovely Marya. Such a beautiful name."

Marya smiled coldly. "You have the car?"

"*Ja*, not far from here." Dieter reached to take Marya's bag but she pulled away sharply. He shrugged his shoulders, turned, and headed down the street.

Marya stood for a moment, annoyed by the man's abruptness. Shouldering her bag again, she followed after him, managing the cobble stones with some difficulty in her heels. She chided herself at not having worn more comfortable shoes. They turned down several more streets and the bag was growing heavier and heavier.

"How much farther?" Marya called out, feeling a blister beginning on her heel.

Dieter motioned mutely for her to come along and turned down into a narrow side street. Marya followed as quickly as her shoes would allow. She wondered if the bag was making a permanent indentation in her shoulder. At the entry to the side street, Marya slowed. Windowless buildings rose on both sides giving the impression of a long tunnel. The small hairs on her neck rose with a sudden wave of apprehension.

Dieter strolled quickly to a small Volkswagen parked at the side. He opened the driver's door and waved to Marya, displaying his near-toothless grin. Marya sped up her pace, dismissing her previous doubts for claustrophobia. She rubbed her cold-numbed fingers and rushed for the protection of the automobile from the resurgent wind. Dieter stood holding his door, nodding his head, and motioning her in.

Marya circled the small car and reached for the passenger door. She carried a pistol in her coat pocket but she wasn't quick enough. A figure sat up in the back seat of the automobile the moment she opened the door, firing a shot at her point blank. Marya was thrown back against the building. The impact against the brick wall hurt more than the sharp sting she felt in her upper chest. It didn't last long. A creeping numbness took the strength from her legs and she collapsed down the wall onto the damp street and into unconsciousness.

The other man crawled from the car and knelt beside the body. He tore the bag from her shoulder and rifled through it savagely, searching. "*Ist hier!*" he cried out excitedly. He took the bag and stood to face Dieter, his gun raised.

Dieter merely grinned his toothless grin, showing his own weapon pointed directly at the man's chest.

The other man smiled, shrugged, and lowered his weapon. "*Das Geld?*" He nodded toward the car.

"*Bitte*," Dieter replied evenly.

The man returned to the car and opened the trunk. He pulled out a black valise and offered it silently to Dieter. Dieter accepted the case and threw it on the roof of the car for a look inside. He kept his gun aimed casually at the other man while he flipped the latch on the valise and raised the lid. So much money. Dieter swallowed hard. He had done the right thing, for himself anyway, no matter what. He looked back at the other man who stood shifting his weight impatiently in the cold.

"*Danke, Herr Schloss,*" Dieter said jovially, pulling down the case and stepping back from the car. "*Auf wiedersehen.*"

Schloss took the bag and climbed into the car behind the wheel. He revved the engine slightly before pulling out onto the main street. "*Schmutzig russisch,*" Schloss muttered loud enough for Dieter to hear as he pulled away.

Dieter suppressed a laugh. Filthy Russian, indeed! He hummed softly to himself as he strolled in the opposite direction. Schloss was a fool in more ways than one, Dieter thought, glancing back at the woman's body and the spreading pool of blood. He patted the valise. The money was his now. He would give Schloss' name to The Family later and make up a nice story. He would have the money and The Family would still have what they wanted. Everyone would be happy—except for Schloss. Dieter laughed joyously unable to contain it any longer.

Chapter 7

"Dammit, Madelyn. It was a family heirloom. It has been in my family since it was made almost hundred and years ago."

"Yes, Robert, but thirty-seven hundred dollars."

"That's the appraised value. It was destroyed as a direct result of this . . . inquiry you insisted that I be a part of." He leaned across the desk poking at his expense voucher. "It is a legitimate expense claim."

"Oh, Bobby," said Noah, standing over in a corner a safe distance away. "Don't make such a big deal. Just put in a claim on your homeowner's insurance. You know . . . a robbery attempt and all that."

Robert turned on Noah who moved back farther into the corner. "I don't have insurance," Robert said, glaring. "I can't afford insurance. Before I met you I didn't need insurance."

"All right, Robert. All right, calm down," said Madelyn. "I'll submit your voucher. I'll make no promises but I'll submit it."

Robert sat down in the chair facing Madelyn's desk. "And I want *off* this assignment."

"Whoa!" Noah intervened, coming out of his corner. "Things are just beginning to break on this story. You can't quit now."

"Nowhere in my job description does it say I have to be assaulted and shot at. I want out of this."

"Now, Robert, you're overreacting," Madelyn said.

"Under-achieving if you ask me," Noah muttered.

"No one did," Robert retorted. He turned to Madelyn. "Does he have to be here?"

Madelyn sat back in her chair with a sigh. "Noah, dear, why don't you run down a little more research on all this while I talk to Robert? Use whatever resources you need—carte blanche."

Noah stood for a moment, hands on hips, staring at the two of them. "All right. I'll go." He leaned over and spoke into Robert's ear. "Chicken!"

Robert took a deep breath, repressing the urge to pull the boy across his knee. "Go away," he said firmly.

With a smirk, Noah left the office for his own.

"Now, Robert . . ." Madelyn began.

"I don't want to hear it, Madelyn," Robert said, interrupting. "I want off this assignment. I'm a historical researcher, not an investigative reporter."

Madelyn smiled. "Robert, around here what's the difference? We are all required to wear several hats. The important thing is to get the story. You and Noah are the ones on top of this news. You are the ones who should follow it through."

"He is not professional . . ."

"What do you know about Noah?" Madelyn's voice had an edge Robert was not familiar with. "You think I employ incompetent people here? Noah Taylor has almost as much education as you have. Not everyone had the resources at their disposal to play student as long as you did. That young man pulled himself up and out of deep-south dirt and made something of himself. Despite a hick family that disowned him. He worked, went to school, snagged this job, and is still paying off student loans. You think working hard is earning enough to keep up that million dollar albatross you call home."

"I finished my education as a grown man," Robert insisted. "And I did it without my family's help."

"But certainly with a little help from the government, right?" Madelyn sat back. "Noah is an expert in his field just as much as you are in yours."

"Madelyn, he's just a kid!"

"He is not a kid!" Madelyn tapped her gleaming nails on her walnut desk. "He's a man. A younger man." A strange smile crossed her face. "I'm trying to find out which one of those bothers you more."

"What's that supposed to mean?" Robert didn't like the way things were going. "What are you implying?"

"Don't be so sensitive, Robert dear." Madelyn voice was syrupy. "Noah is young and needs some seasoning, but he's ambitious, passionate," she smiled that strange smile again, "and willing to learn. You can teach him the ropes."

"What ropes? Dammit Madelyn!" Robert could feel himself loosing. "We can't work together. He drives me . . ."

"Crazy! Yes, I can see that, Robert. But you're the one who wants to quit!" Madelyn sighed. "He's sticking with it."

Robert felt stung. "That's neither here nor there, Madelyn, and you know it. I was hired as a historical researcher. That's what I do best and it's what I want to do."

Madelyn pulled a file from her desk and flipped it open in front of her. "Your resume is more extensive than that, Robert. And you were hired on the basis of your over-all experience, not just on that one facet."

Robert sat forward sharply. "What do you mean?"

"I mean you were Special Forces in the Gulf War, served a stint with the CIA . . . ."

"As a research specialist." He didn't like the turn of the conversation one bit. "A desk jockey."

"That's not what my sources tell me," Madelyn responded with a raised eyebrow.

"Your sources?" Robert jumped up from his chair. "What the hell's going on here, Madelyn?"

"Now don't start ranting again, Robert." She was clicking her nails together, which Robert found particularly unnerving. He began to pace.

"Madelyn, I just want off this assignment." He tried to sound more reasonable. "I'm not good at this sort of thing. Assign someone with more experience in this. I'm sure Noah would get along much better . . ."

"But you are good at this sort of thing, Robert," Madelyn countered. "Don't be so modest."

He looked at her, hard. She knew something. "Let's cut the crap, Madelyn. What's the deal?"

Madelyn sat forward and studied the file before her with a self-satisfied grunt. "I know more about your background than you think, Robert. That's why I hired you. I thought your inside knowledge and contacts would be particularly useful in the research you do here. You have other talents too, which I never thought I'd ever have use for. But, here we are. I want this story and Noah is right. There is a major story to be had. I want you to get it for me. Like I said . . . carte blanche, anything you need. And, if we break this story, there'll be a corporate vice-presidency waiting for me."

Robert dropped back into his chair. "What do you mean, inside contacts? What do you know, Madelyn?"

She smiled. "You weren't a desk jockey, dear. You were a field agent. One of the Company's golden boys. As I understand it, you worked most of Western Europe for several years, doing all those nasty little things the CIA always denies."

"Who told you these lies?" He protested, standing again.

"Park it, Robert." She stood up angrily. "They're not lies and you know it."

He sat back down, taken by surprise.

"I have quite a few Washington contacts, Doctor. I had a dossier on you faxed to this office within an hour of having read your application." She slipped on her reading glasses and glanced over the file. "It was a limited dossier, I admit, but sufficient information to hint at your ... value as a potential employee of this corporation. I don't know why you resigned the Agency, Doctor. The file says it was for personal reasons. But unless you plan to resign your employment here you will continue on this assignment and get me this story."

Robert sat silently looking at her, feeling trapped. "So . . . I have no choice."

"None."

"You'll have my resignation in the next ten minutes." He stood to leave.

"Oh, Robert, sit back down. Jesus Christ! Why are you such a stick in the mud sometimes?" Madelyn's attitude softened with chameleon-like ease. "Now, what's the problem? Really, why won't you do this?"

Robert stood with his back to her. "Madelyn, sticking my nose in where it doesn't belong is a part of my life I have left far behind." He turned to face her. "You can't even begin to understand. Have you ever killed anyone before, Madelyn?" He pressed in on her. "Seen anyone killed? I mean, seen their brains blown out? Anyone you loved?" He tried to push back the plague of memories festering from their hiding places in his subconscious.

Madelyn shuddered. Robert's eyes suddenly held something that made her very uncomfortable.

"If you had even an inkling," Robert continued, "of what danger really felt like, you wouldn't sit there so smug and expect everyone to jump in on your command."

She tried to dismiss his words with a wave of her long finger nails. "Don't be so melodramatic, Robert. I'm asking you to investigate a news story, not overthrow a government."

"And what about Noah? Asking me to march in to this is one thing, but that kid's got no idea what this is all about. Are you going to accept responsibility for him?"

Madelyn looked at him hard. "Noah Taylor is an adult. He knows the subject you're investigating. He's certainly old enough to make his own decisions and accept the consequences."

Robert slammed his hands down on the desk in exasperation.

"Robert, let's be realistic," Madelyn continued. "You need this job. What's more, you can do this job. I have every confidence that you can look after Noah." Madelyn took her seat again. "I want this story, Robert. I need this story. I gave you a job when you needed it, Robert. I don't think this is asking too much."

Robert shook his head. "Throwing out this little guilt ploy is beneath you, Madelyn."

"I need this story, Robert."

"I'll have to think about it."

"That's fine. Take a little time on it. See what Noah has dug up and get back to me."

Robert left her office without another word. Madelyn watched him leave, clicking her nails together thoughtfully. She smiled to herself. She had him. She felt sure of that. But something was bothering her . . . something Robert had said. She closed her eyes and shook it off. The story was the important thing.

Noah bounced excitedly. "Bobby, you won't believe the luck." He looked up from the floor as Robert came into the cubicle. "God, you look awful. Well, no worry. You'll feel better after you hear this."

Robert pulled a chair in from outside the cubicle and sat down heavily. "All right. What have you got?"

"Well, we're dealing with a stolen art object, right?"

"Right."

"So, I phoned up a few fences I know."

"Fences!"

"Yeah, dude, fences," Noah said with his most self-possessed look. "You know. Those people who buy stolen goods from thieves at wholesale."

"I know what a damn fence is," Robert said, annoyed. "I'm just surprised you know any."

It was Noah's turn to be annoyed. "This is my field, Bob, old boy. I know fences on every continent."

"Do tell."

Noah broke into a smile. "As I was saying, I phoned a few fences I know to see if there have been any rumblings in the Russian antiquities market."

Robert shook his head in amazement. "I have to admit to being impressed."

Noah brightened. "Well, it seems that several of the bigger and, I might add, more nefarious collectors have been making inquiries about a collection of icons being offered for sale by a dealer in New Orleans."

"So?"

"The collection's appraised value is eleven million dollars."

Robert let out a whistle. "That's a lot of icons."

"No joke."

"So, what's this got to do with our problem?"

Noah smirked. "There aren't enough icons in the State of Louisiana to fetch eleven million dollars, and this collection consists of only three."

"I see." Robert rubbed his chin thoughtfully. "And what do you think could fetch such a price?"

"One thing I can think of offhand," Noah said. "A singular and rare, the last one made, stolen Fabergé Imperial Easter Egg."

They sat looking at each other.

"I thought such a thing would be difficult to sell," Robert said finally.

"We underestimated the greed of the private collector," Noah responded.

"There is still no connection with Kozlovsky."

"I know," Noah said, frowning. "But these events are too closely tied to be dismissed as coincidence. I'm sure they are connected in some way."

Robert sat silently, weighing his options. "It's been a long time since I've been to New Orleans."

Noah jumped up from the floor. "New Orleans. Oh, how wonderful! I love New Orleans."

"You've been?"

"No."

Robert laughed. "Madelyn will never agree."

"She said we'd have carte blanche," Noah reminded him.

"Madelyn said a lot of things."

"Oh, Robert, we can do this," Noah pleaded. "This is so exciting. If we get this story we can write our own ticket out of this dump."

"If that means finally being left alone, I'm almost convinced. By the way," Robert said with sudden realization. "You called me Robert."

"Oh, I'm sorry, Bobby," Noah said with a wave of his hand.

"No, I—"

"I've got to pack!"

"You don't understand. I want you to—"

"Oh, damn! I hope my luggage is still good."

"You're not listening to me, Noah. My name—"

"Be a dear, Bobby," Noah said, grabbing for his messenger bag, "and clear all this with Madelyn. We haven't much time. I've so much to do."

"But—"

"I'll phone later."

"Noah!"

Noah blew out of the office in a cloud of flying paper, leaving Robert still sitting. He sat back with a sigh. "Never mind."

Chapter 8

A wet, lazy breeze lumbered off the Mississippi River, spreading its torrid moisture over the sweltering crowd milling through Jackson Square. Noah stretched like a waking cat from his perch over the Toulouse Street Wharf, basking in the humidity and hot sun. He had forgotten what the sultry Gulf climate felt like. He turned at the sound of rustling paper to find Robert scaling the steps up to him, carrying a small white sack of beignets and another of coffee.

Robert wiped the sweat from his brow with the back of his hand. "Damn this place!" he muttered, breathless. "Damn this heat! Damn this humidity!"

Noah laughed. "Don't be such a carpetbagger," he admonished. "Isn't this just absolutely romantic?" He swept his arms from the spires of St. Louis Cathedral out to the muddy river beyond.

"If you like being kissed by a mosquito," Robert said, dropping the sack to take a swat at the back of his neck.

Noah took the coffee from him and sat at one of the benches lining the river promenade. "I'm surprised you don't have an ulcer by now. Can't you even pretend to enjoy anything?"

"Enjoy?" Robert asked, suppressing a yawn. "I hate long plane rides. And then, after we finally got here, I'm kept up half the night by one drunken street brawl after another."

"They weren't street brawls. They were just people having fun. For crying out loud! This is the French Quarter. You know, Bourbon Street and all that." Noah took a sip of coffee. "It's an exciting place, full of interesting people all having a good time. Apparently, you resent people having a good time."

"Here we go again." Robert sat down beside the boy. "Just because I didn't want to go out bar hopping with you at midnight last night does not mean I don't like to have a good time. I was tired."

"I said nothing about bar hopping," Noah protested. "I just thought, maybe, it would be fun to go to a jazz club or two. You know, soak up a little of the atmosphere New Orleans is famous for. God! You'd think I'd asked you to go roll hookers in the park."

Robert watched in annoyance as powdered sugar from his puffed, hole-less donut sprinkled down on his navy trousers. "Just remember we're here on business, Noah. Let's try and keep expenses down a little. I'm already out a small fortune because of this little treasure hunt."

"Oh, God! Not that damn plate, again?"

"It was a priceless family heirloom."

Noah let loose with an loud and exasperated yell. Embarrassed, Robert looked about. It was too late to pretend he didn't know the boy.

Noah noted his discomfort with satisfaction. "I don't want to hear about this anymore," he said. "Not one more word. Every time you mention that stupid plate I'm going to scream. I don't care where we are or what we're doing. I'll scream bloody murder!"

"All right, all right," Robert said in a whisper. "Jesus! Finish your coffee."

Noah sat quietly for a moment, trying to recapture his mood. "How far is the auction house from the hotel?"

Robert chewed the last of his beignet and brushed at the sugar on his pants in vain. "A block or two." He looked at his watch. "It should be opening up before long."

"What's our cover?"

"Our what?"

"Our cover. You know. Maybe you could be a fabulously wealthy collector or maybe I should be the scion of a family fortune out to sell the family jewels . . ."

"Oh, for heaven's sake, Noah. This is the real world, not a romance novel."

"How else will we get inside and uncover anything?"

"We're with a major news organization, Noah," Robert said with a sigh. "We heard about the icons and we're there to ask a few questions, both about the icons and the Abdication Egg."

Noah looked aghast. "Just like that? Right out in the open?"

"It would seem reasonable."

"That's pretty naive, Bobby. They're not going to tell us anything."

"Probably not," Robert said. "But at least we will have stirred the water. The secret to questioning people, oh young one, is to catch them off guard. Study their reactions. People give themselves away with more than just statements of fact."

Noah thought on this for a moment. "Well, maybe, but still . . ."

"It beats wasting time keeping up some ridiculous cover that can be shot to hell with one phone call."

"Okay, we'll do it your way," Noah said, brightening. "Let's go to work."

"Finally." Robert deposited the sacks and Styrofoam cups in a nearby receptacle. "Let's see if we can find a taxi."

"Don't be silly," Noah said taking his arm. "The hotel's just a block from the Cathedral and the auction house no more than another block. It's such a beautiful day. Let's walk." He tugged Robert down the steps to the square.

"It's too damn hot," Robert complained, pulling at his tie.

"I can't believe you don't own a short-sleeved shirt. And that tie! People aren't that dressy here. Especially in the heat of the day. Loosen up, Bobby."

"I don't criticize the way you dress," Robert said, his brow furrowing at his companion's choice of hip-hugging, skin-tight jeans, sneakers, lilac linen, band-collared, also skin-tight shirt. "So don't complain about mine."

"What's wrong with the way I'm dressed?"

Robert ignored him and hurried around the side of the Cathedral to St. Ann Street, hoping the buildings surrounding the narrow street would provide some shade from the sweltering sun. Robert tried to keep up a fast pace but the heat seemed to drain his energy.

They turned onto Royal Street and Robert had to pause a moment to catch his breath. He daubed the sweat from his face with a tissue pulled by Noah like a rabbit out of a hat, out of his ever-present messenger bag. The four blocks they walked seemed a mile to him, and even longer as he had to keep backtracking to retrieve Noah from the various boutiques that lined the streets on the way.

"Don't you just love this place?" Noah said, attaching the two *fleur de lis* earrings he had just purchased onto the pocket of his shirt. "The architecture, everything is so continental. It's like being in another country."

"I'd hate to have to pay the electric bill for an air conditioner around here," Robert complained as they approached the auction house.

"Dude, you are such a romantic at heart aren't you?"

"There's the auction house," Robert said, ignoring the boy again.

Before they could get across the street, Noah grabbed at his arm. "Bobby, I forgot!"

Robert turned to him testily. "What now?"

"What about identification?" He asked in a panic. "We don't have a press card or anything?"

"My private investigator's license is registered in the company name," Robert answered, continuing across the street. "That ought to be sufficiently impressive."

Noah giggled with excitement. "That's right. I forgot that too." He caught up to Robert. "That should really shake them up."

They entered the auction house through a pair of vaulting French doors and found themselves in a modestly appointed reception area.

"Doesn't look like a place one would auction off baseball cards much less a multi-million dollar icon collection," Robert whispered to Noah as they approached the reception desk.

"It has atmosphere," was Noah's response.

Robert sniffed disapprovingly. "That's for sure."

"May I help you?" asked the receptionist. She was an older, black woman, slim, with grey and white streaks through once jet-black hair. Her wrists were wrapped in a myriad host of silver bracelets and about her neck hung a primitive necklace of unpolished jade and amber.

Robert stepped forward. "Yes, my name is Dr. Robert Tate and this," he gestured to Noah, "is my assistant, Noah Taylor. We're with the McNaughton News Corporation out of Boston." He gave her his card. He didn't like to use the title doctor, but it held a certain force in situations like this. "We would like to see the Russian icon collection you're preparing to auction."

"That is impossible," said the woman in a striking Creole accent, folding her hands over the desk. "The collection is for not for public viewing."

Robert smiled. "Then perhaps we could talk to the house manager."

The woman's eyes narrowed at his breach of her authority. She pushed up from the desk and darted through the door behind her without a word, taking his card.

Noah looked up at him. "Assistant?"

"Don't quibble."

"Yes, sir!" Noah sneered at him.

"Fine," said Robert with a sigh. "You want to be in charge? I'll step back and you can deal with the voodoo priestess."

Noah giggled and glanced back into the door to be sure they were not overheard. "Why is it that people who have jobs working directly with the public are always the last ones who should?"

Robert merely smirked.

"I'll bet you lunch," continued Noah, "that the manager refuses to see us."

"You're on," said Robert. "He'll see us. Merchants never wittingly offend the press, especially international wire services. Besides, he'll probably be thinking more about all the free publicity his store might reap by cooperating."

"Perhaps," said Noah. He smiled thoughtfully. "But a man selling stolen art objects for millions of dollars might also be thinking that publicity is the last thing he needs."

Robert nodded. "You may have a point. We'll know in a moment at any rate."

The tight-lipped receptionist emerged from the door followed by a portly gentleman in an ill-fitting polyester suit and a well-oiled Elvis hairstyle. The man looked up from the card and smiled broadly. He held out his hand to Robert.

"Dr. Tate. A pleasure." He shook Robert's hand vigorously. "I'm Leldon Arceneaux, manager of this auction house."

"Mr. Arceneaux," Robert acknowledged.

"And who is this handsome young man?" Arceneaux asked, beaming at Noah.

"Noah Taylor," Noah responded, extending his hand. "I'm Dr. Tate's . . . assistant." He batted his eye-lashes at Robert.

"A pleasure to meet both of you," said Arceneaux. "It's not often we have such distinguished visitors from the press as our guests. What can I help you with?"

"We're interested in the collection of Russian icons you're putting up for auction," Robert said.

"Russian icons?"

"Yes. We're doing a series on the theft of one of the Fabergé Imperial Easter Eggs from the Kremlin." Robert studied the man's face. "Perhaps you've heard of it?"

Arceneaux nodded. "Yes, of course. Read about it in the papers. I can't imagine why people do such things."

"Usually for money," Noah interjected.

"Yes, son," Arceneaux said solicitously. "But such a venture is so risky. And such a well-known object is almost impossible to sell."

"At any rate," Robert said, "we wondered if we could see your icon collection. Since they are also valuable Russian art objects we are considering a story on them as a sidebar to the theft of the Abdication Egg."

"I see, I see," Arceneaux said. "Regrettably, I must refuse your request. Understand that this is a private auction of a private collection. I have a responsibility to protect the interests of my clients who, in this case, not only wish to remain anonymous but also wish to keep the value of their sales and purchases a confidence as well."

"Perhaps one of your clients would grant us an interview," Robert said, "provided, of course, that they be allowed to remain anonymous to our readers." He smiled reassuringly. "We would be interested in a collector's perspective on this theft."

"No, no. I could not allow it." Arceneaux shook his head firmly. "I'm sorry. I wish I could be more help to you."

"No problem, sir," Robert said. "Tell me, Mr. Arceneaux, exactly how would the thieves go about unloading such a priceless work of art?"

Arceneaux's eyebrows shot up. "I really would have no idea Dr. Tate. The police would be more help to you there."

"Yes, well, thank you for your time, Mr. Arceneaux."

"It's been a pleasure, Dr. Tate. Mr. Taylor."

"One more thing, Mr. Arceneaux," Noah said, shaking the man's hand. "Our sources inform us that the starting bid for this icon collection is somewhere around . . . eleven million dollars?"

Arceneaux blanched. "I cannot discuss such matters."

"Still, wouldn't you consider such an asking price to be highly inflated?" Noah persisted. "Especially considering that there are only three icons in the collection."

Arceneaux handed Robert's card back to him. "Sorry I cannot be of more help," he said, completely ignoring Noah's question. He turned to leave. "I hope you enjoy your stay in New Orleans." He disappeared through the door at the back.

Noah and Robert retreated back out the French doors to the street under the watchful glare of the receptionist.

"Well, that was really informative," Noah quipped.

"He's certainly hiding something," Robert said. "What, I don't know."

"What do we do now?"

"Go back to the hotel."

"Oh, not just yet. I'm hungry."

"Hungry!" Robert couldn't believe his ears. "We just ate breakfast."

"Big deal," Noah said, "a square donut and coffee. What a breakfast!"

Robert sighed.

"We'll find a nice quiet place to eat and plan our break-in," Noah continued, "and then go back to the hotel for a nap."

"Whoa!" Robert said, spinning Noah around to face him. "What do you mean, plan our break-in?"

"We've got to see what's in that auction house," Noah responded, matter-of-fact. "We'll go in tonight and have a look around."

"You are a damn space cadet," Robert said, almost shouting. "We can't keep resorting to breaking-and-entering to get this story."

"We're just going to look around."

"Tell it to the judge!" Robert paced around Noah in the street. "We are going back to the hotel and then back to Boston."

"No way!" Noah hit him in the shoulder with his fist. "We're not going anywhere until we get to the bottom of this. Besides, I have every confidence you'll get us in and out unnoticed."

"The hell I will!"

"Let's talk about it while we eat," Noah pleaded, starting down the street. "I want to eat crawfish, gumbo, étouffee . . . for some reason, I'm in the mood for anything authentically Creole."

"Creole cuisine? At this hour?"

"Well," said Noah casting a glance back over his shoulder. "We can go back to the hotel it you want . . . I do have other appetites."

"Creole it is," Robert responded, pushing his young companion down the sidewalk. "But it better not be far."

Noah smiled triumphantly. "I know just the place. We passed it on the way. There were troughs of fried shrimp and every size bottle of Tabasco sauce!" He grabbed Robert's arm and pulled him along.

"Dear God!" Robert could feel the fire rising in his throat and started after the boy, holding his stomach.

Chapter 9

Sundown in the French Quarter is an open invitation to revel. The streets are cordoned off to allow only pedestrian traffic and all the streets congeal into one giant nightclub. The air vibrates with the combined force of each club's jazz or Dixieland band and spirits of every kind pour freely through the narrow lanes where every corner hosts its own independent street performer.

Noah and Robert wove their way through the hundreds of revelers who danced, chatted, drank, whooped, hollered, peed in the gutter, and otherwise enjoyed themselves. The two seemed an unlikely pair—Robert, the reserved Bostonian, walking erect with an even stride, and Noah, dancing through the streets beside Robert, balancing a drink like one of the natives.

"Loosen up, Bobby dude," Noah sang, clapping his hands to the music around them.

"Loosen up, he says," Robert shouted above the din to no one in particular. He dodged around a small group trying to form a conga line. "I'm on my way to commit yet another first degree felony and he wants to loosen up." He shook his head at Noah. "I can't believe I let you talk me into this."

"Oh, don't be such a worry wart," Noah said, laughing and dancing. "You obviously know what you're doing when it comes to breaking and entering."

"Spare me the compliments."

"How are we going to get in? These buildings are all attached. There aren't any nice secluded alleys to work in."

Robert shrugged his shoulders. "There's always the back door."

"And where is that? These buildings are attached, at the sides and the back."

Robert studied the outside of the auction house. "Do you see a fire escape or anything?" he asked.

"Maybe we could go through the roof," Noah suggested.

"Don't be ridiculous."

"You asked for ideas and I gave you one," Noah said.

"I was looking for something more useful." Robert walked around to peek in a small café next to the auction house.

Noah put his nose up to the glass in the large French doors and tried to see anything in the darkness beyond. He reached down automatically and gave the door knob a turn. The door gave way easily. He shut it back immediately, looking around to see if anyone had noticed. "Bobby," he called out, stepping away from the door. There was no answer.

Noah zigzagged his way through the crowd to the small café and ducked inside just in time to avoid the crush as people jumped out of the street to make way for a horse-drawn buckboard, listing with intoxicated revelers. He stood for a moment in the doorway and watched the drunken procession go by. A hand grabbed his shoulder.

"Shit!" Noah said, spinning around, wide-eyed and mouth agape.

"It's just me," Robert assured the startled boy. Noah started to speak but he interrupted. "We might as well forget about this. It looks like the front door is the only way in or out."

"Then let's go in the front door," Noah said cockily.

Robert brushed by him to the café door. "You're a lot of help."

"No, I'm serious, you don't . . ."

Robert glared back at him. "Jimmying the front door lock in this crowd of onlookers is a sure-fire way to end up in a Louisiana jail."

"Listen to me, the—"

"I'm tired. I'm going back to the hotel."

Noah all but tackled him before he got to the door. "The front door is already open." He shook Robert. "Listen to me! It's already unlocked. I tried it. The door is open."

Robert gave Noah a funny look as if refusing to understand or take him seriously. The look Noah gave him back helped to change his mind. "Are you serious?"

Noah threw up his hands. "I'm going to scream!"

"All right, all right! I believe you." He grabbed Noah by the arm and pulled him out the door. "Come on or we'll be all night."

They pushed through the crowd back to the front of the auction house. For a moment they simply stood in front of the door with their backs to it. Feeling rather sure that no one was paying particular attention to them, Robert reached behind to the doorknob and opened it.

"Let's go!" He slid through the door pulling Noah with him. He shut the door quickly and engaged the dead-bolt just in case.

"That was easy," Noah said squinting his eyes in the darkness. "Where's the light switch?"

Robert caught the boy's hand before he could turn on the lights. "Are you crazy? No lights. At least not until we get to the back. There are too many windows here."

"Okay, but you'll have to lead the way. My night vision is not very good."

Robert took Noah by the hand. "Door's over here."

They inched along aided by the dim light from the streetlights outside, glowing through the small square panes of the French doors. The door from the reception area back into the auction house was also unlocked. Robert led Noah into the large, warehouse room beyond and flipped on the lights after shutting the door. They stood surveying the room and its contents. At the center rear of the room a small platform had been erected upon which a podium with microphone was attached. Folding chairs had been set out in rows in front of the platform. Surrounding this, stacked up along the walls, were various items of antique furniture, paintings, and knick-knacks.

"Mostly looks like a bunch of junk to me." Noah stepped over to examine a hodge-podge of disassembled furniture. "Nothing of any real value."

"There are some paintings over here." Robert knelt for a closer look.

Noah could tell their worth even before a close inspection. "Unexciting, run-of-the-mill, turn-of-the-century, sofa art," he commented dryly. "Most of this stuff would be better displayed in an upper middle-class garage sale."

"Hardly a fitting repose for a multi-million dollar collection of so-called Imperial Russian icons, is it?" Robert commented.

"Perhaps there is another room, or better yet, maybe the owner has a warehouse somewhere." Noah said.

"I doubt it. We're probably at a dead end here." Robert ran a hand through his hair. "I'll be willing to bet our Mr. Arceneaux is merely fronting for someone else."

"The West German lead."

"Most likely. I seriously doubt the real merchandise is even here in the States."

Noah's brow knit. "I can't imagine that a serious collector would even consider bidding as high as eleven million dollars on merchandise they haven't seen."

"Yes, true. Unless, of course, the collector is already very familiar with the object in question."

"The Abdication Egg," Noah said with a self-satisfied smile.

"Possibly, but we can't be for certain at this point," Robert answered.

"What next?"

Robert thought a moment. He glanced at a small staircase to the rear of the large open space which led up to a small room with large picture frame windows, perched like a tree-house, overlooking the auction area. "I think we should have a look at the office."

Noah thought of the last office search they had made. "I hope we have better luck with this one than we did with the last."

They picked their way through the chairs to the staircase and made their way up its steep angle to the small office.

Robert tried the door. "Locked," he said in disgust, giving the door knob a shake.

"So, pick it," Noah said.

"Oh, just like that."

"You did it before."

"This is a different kind of lock." Robert gave the handle another shake. "You can't jimmy a dead-bolt with a credit card."

Noah leaned back against the wall, tapping his foot on the stairs. "Now what?"

"Give me a minute!" Robert ran his hands over the door. "I could use a screwdriver and a hammer."

"Oh, sure, got 'em right here in my bag," Noah retorted.

"Don't be cute. See what you can find."

Noah climbed back down the stairs and rummaged about in the stacks of merchandise. "There are no tools around," he called up. "I found a large, rather rusty nail, but that's about it."

"Bring it. I think I can make it work."

"What are you going to do?"

"I can do it in the time it takes to tell you about it. Hurry!"

Noah pulled himself back up the stairs and thrust the nail at Robert, panting. "Take it before I stick it somewhere else," he said with a peculiar glint in his eyes.

Robert ignored him. "Give me your shoe."

"Why?"

"I want to use it as a hammer."

"Use your own damn shoe."

"These are expensive, Italian—"

"You're not getting my shoe." Noah backed down a few steps.

Robert sighed. "All right, all right." He slipped off his shoe and looked at the leather soles with a forlorn expression. "If I ruin this shoe . . ."

"Just hammer and get on with it. What are you gonna do."

"Most inside doors are set with the hinges on the side of the door that pulls away from the jam. Exterior doors are made just the reverse for more security. If I can knock the pins out of these hinges we'll be able to lift the door out."

Noah clapped his hands together. "Ingenious. I love it!"

"Don't get too excited until we see if I can do it."

Robert braced the nail up against the top hinge pin and hammered it hard with his shoe. The pin gave a little and he increased the angle of his strikes, slowly raising the pin from its tight mooring. When it was almost out, Robert switched to the bottom hinge. In no time he had both pins out and slipped them in his coat pocket. "Give me a hand," he said, slipping his shoe back on.

"What do I do?"

"You pull out from the bottom and I'll get the top."

"No sweat." Noah dropped to his knees and slipped his slender fingers under the door in the ventilation space.

Robert got a grip on the upper hinge. "Okay, now. Give it a good tug," he said, rising to his tip-toes for better leverage. "One . . . two . . . three!"

The door pulled out with unexpected speed. Noah's zealous tug whipped the bottom of the door up and into Robert's shins.

He fell backwards over Noah, pulling the door down with him. "Damn it to hell!" he managed to cry out on his way down.

Noah reached around and grabbed him about the left leg preventing him from catapulting down the stairs. The door flew over their heads and crashed in slow, comic ballet of somersaults down the stairs. The noise was deafening. Noah and Robert lay still at the top of the stairs—Noah holding on to Robert's leg, and Robert grasping the stair rail.

"Wow!" Noah managed.

"Well, I'm sure no one heard that," Robert said sarcastically. He pulled himself up, breaking away from Noah's death-grip.

"Don't worry," Noah assured him. "With all the noise outside we could set off a bomb and go unnoticed."

"The only thing I'm worried about is your killing me before someone else does."

"Ha, ha!"

Robert brushed off his coat and pants. "We'll have to get that back up here," he said, nodding down to the door which had landed up against a stack of boxes.

Noah laughed. "With our luck those boxes were probably full of crystal."

"Let's get a look in this office while I can still walk," said Robert, limping slightly through the open door.

"Are you hurt?"

"No, just a little stiff."

"I meant your leg, not your disposition."

Robert looked back at the boy and rolled his eyes. "Being your straight man is getting a little old."

Noah pushed in and embraced Robert from behind. "But you're so good at it, Bobby, old man. Besides, joking around keeps me from being nervous."

"All right. Let's cut the chatter and get to work." Robert broke free of Noah and flipped on the lights in the office.

It was a long, narrow room, lined with file cabinets and more stacks of cardboard boxes. Two desks were pushed up against the over-sized picture windows overlooking the auction area below.

"Same procedure as before," Robert said. "I'll take the file cabinets, you tackle the desks."

"Yes, boss," Noah responded.

Robert merely turned his back on the boy and grunted, pulling out the first file drawer. He heard Noah gasp behind him. "Find something?" he asked.

"Uh . . . Bobby . . ."

"Well?" Aggravated, Robert turned from his digging.

Noah stood frozen, hands clasped to his chest. A hand extended from under the desk pointing an ugly looking, black luger pistol at them. Its aim was steady.

"What the hell . . ." Robert managed, moving slowly up to Noah's side. "Who are you?"

He eyed the polished, manicured nails gripping the pistol and traced the feminine line of the arm to its owner crouching under the desk. The woman eased from her hiding place, keeping the pistol leveled at Noah and Robert.

Robert forgot the pistol when he saw her face, her flawless skin so pale it almost glowed in the soft, fluorescent lighting. Black hair, cut short in a French bob, perfectly framed her dark eyes. He admired the svelte line of her thin, model's body, standing tall, unafraid, and heavily armed before him.

Noah looked from one to the other. "What are we gonna do, stand here all night?"

"I will ask the questions," the woman said, sitting down on the desk top.

"Eastern European," Robert muttered to no one in particular. Noah's eyes widened.

The woman continued, "It is obvious you are both not employees here." She crossed her arms, waving the gun absentmindedly under her chin. "Thieves perhaps?"

"Look who's talking," Noah began.

"Quiet!" Robert snapped between clenched teeth. He relaxed his posture perceptibly and gave the woman a casual once-over. "I think it's obvious none of us have permission to be here. You're looking for something and so are we. I wonder if it might not be the same thing."

"Perhaps," the woman said with a slight smile. "Who do you work for?"

"McNaughton News Corporation," Robert answered.

She raised an eyebrow.

"I have identification."

She shrugged permission for him to take out his wallet. "Slowly," she warned.

He reached carefully into his inside coat pocket and extracted his wallet. He flipped it open to the laminated P.I. license and held it out for her inspection.

"Private Investigator?" she said, nodding. "Interesting, Mr . . . Tate?"

"Dr. Tate," Noah corrected her cattily.

The woman merely raised an eyebrow and returned Robert's casual once-over.

"Now, how about telling us who you are," Noah demanded.

"The side of the gun I am on does not require me to answer your questions," the woman said.

Robert stepped forward. "This is ridiculous. It's reasonable to assume we're all looking for the same thing. May we assume you to be FSB?"

The woman laughed with uninhibited enjoyment. "FSB! That is a good joke." Her eyes flashed with amusement. "No, you may not assume I am FSB." She stood up from the desk and walked up to Robert, still maintaining a cautious distance with the pistol. "I represent a . . . private interest."

"Might we assume then, a private collector of Imperial Russian art?" Robert asked.

"Perhaps."

Robert decided to play his hand. "If you work for a collector who is interested in bidding on merchandise here, I don't understand the need for breaking and entering. Just attend the auction." He watched her face. "Unless, of course, this collector was not invited to attend this auction. Perhaps your employer is not a collector of Russian icons at all."

The woman smiled and shrugged her shoulders. "What do you think he collects then?"

"Fabergé Easter Eggs?"

The woman's eyes flashed and her smile disappeared for a split second, enough time for Robert to get his answer. He turned to Noah. "You were right about this place all along. Congratulations."

Noah raised an eyebrow. "Thank you for remembering I'm still alive."

Robert looked at the boy puzzled for a moment before returning his attention to the dark woman. "May I propose a sharing of information for our mutual benefit? You want the egg, we merely want the story."

The woman lowered the gun to her side and paced away from them. She stood looking out the window over the auction room. "So, you know about the egg."

Robert nodded. "We know some. More than we know about you."

The woman laughed. "I am Marya Dmitrievna."

"Russian?" Robert sounded not surprised.

"Actually I was born in Copenhagen."

"Your accent isn't Danish."

"Neither is my family."

"Immigrants?"

"Exiles. We are a close-knit community within Sweden and Denmark. Our elders felt it important to preserve our language and culture."

"The collector you represent is also a White Russian exile?"

"Yes." Marya nodded at Robert's grasp of the historical context. "A distant relative." She turned back to Robert and Noah, gun still in hand. "That is all I will tell you about myself and the one I represent."

"It isn't that important anyway," Robert assured her. "What brought you here?"

"I traced the egg from its German source."

"German? West German?"

"Yes. I had hoped that perhaps the egg had been transported out of Europe to here."

"We were obviously all wrong on that point," Noah said. "Arceneaux is just a middleman in this sell."

"That would appear to be the case," Marya agreed.

"About this West German connection," Robert pressed.

Marya raised a hand. "Please Dr. Tate. If all we're going to do is talk, let's take it someplace else. We're taking an awful risk for conversation."

"Yes, you're right. Where are you staying?"

"With friends of my family."

"Shall we meet at our hotel?"

"No," Marya shook her head. "You are being watched."

"Watched!" Noah jumped between them. "What do you mean, watched?"

"The senior couple, a heavy-set man and woman," Robert said calmly.

"Yes." Marya raised an eyebrow as if surprised by his perceptiveness. "FSB."

"FSB." Robert cocked his head to one side. "Not SVR?"

"FSB!" Noah was beside himself. "Would someone please tell me what the hell you're talking about? What FSB?"

"Federal Security Service," Robert replied. "Of the Russian Federation. They replaced part of the KGB."

"And SVR?" Noah asked.

"Foreign Intelligence Service," Robert stated flatly. "The other part of the former KGB."

"You interest me, Dr. Tate," Marya said moving close to him. "Why would FSB be interested in you?"

Noah stomped his foot. "Damn it to hell!"

"We were . . . unwitting witnesses to a murder," Robert said.

"Really?"

"Vasily Kozlovsky."

Marya's eyebrow went up again. "We do need to talk, Dr. Tate."

"When and where?"

Marya started for the door. "Let us say tomorrow at two . . . at the Museum of Art."

"The Museum of Art."

"Yes." She motioned to the door lying at the foot of the stairs. "You need any help?"

"We'll manage."

She disappeared through the door and down the stairs.

"Damn it, Robert!" Noah slugged him on the side of the arm.

"Ow! What was that for?"

"You know damn well! Why didn't you tell me about the goddamn VGB!"

"FSB," Robert responded, retreating for the door. "Come on. I'll explain later. Let's hurry and get this mess cleaned up."

Noah stood stubbornly fuming at him. "All right. But when we leave here you're taking me someplace to get something to eat."

"At this hour?"

"Yes! And you're going to explain this mess if it takes all night."

Robert moaned and started down the stairs.

"And I want Cajun food tonight!" Noah called after him, "crawfish and Tabasco!"

Robert fumbled in his pockets for his roll of antacid.

Chapter 10

"But we haven't even had breakfast yet," Noah complained. He slammed the car door shut.

Robert yawned. "There was no time to stop if we were going to lose those two agents who were tailing us. Besides, you ate at two o'clock this morning. You ate fried crawfish at 2 o'clock this morning." He smacked his lips, trying to dissipate the hours-old taste that continued to defy his mouthwash. "You kept me up for another two hours griping. Now, I don't want to hear anymore about it."

Noah started up the sidewalk leaving Robert dragging behind. "If you'd bother to eat a good meal on occasion you'd have a little more energy. Food is fuel—fuel for the mind, fuel for the body, my daddy always said."

"Obviously your father didn't have red pepper, flavored with crawfish, at two o'clock in the morning."

Noah chuckled. "I hope you weren't too uncomfortable, what with my falling asleep like that . . . you know . . . in bed with you."

"What goes on in your head?" Robert signed. "I've slept in the same bed with other men before."

"Do tell!" Noah took Robert's arm. "Sounds hot!"

"It was in a theater of battle in Afghanistan," Robert said quickly—a little too quickly perhaps.

"You were in Afghanistan?" Noah looked up at him. "During the war?"

"Yes."

"I didn't know you were in the service," Noah said. "Was it horrible?"

Robert rolled his eyes upward, smiling at the clouds overhead. "Well, probably not as dangerous as one of your rave's on Fire Island, but it had its moments."

Noah ignored him and took in a deep breath. "Oh, smell those roses. What a beautiful park."

Robert merely grunted behind him.

Noah waved his arms at the impressive building they were climbing the walk towards. "This makes me feel just like I'm on an Old South plantation. Did you notice all the Spanish moss hanging from the oak trees? I can't wait to get inside. They have a fabulous collection of early American paintings. One of the best—Oh . . . my . . . God! Are those gardenias?" He leapt off the sidewalk to the flower bed beyond. "These are wonderful, Bobby. Come and smell them. This is so perfect. Now if we could only find a magnolia tree in bloom. Do you think they'd mind if I picked one?" He looked back at Robert excitedly. "Bobby, are you listening to me?"

Robert paused in his climb up the walk and sagged, sighing with his most long-suffering look. "I have to have at least twelve hours uninterrupted sleep before I can deal effectively with you."

Noah climbed out of the flower bed with his gardenia and huffed past Robert up the walkway. "My, we do miss our cup of coffee in the morning at your age, don't we?"

Robert sneered and grunted again, climbing up the steps to the museum door.

"Here, let me get the door for you," Noah said, pushing open the heavy door. "I wouldn't want you to tax yourself further."

"Let's not quarrel anymore, please," Robert said. He moved past the boy into the cool of the museum. "Air conditioning. Thank God!"

"I'll bet you had all those beautiful Afghan boys fanning you at night."

Robert considered how easy it would be to hide the gypsy boy's body in the swamps and bayous about the city. "We have a meeting here. It's important. Let me do the talking," he said in a tired monotone.

"Do you really think that woman is going to show up?" Noah asked, taking a guide book from the reception desk.

"You mean, Marya?"

"You remembered. How sweet."

"What are you talking about?"

"Where do we find her?"

Robert tried to shake the sleep from his mind. "You are exhausting." He looked around the vaulting, marbled room. "We're on time. We'll wait here for a . . ." He noticed the receptionist looking strangely at him and realized that Noah had disappeared. "Great, now I'm talking to myself." The receptionist smiled at him nervously. Robert merely shrugged.

Noah came racing out of one of the exhibit rooms. "Dude, they have the most exquisite primitive murals over here. You have to come have a look."

Robert's expression brought Noah to a stop. "Can you manage, just for once, to focus your attention in one direction, at least for this morning? We have work to do. Art appreciation will have to come second."

Noah looked at him wounded. "That's not fair. I was just having a look around while we wait for that . . . that woman." His eyes grew fiery. "Where is she?"

"I don't know." Robert rubbed his eyes. "Let's think. Why would she want us to meet her here? Why the Museum of Art?"

"That's simple enough," Noah said with more confidence than he was feeling, "the Fabergé collection."

"Here?"

"Yes, remember? I told you they have a current exhibit of part of the Forbes Collection that was repatriated to Russia. It includes a few eggs on display."

"Find that collection," Robert said indicating the guide book.

Noah skimmed over the book's contents. "Here it is. Second floor. Come on."

"Don't they have an elevator?" Robert eyed the cascading grand staircase Noah was heading for.

"Wimp!" Noah called over his shoulder with a laugh as he vaulted the stairs, two at a time. "You could use a little gym time."

Robert psyched himself for the climb and started after the young fire brand. They circled the mezzanine level, reading the names and notices on the various doorways leading off into the exhibit rooms.

"That must be it down there," Noah said, pointing to the far corner.

The room was comparatively small with built-in displays, like jewelry store windows, lining the four walls. In the center, circled by the narrow walkway, were several block pedestals supporting three-tiered glass cases.

The display cases glowed, reflecting the spotlights aimed at them.

Robert could make out Marya's tall, dark and slender form in the doorway where she stood motionless, transfixed behind one of the pedestal cases. She wore dark, pleated slacks and an emerald green, silk blouse that accentuated the white of her skin plunging in a "v" from the neck to a well-placed button at the cleavage-line. There was no one else within the room.

"Ms. Dmitrievna," Robert said softly, entering the room.

Marya smiled up at him from behind the case. "Dr. Tate." She motioned to him to join her. "I must call you Robert and you must call me Marya. It makes things much simpler."

"I agree completely," Noah said, pushing in between them. "And you must call me, Noah. There. First names and no guns. Isn't this cozy?"

Marya blinked at the boy and then walked back around to Robert's side. "What do you think of it, Robert?" she asked, nodding at the display case.

A blaze of precious stones embedded in gold flashed up at him from within the case. "It's beautiful," Robert said, admiring the small, pink-enameled, ruby-encrusted egg. "Is it from the Imperial House?"

Marya smiled and shrugged. "It belonged to a member of my family. They sold it to the museum back in the fifties."

"What a shame to part with something so exquisite," Noah whispered, enthralled by the object.

"Money was tight," Marya said evenly. "Survival was more important than heirlooms."

Robert inclined his head at Noah, motioning him to the other side of the room. Noah glared back at him but moved over to the wall display cases without argument.

"You were going to tell us about this West German connection," Robert said, returning his full attention to Marya.

"Was I?" Marya smiled up at him.

"Yes," Robert replied. "And I believe you were interested in a certain Vasily Kozlovsky?"

Marya circled the case, studying it. "What do you know of Kozlovsky?"

"What do you know about the West German dealer?"

"You first," Marya said. Her eyes smiled up at Robert from under long, dark lashes.

Robert followed her around the case. "You knew, of course, that he was murdered?"

"I do now."

"Did you also know that he was still in the business of creating these things?" He pointed to the egg in the case.

Marya only shrugged. "Who killed him?"

"I don't know. I didn't see them, but I recognized a British accent from one of the men and another was definitely east European, possibly Russian."

"FSB."

"Why do you say that? What interest would they have with Kozlovsky?"

"Trust me, Robert."

"Tell me something that will give me reason to."

"In due time. Let's finish with this."

"Very well," Robert conceded. "It appears that Kozlovsky had performed some sort of service for them. I heard one of the men referring to payment having been made."

Marya stood silently, studying the object in the case.

Robert said, "If you don't have any more questions then, how about mine?"

"The West German dealer?"

"If you don't mind?"

Marya smiled up at him. "I know that there is one, but I do not know his name or location."

Robert looked annoyed. "You said you traced the egg from a West German dealer to here."

"That was not entirely true."

"Oh, thanks!"

"But Robert," Marya said, placing her hand lightly on his shoulder, "I could not trust you before."

"And now?"

She smiled and stroked his cheek with her index finger. "Now is different." She moved closer.

"You must have some sort of lead." Robert backed away slightly.

"You are shy." Marya laughed soft and throaty. "I like that." She stepped in on him again.

Robert sighed with exasperation. "The dealer, Marya. What about the dealer?"

"Ah, him." She rubbed her shoulder gingerly and turned back to the display case. "I will find him." Her features darkened ominously. "I know someone who knows him." Her eyes narrowed into bright slits reflecting the white light from the case.

"Give me something better than that to go on, Marya. This isn't a very fair exchange."

"Let's have a bite to eat." She hooked her arm through Robert's. "There's a small café downstairs."

Noah appeared beside them. "Did I hear someone mention food?"

"Yes, dear Noah, you must join us." Marya grabbed Noah's arm and hooked it through Robert's in place of her own. "You two go ahead and get us a table. I'll just be a moment."

"How long's a moment?" Robert asked, suspicious.

"Robert, trust me." She winked coyly at him. "I would just like to be alone with these beautiful treasures again. They make me feel my heritage so much stronger. Please?"

"Come on, Bobby," Noah said, pulling at his arm. "We can finish our talk over a little lunch."

"All right, all right!" Robert turned back to Marya. "We'll wait for you downstairs."

Marya waved them off and returned to the display case.

"So? What's the scoop?" Noah asked, batting his own long eyelashes at Robert mockingly as they descended the stairs.

"What's that supposed to mean?"

"Don't give me this dumb jock routine," Noah snapped, giving him a little push down a step.

Robert caught his balance easily and looked back at the boy with questioning annoyance. "You go without eating for more than four hours and you really do have fits, don't you?"

"All right, all right, we'll play the game if you like." Noah caught up to him. "Did you at least get some information while that woman was drooling all over you?"

"I don't know what you mean, and no. She didn't have that much information to give."

"God, Bobby! I hope you didn't buy that line."

"At least she gets my name right."

"Oh! You would, perhaps, prefer a Russian accent," Noah said in a mocking cartoon voice.

Robert threw up his hands. "Give me a break!"

"What, in God's green earth, did she tell you?"

"She has a lead of some sort to the German dealer. We'll see what she has to say over lunch." Robert paced about the lobby looking for a sign giving directions to the café.

"Can't we go on in and find a table?" asked Noah.

"No. Not just yet. I want to watch for her here."

"Oh, then you don't trust her."

"It's not wise to trust anyone more than you have to."

"Thank you, Socrates." Noah headed for one of the exhibit rooms. "Well, if you're gonna stand there and wait I'm going in to have a look at some of the other exhibits."

"Can't you wait till later?"

"Oh, all right!" Noah moped over to the window by the front door and slumped into a chair in front of it. He stared out the window at the sloping, circular drive and gardens beyond, trying to regain his cheerful mood while Robert paced at the bottom of the stairs. A dark figure raced across Noah's view toward a white, Japanese-import sedan parked along the drive.

"Bobby!" Noah called out, startled.

Robert turned to him quickly as Noah's voice echoed across the marble room. "Shhhh!" he shot back. He gave the receptionist an apologetic look on his way by the desk. "What are you hollering about?" he asked Noah.

"She's out there!"

"What?"

"That woman. She's getting in that car!" Noah bounced in the chair pointing out the window.

Robert squinted through the glass in time to see Marya's dark hair disappear into the automobile.

"Goddamn it!" He dove for the exit door and yanked it open. The car was already speeding down the long drive. "Come on!" he called after Noah.

The whole building suddenly shook with the clamor of an alarm going off. "You there!" a security guard shouted, racing down the stairway behind them. "Stop!"

Noah and Robert froze at the door.

"Is there a problem, Officer?" Robert asked the panting guard.

"I'm sorry, sir!" the guard answered. "You'll have to remain in the museum. No one will be allowed to leave."

"What! Why?"

"There's been a robbery, sir. Will you come this way please?" He took Noah's arm. "You too, sir."

"A robbery?" Noah piped. "Oh, my god! When? What was stolen?"

The guard escorted them over to an office off the lobby. "We'd just like to ask a few questions, sir," he said. One of the museum curators appeared at the door.

"How long will this take, Officer?" Robert asked with undisguised annoyance. "We have an important meeting to make."

"We have to wait for the police to arrive, sir," the curator said politely. "This is a very unfortunate business for everyone."

"Sir, I need to have a look at your purse," the security guard said.

"My purse?" Noah's voice rose. "It's not a purse, you ass, it's a messenger bag."

"Yes, sir. Please."

Noah handed the bag over to the guard. "You still haven't told us what was stolen."

The guard rummaged through the bag.

Robert turned to the curator and flashed his identification. "Can you please tell us what was stolen?"

The curator studied Robert's identification with surprise. "One of the eggs from the Fabergé collection upstairs," he said.

Noah gulped audibly. "An egg?"

The curator nodded. "Thankfully, it wasn't one of the best pieces in the lot. Our thief wasn't very bright."

Robert cursed softly to himself.

Chapter 11

Noah burst into the hotel room in a flurry of arms and legs.

Robert looked up from the bed where he had been punching data into his cell phone for five minutes, looking for a cheap flight. "Well?" he asked watching Noah tear off layers of clothing.

"You're right! It is god-awful hot and humid down here," Noah said, kicking off his shoes and working to unbuckle his belt.

"What are you doing?" Robert lowered his cell phone.

"I'm gonna take a shower."

"We haven't time!"

"I'm making time," Noah said not bothering to hide his annoyance. "He tossed his pants onto the bed.

"Is there a reason you're not taking a shower in your own room?" asked Robert.

"Oh, excuse me," Noah responded. "But the shower head in my room is busted. It only gets a trickle. You know what that's like."

"What's that supposed to mean?" Robert stretched back onto a pillow.

Noah shot him a snarling grin. "Nothing." He stripped off his boxers and stood hands on hips, facing Robert. "Just making conversation. Oh, yeah, I forgot. You don't do that." He spun around and padded across the carpet to the bathroom.

Robert watched him. The boy was undeniably beautiful . . . perfectly proportioned and, while not muscular, was flat-stomached and lean. Robert caught himself staring at the boy's rounded buttocks. He shook himself and closed his eyes. The attraction was physical and Robert knew himself . . . knew that temptation was something he had long ago learned to overcome.

"Do you have any shampoo?" Noah called out from the shower.

Robert sighed and got off the bed. He stretched and looked about for his shaving kit, remembering that he had deposited it on the countertop in the bathroom. "It's by the sink," he called back.

"Can you get it for me?" Noah whined. "I'm kinda in the middle of something."

"Insufferable little . . ." Robert headed for the bathroom. Instead, he grabbed the travel-size shampoo left by the maid on the sink and shoved it through the shower curtain. "Here!"

"Thanks."

Robert thought he heard Noah chuckle. "Hurry up in there," he said. "I want a shower and some hot water too if you don't mind."

Noah's head popped through the shower curtain. "You said we didn't have time."

"I changed my mind."

"You are so full of shit!"

"And you look like a chia pet," Robert responded, nodding to the mound of lather over Noah's hair.

Noah pulled back into the shower. "Too bad. I never rush a shower."

"I'm serious," Robert said, "I want some hot water left for my shower."

"If you want hot water, you'd best hop on in, because I'm not getting out anytime soon!"

"Goddamn it!" Robert leaned back on the counter. He watched the silhouette of Noah gracefully dancing in the water behind the clear shower curtain. "That does it!" He stormed back into the bedroom, pulling off his own clothes. He paused in front of the dresser mirror to check out his own profile. He was still in shape, but . . . He frowned at the barest hint of a belly he hadn't noticed before. "Fuck it!" he muttered to himself.

He returned to the bathroom and stood for a second in front of the curtain. He could hear Noah humming. "You asked for it," he said pulling back the shower curtain. He stepped into the large tub and shower combo, and stood waiting for some sort of negative reaction from Noah.

Noah stood with his back to Robert, face up into the steaming spray of water. He busied himself rinsing his hair. "Don't know where the soap is," he said lightly. "Think I dropped it."

Robert smiled . . . *smart-ass kid*. He stepped in closer till he could feel the warmth radiating off the boy's body. Noah didn't budge. Robert reached out, lightly caressing Noah's shoulders and down the sides of his arms. It sent a shiver through both of them.

Noah leaned back into Robert. He turned slowly, tightening Robert's arms about his slim waist. "Well."

Noah looked down at Robert's rising hardness. "I guess someone's not as old and straight as I thought."

Robert glanced down at the object of Noah's attention. "Careful, kid." He reached up and took Noah's head in his hands. "I usually don't succumb to temptation . . . but when I do . . ." He pulled Noah's lips to his own.

Their tongues entwined, wrestling for supremacy, until Robert pulled away. He stared into Noah's eyes, and could see the boy's desire all but matched his own, and he enveloped Noah's smaller, lithe body in his arms. He ran his tongue down the side of Noah's neck.

"Careful, old man," Noah muttered hoarsely. "I *always* succumb to temptation."

Noah paused at the dresser mirror to adjust his cap. "I thought I'd never get that call to go through." He plopped down beside Robert who was still half dozing in the bed. "Madelyn was quite pleased I think. Wouldn't it be something if we got a by-line?"

Robert's eyes opened. "Just so long as you got her the story," he said with a yawn. "Maybe that will justify some of the expense we're charging up to the company."

"Did you finish your call?"

"I got through while you were out having your after-breakfast brunch," Robert said.

"Nothing yet, then?" Noah asked, ignoring him.

"Not yet. Did you get anything on our latest piece of stolen property?"

"You're not going to like it." Noah's eyebrows bobbed up and down.

"Why?"

"Because it's gonna open a whole new can of worms." Noah pulled his small notebook from his bag. "I know how you hate complications."

Robert rolled his eyes. "FSB, wealthy Russian exiles, murder, burglary, breaking and entering . . . I don't see how things can get more complicated."

Noah read from his notes. "This most recently stolen egg is undated but assumed to be of the Imperial period . . . Fabergé . . . sold at an auction to one of the Vanderbilts in the 1950s and then to the Forbes in 1966. It was supposedly a gift to the Tsar's daughter, the Grand Duchess Anastasia, but that is undocumented."

"Nothing unusual in any of this," Robert said. He sat up on the bed.

"Perhaps," Noah replied. "But let me go on." He flipped a few pages in his notebook. "In order to properly authenticate a acquisition, it is standard practice for a museum to trace ownership of a piece, as closely as possible, from creation to museum display. Although the piece is, without question, an original Fabergé creation, it remains undated as to when it was made."

"So?"

"When these pieces are made they are stamped by the head workmaster of the shop of the period with his signature seal."

Robert grunted that he was listening.

"Here is a photo of the egg in the guidebook along with a blowup of the signature seal."

Robert glanced at it wearily. It consisted of a small, square, rune-like cryptogram of Russian letters.

"The owner of this seal was unknown to the museum archivists and is the reason it could not be dated. However, I recognized it immediately."

"You're so clever." Robert said, unimpressed.

Noah smirked at him. "See for yourself." He lifted the medallion hanging on one of the silver chains about his neck and held its back up for Robert's inspection.

Robert studied it with disinterest until Noah held up the picture from the museum's guidebook. "What the . . ." He was interrupted by the phone. "Yes, I'm sorry, what did you say," he stuttered into the phone, staring at Noah in stark surprise. "Yes, I have it. You're sure?" He grabbed for Noah's pen and jotted a note on the back of the phone book. "Yes, thank you very much." He hung up and sat staring across the room.

"Fascinating, isn't it?" Noah said with airy self-satisfaction.

"Kozlovsky." Robert shook his head. "It couldn't have been him. He would have to be well over a hundred. It's not possible."

"It was his father. Kozlovsky just continued the tradition of using his father's seal," Noah said. "You may not know it, but you've hit on the most interesting aspect of the whole mess. We can't deny that the Kozlovsky angle is true. All the workmasters of the Imperial period are well known. While Kozlovsky's dad was a fabricator in the Fabergé shops, he was not recognized as associated with eggs."

"But I thought it was supposed to be a present from the Tsar to his daughter. They were all murdered during the revolution. How did the egg get out of Russia?"

"Murdered? Were they?" Noah asked.

"Oh, come on! Not that old hat again. Their deaths were too well documented."

"That's where you're wrong. There were no bodies found; only fragments of bone, clothing, and jewelry. That one or more of the family members might have escaped has always been a possibility."

"You've been watching too many movies."

"You think so?" Noah flipped a few more pages in his notebook. "Not only was there a gap in the dating of the egg in the museum's records but there was also no mention of the owner who originally sold the egg or even how they came to possess it."

"Okay."

"The agent who put the piece up for auction when the Vanderbilts bought it was a Mr. Jeffrey Hauser in Manhattan. I telephoned him at his office. He said he was not supposed to release the name of the person who sold him the egg as a condition of the sale. But that person was now deceased and so he guessed it would be okay."

"And the mystery person is?"

"A Mr. Alfred Gilroy of Houston, Texas."

Robert thought about the name but shook his head. "Means nothing to me."

"I felt the same way. But, just in case, I called Gillie back at the office and had him check the name in the computer on the off chance that it had come up in the news at some point."

"And?"

"Bingo! Mr. Gilroy was in quite a few news articles from the 1950s up until about twenty years ago."

"Still doesn't register."

"It wasn't really Mr. Gilroy, but his wife who was the subject of the articles."

"This is taking forever, Noah." Robert sighed. "Get on with it."

"Just listen." Noah referred back to his notes. "Mrs. Gilroy was originally Elly Edmundson."

Robert knitted his eyebrows. The name was familiar.

Noah watched his reaction. "Let me put that with another name for you. Anastasia."

The connection registered for Robert at last. "Now I remember. She was one of those Grand Duchess Anastasia wanna-be's. There was something about a lawsuit filed in the West German courts to establish her rights to certain bank funds."

"Yes, that was the reason for the suit on paper. Actually it was more to have her true identity recognized by a government and thus settle the issue. She died before it could be settled."

"That was almost fifty or more years ago, wasn't it?"

"Right."

Robert scratched his chin. "But I thought the deaths of the Tsar and his family were all settled with DNA testing or something of the sort."

"No, no." Noah shook his head. "Mrs. Gilroy was cremated long before there was anything like DNA testing."

"Is the husband still alive?"

"Alive and well. He was considerably younger than his wife. He still lives in the same house. A used bookseller or something like that, but now very old himself."

Robert sat on the bed thinking. "All right. I have a line on our so-called Marya Dmitrievna. A man at Customs and Immigration at the airport remembered a woman of her description boarding a flight to London. According to his list the name on her Norwegian passport was Olga Holsted."

"Norwegian?"

"Probably a false passport. Either way there's a Lufthansa flight out in an hour. I'm gonna be on it."

Noah looked disappointed. "What about me?"

"Get yourself on a flight to Houston, Texas as soon as possible."

"Oh, I see. You get to go to Europe and I get to go to Texas."

Robert rolled his eyes. "I know Europe and I know people there who can help. We'll keep in touch through the office. Find out as much about this egg and this woman as you can, then join me wherever I am."

"No problem," Noah said, sounding peeved. "After all I am just your assistant, remember?"

Robert sighed. "One other thing. Keep out of contact with our friendly neighborhood FSB."

Noah sat up, worried. "I forgot about them. What'll I do?"

"Make your plane reservations. Leave plenty early so you can drive around a while and lose them."

"Just like that?"

"You can do it. Just use your head." Robert jumped up and pulled his suitcase off the chair. "I'm already packed, so I'll be off. But first you have to provide me a little diversion."

Noah's eyes widened with excitement. "A fight in the bar? Scream and faint at the desk?"

"Nothing so dramatic," Robert said with a sigh. "Just keep the two Ruskies busy so I can sneak out unseen."

"Like, how?"

"Go for a walk, run down the street, anything like that. Just look like you're up to something very important."

"Now?"

"What's wrong with now?"

Noah shrugged. "Well. I thought . . . maybe . . . there'd be time for . . . "

Robert stood and took Noah in his arms. "Why is it guys your age only have one thing on their minds . . . all the time?"

"Because we can," Noah said, wrapping his arms about Robert's waist, "all the time!"

Robert leaned over and kissed the boy, a lingering kiss. Noah seemed to melt against him. "Whoa there, my little fashion porn star," Robert said, caressing Noah's cheek with his finger. "We have work to do."

"I repeat . . . *now?*"

Robert nodded.

Noah sighed. "Okay, you're the boss."

"Give me about fifteen minutes. That ought to do it."

"You'd better call." Noah started for the door. "I want to be in on this West German thing." He opened the door and turned back to face the older man. "If you screw me on this and I don't get to go to Europe, you might as well not come back." He donned his fiercest expression. "Because your life will be a living hell if I have anything to do with it, and I will." He smiled at Robert suddenly, fluttering his eyelashes and spun out the door. "Give my best to Marya," he called out, slamming the door shut."

Robert pulled his carry-on bag out of the closet and threw it on top of the bed. He had already packed it for the most part, but made a little room for his shaving kit, which he retrieved quickly from the bathroom. He stood at the well-organized suitcase contents for a moment, shaking his head. What was he thinking? Hadn't he learned anything? He knew better than to get involved with people he worked with, especially after the Baltic fiasco that had precipitated his break with the Agency.

He closed his eyes, trying to will the memory out of his consciousness . . . Daniel . . . The name alone seemed to open up old wounds he thought he had healed . . . but the pain was as fresh and new as if it had all happened yesterday.

Robert zipped the suitcase shut and, spotting his bottle of water on the bureau by the window, grabbed it up to take a deep swig. He blinked through the blinds, just able to make out Noah's cap, jauntily askew, moving out into the street below. Robert smiled down at the young man's fluid way of moving . . . energetic and uninhibited. The kid was much too young for him. Well . . . only by ten or eleven years. They had nothing in common.

Robert lifted the small valise onto the floor and extracted its telescoping handle. The thought of Daniel returned—wreckless, smart-mouthed, sloppy . . . Robert almost laughed. He sure knew how to pick 'em.

His smile left as quickly as it came. Daniel had been the loser in it all . . . not Robert. The kid had taken a bullet, and Robert had lost what he thought was his one, real chance at love. It just wasn't meant to be. He'd have to cool this thing with Noah. History has a way of repeating itself. Robert jerked the wheeled suitcase along behind him out the door.

Noah flew down the stairs to the front desk, trying to keep his heartbeat down to a rapid flutter. Never in his wildest dreams had he ever supposed he would be mixed up with murder and the Russian FSB. It was more than he could ever hope for. He played with the tourist brochures on the desk for a moment, using the time to look about for the older couple who seemed to always be nearby. He caught sight of them sitting out by the pool in the courtyard. They were sitting, having tea at one of the patio tables in front of the large, plate-glass window that overlooked the hotel lobby. Perfect vantage point from which to watch the stairs, Noah thought.

Inspiration struck and he picked up the desk phone and pretended to punch in a number. "Hello, Robert?" He said loudly into the dial tone. "How much longer are you going to be there? No! I can't believe it! You don't mean it? Don't worry, I'm on my way. Give me directions? Yes . . . Yes . . . Yes . . . Got it!" He slammed the phone down excitedly and ran for the exit to the street. He paused at the door to bend over and pretend to adjust a shoelace, and caught a glimpse of the couple getting up quickly from their tea to follow him.

Noah smiled to himself and headed off down the street toward the cathedral with the two Russian agents in tow. He checked his watch to gauge how long he needed to keep them on the run so Robert would have enough time to get to the airport. It was all he could do to keep from laughing. The whole situation was so comedic to him. The couple kept a discreet distance, stopping when Noah stopped, ducking into doorways whenever he turned around. He loved every minute of it.

To keep from wasting time, at one point, he paused to pull out his Blackberry and make his own plane reservation to Houston. The Russians immediately turned into one of the street artists exhibits and stood admiring the various nudes and other displays of Western extravagance.

Noah checked his watch again and noted with some amusement that the fifteen minutes were up. He started strolling for the artists' exhibits wondering if he really had the chutzpah to do what he was wanting to do. Before he could change his mind he walked up to stand by the couple who were being less than successful at ignoring his presence.

"Hi! My name is Noah Taylor," he said confidently to the couple, extending his hand to them.

The older gentleman shook Noah's hand and looked at his wife in confusion.

"I work for the McNaughton News Corporation," Noah continued smiling broadly. "I understand the two of you work for the Soviet KGB." He was speaking loudly enough that the people around them were beginning to stare. "Actually that would be the Russian FSB, now wouldn't it, what with the Berlin wall brooha and all? I've never met a KGB . . . I mean FSB agent before, let alone two, so you can imagine my surprise when I found out that the two of you were staying at the very same hotel as I am."

The couple began to back away from him as if he had the plague.

"You must let me interview you," Noah said, taking out his notebook. "Imagine what a story this would make. My readers would be fascinated."

The couple turned to walk away, their faces ashen.

"I mean do you work out of the Russian Embassy or is this just a little something you do on the side for extra bread-and-butter money?"

The two clung to each other and began to shuffle for the nearest side street out of the square.

"Maybe we can have lunch," Noah yelled after them. "Inquiring minds want to know!"

Chapter 12

Noah vowed he would never take another shuttle flight as long as he lived. The taxi ride from the airport had been almost as harrowing, and so he had spent the better part of the last hour and a half with his eyes closed, clutching on to anything solidly handy. He was also upset that he had not been able to appreciate any of the city sights along the way, but he could not bear watching the outdoors careen past him as the driver, obviously trying to set some new record, hurdled toward the small house in the Houston suburb. Noah wondered if the man was the only taxi driver in town.

When the cab finally arrived in front of the small tract home, Noah was ready to get out anywhere. He paid the driver and sent him on his way. It would be better to return to the hotel on foot rather than risk another ride on that roller-coaster. If only he had learned how to drive, he could have booked a car rental.

He stood at the end of the sidewalk a moment to get his bearings and try to recover his land-legs. Except for the chain-link fence surrounding it, the house looked as plain as the rest on the street. The grass was a little too high and, from the look of the paint peeling about the windows, upkeep was not a priority. Noah opened the gate slowly and proceeded up the uneven walk, climbed the concrete steps to the covered, wood-plank porch and rang the doorbell. He listened for the sound of life inside, and wondered at what circumstances could have brought a daughter of one of the wealthiest and most powerful monarchs in the world to such a fate—the alleged daughter anyway.

Noah heard the rattling sound of locks and chains being disengaged. He reached down to pull open the warped screen door as the other door beyond swung inward. An ancient man, approximately in his late eighties or more, stepped into view. He was thin, not particularly tall, with a prominent, almost pregnant paunch at the midriff, and his white hair thinned to non-existent at the crown. Three or four cats of varying breed and parentage nosed around his legs cautiously.

"Yes?" The voice was a cultured one, strong and showing none of the usual signs of age. He peered down over his reading glasses at Noah and began to roll his sleeves down to button them at the cuff.

"Mr. Gilroy?" Noah tried to look at him and not at the growing population of cats at his feet. "I'm Noah Taylor. We spoke earlier on the phone. McNaughton News?"

The old man's eyes brightened. "The press! Yes, yes, young man, come inside, please." He stepped back inside and held the door open. "Move back, children, and let the boy in." He nudged the rug of squirming cats with his foot.

What struck Noah at first was the smell. He could not decide if it was the cats, the clutter of food and garbage on the dining room table, litter boxes scattered about each room, or any combination of these. He longed to find an open window to sit by.

"Please pardon the mess," said Mr. Gilroy escorting Noah to the sofa at the center of it all. "I spend most of my time at the bookshop. Besides, I never was much for house cleaning."

Noah tried to look sympathetic. "I'm sure things have been difficult since your wife died."

Mr. Gilroy seemed unconcerned. "No, no, not really. In any event that was thirty-two years ago. The duchess wasn't much for housework either. The cats are all descendants from her brood of pets." He pushed several off the sofa to make a place for Noah. "I've tried to get rid of them all but it's very difficult. One does want to find them a good home, you know."

"Of course," Noah replied.

"We haven't had many visitors in a while. Most of the attention always centered on Elly." There was no bitterness in his voice. If anything he spoke his wife's name with admiration and a touch of awe. "Elly didn't care much for all the attention, though. It was usually all I could do to get her to sit for an occasional interview. I think that's one of the reasons I believed so strongly that her story was a true one. If she were a fake she certainly would have sought the limelight more, or else, why bother making up such a tale. And, too, she could have made a lot of money . . . a lot of money exploiting the media attention." He talked like one used to the job, speaking as if he and Noah were old friends.

"Tell me, Mr. Gilroy . . ."

"Please, call me Alfred."

"Alfred, how is it that you and your wife came to be in possession of an Imperial Fabergé Easter Egg? I'm talking about the one you put up for auction some years back." Noah pulled his small note pad from his messenger bag.

"Ah! Elly's treasure." Gilroy pulled off his reading glasses and polished them on his shirt. "Yes, we were needing money at the time. I made enough at the bookshop to take care of our day-to-day existence, but what with the legal expenses, the travel, and all, at the time we were hurting pretty badly. Back then, Elly was surprisingly keen on proving, or at least legally establishing, her rights and her identity." He returned the glasses to his nose. "We came so close." His eyes seemed to stray into the distance. "So very close."

"About the egg, Alfred."

"Oh, yes. Sorry. That was back in about 1958. I usually never discussed money matters with Elly . . . she seemed to have so little grasp of them . . . but things were getting desperate. When I finally broke down and told her the bad news, she told me of a safety deposit box she had in a Swiss bank. She wouldn't tell me anything further about it, which, of course, made it even more exciting. I had visions of Imperial jewels and gold."

"And?"

"Just that one egg."

Noah looked up from his notes. "The egg, and that was all?"

"Exactly."

"No papers or other identification?"

"Nothing. Just the egg. Still, that was no small find in and of itself."

"True," Noah said. "May I ask how much you got for it?"

"About a hundred and thirty thousand." He winked at Noah. "In 1958, that was a small fortune."

"It's nothing to laugh at now."

Alfred kicked absent-mindedly at one of the cats. "Of course, it's all gone now. We spent it all on legal maneuvering and travel expenses. That and then some."

"She never said where she got it?"

Alfred smiled. "To her, such things were obvious. She was the Grand Duchess Anastasia. Why shouldn't she have such a thing?" He gave Noah a curious look. "Why all this interest in that egg? It's on display in a museum somewhere, I believe."

"Was in a museum, Alfred. The New Orleans Museum of Art. It was stolen today."

"Stolen? Ah, now I understand."

"Oh?"

"Well, we haven't had visits from the press in a long while. Now all this makes sense."

Noah patted his hand. "Alfred, do you really believe that your wife was the Grand Duchess Anastasia?"

"Completely." Alfred's look was naively serious. "You had to know her as I did. Yes, she was a bit schizophrenic . . . or paranoid . . . or both, but who wouldn't be, after having gone through what she went through. She was quite genuine—of that I am sure."

"It is a shame that she had to sell the egg," Noah said. "If it was truly a gift from the Tsar, it must have meant a great deal to her."

Alfred shook his head. "On the contrary. The egg seemed to hold little significance for her. She gave it up without an ounce of regret. It was the little crucifix inside that she could not bear to part with."

Noah sat up. "I beg your pardon?"

"Oh, didn't I mention that?" Alfred polished his glasses again. "Yes, there was a little crucifix inside. All those eggs contained some sort of toy. This one was a little cross. Quite an unusual design, rather *avant garde* for that period."

"She kept it?"

"Oh yes. Wore it on a chain around her neck day and night." He frowned. "As a matter of fact, I believe it was then . . . yes . . . I'm sure of it. It was after that point that Elly seemed to lose interest in the legal proceedings. Regaining her lost identity was no longer as meaningful to her as before. She drifted farther and farther into nostalgia and remembrances, seeming to retreat more and more into her own little world."

Noah tried to maintain calm. "Where is this crucifix now, Alfred?"

For a moment he seemed lost in the past himself. "Oh, I'm sorry. The cross. Oh, it's around here somewhere. That and these cats are all I have left of her."

"May I see it?"

"See it?"

"The crucifix, Alfred."

The old man laughed, more at himself than anything. "I'm not usually this slow, I assure you." He stood up. "I guess I'm just a little off balance, what with all this renewed interest, the questions, that other man." He chuckled to himself again and started out of the room.

Noah jumped up to follow. "Other man? What other man? Have there been others here asking questions?"

"Here? No, just you. There were a couple of other phone calls shortly after yours. Newspaper reporters. The usual."

They walked into a room full of boxes and papers. Noah guessed that underneath the chaos was a bedroom, since the large mound of files and papers in the center had a headboard.

"They asked you about the egg?"

"Oh, yes." Alfred began to rummage through things.

"Did you mention the crucifix to any of them?"

"The crucifix? Oh, yes. One gentleman, from the New York Times, I believe, was particularly interested in it. I had forgotten to look for it. He wanted to come by and photograph it."

Noah followed him about, worried. "Did he give his name?"

Alfred stood up from his search and thought. "He might have. I don't remember." He resumed his rummaging.

Noah stood by helplessly watching. "Is there anything I can do to help, Alfred?"

"No, no, young man. It's in here somewhere. I put it in Elly's little jewelry box. I packed . . . Ah!" He pulled a small, wooden box out of the pile on the bed. "I knew it was here somewhere." He opened the box and took out its golden contents, holding it up for Noah to see. "What do you think?"

Noah studied the small, gleaming treasure. "You say it's a crucifix?"

"Best I can tell. As I said it is a unique design."

"May I hold it?" Noah extended his hand.

Alfred looked doubtful. "I suppose that would be all right." He smiled. "You seem somewhat different from the usual run of reporters."

Noah returned his smile. "Why thank you, Alfred. My specialty is art and fashion, so this type of field work is a little new to me." He took the small cross for closer inspection.

"I knew you were different," Alfred said with a laugh. "You're too . . . relaxed to be an ordinary reporter."

Noah laughed as well. He turned the golden object over in his hand. "It's not a very good grade of gold, is it?" He commented, weighing it in his hand. He noted some scratches among the filigree. "Actually this is only gold-plate isn't it?"

"Not very valuable at all, you're right." Gilroy gave Noah a sheepish look. "I had it appraised shortly after Elly died." He looked at his shoes. "There were many expenses. The jeweler said it was just a piece of costume jewelry. I decided to hold on to it. It was something to remember her by."

Noah found the object's shape fascinating. "I don't blame you," he said to Alfred. "The value of some things doesn't lie in their gold content."

"Well said," Alfred agreed with a clap of his hands.

The door bell buzzed loudly from the other room.

"Oh, dear," Alfred said, stumbling through the mess to the living room. "I wonder who that could be." He motioned to Noah and pointed down the hall to the back of the house. "Why don't you head for the kitchen, dear boy, and plug in the coffee pot. I'll get the door."

"All right," Noah said and started off to negotiate the obstacle course that was the hallway. He kept his ears pricked as the older man answered the door.

"Yes, can I help you?" He heard Alfred say.

"Mr. Gilroy," replied a gruff, heavily accented voice.

Noah heard the sounds of a scuffle and the front door slam. He froze in the doorway to the kitchen and listened.

"Where is the cross you spoke of, Mr. Gilroy?" the accented voice demanded.

"Now see here! Who do you . . ." Noah heard Alfred begin.

"Bykov!"

Noah heard a loud slap and a man cry out in pain.

"The cross! Quickly before you are caused further discomfort."

Noah's faced burned with a mixture of fear and rage that someone would strike such a gentle old man. He crept back down the hall to the living room and peeked around through a stack of boxes.

Gilroy was on his knees with a hulking blond giant holding him by the scruff of the neck. Another, short and stocky man dressed in a black overcoat and hat stood in front glaring down at the cowering old man, holding a heavy, chrome pistol.

"Again, Bykov!" the short man commanded.

The giant spun Gilroy around and slapped him across the face again, sending the old man sprawling to the floor.

Gilroy spit blood. "Why are you doing this?" He groaned.

"Silence!" ordered the man in black. "Show us where the cross is or die! We know it's here and we will find it. You can make things easier by telling us what we want to know."

Gilroy looked up from the floor to the hall. He caught Noah's eye through his own swollen ones. Noah gestured to him hastily that he was going to phone for help and retreated down the hallway.

Gilroy turned quickly to the men in front of him before they could follow his line of vision. "The cross? Wait! Let me think."

"Enough!" Noah heard the gruff man thunder. "Kill him."

Noah shoved his cell phone back into his messenger bag and rushed back to the corner just in time to see the giant take Gilroy's head between his massive hands and snapped it around. He felt the blood rush from his head at the sound of bone cracking and pulled himself back out of sight into the hall. He looked down at the object of all the violence resting innocently in his hand. Grasping it tightly he moved silently down the hall and back to the kitchen.

Noah could hear the two men tearing apart the living room as he crept into the kitchen. He breathed a sigh of relief at the sunlight streaming in through the panes of glass in the back door. He heard the sounds of destruction move across the hall into the bedroom and he turned the doorknob silently and gave it a tug. Stuck momentarily, the door suddenly broke free and flew open. Noah stopped it just before it slammed into a stack of empty aluminum soft drink cans. He went out the door without bothering to close it behind him and rushed around the overgrown backyard to the front.

Noah hoped no one would take much notice of him jogging down the street. If anyone had happened to be looking, he would have been hard not to notice, what with bag flying, hands on cap, and silver flashing. He raced for the small grocery store at the corner and ducked inside out of sight. He tried to suppress the sight of Gilroy's face as the old man's head was snapped around. It could just as easily have been him.

Noah felt the panic take hold. He looked around, wondering if he should scream for help. Another feeling—guilt . . . shame—he couldn't tell which was also eating at his stomach. Why hadn't he done something— and then—what could he have done? They would have killed him too.

Tears streaked his cheeks and blurred his vision. Noah tried to peek out the door and focus his vision down the street to make sure he was still unnoticed. He thought of Robert enjoying the sights of London and rubbed his feet. "Wait till I get my hands on you, Bobby Boy," he sobbed, retrieving his cell phone once more.

Chapter 13

Robert glanced down at his watch and finally reset it to the new time zone. He rubbed his eyes wearily, thankful, at last, to be off planes. Unable to get a direct flight, he had to hop two more planes after landing at Heathrow. Provided that he was tailing the right woman, Marya—alias Olga Holsted—had caught a flight out of London's Heathrow to Frankfurt and then yet another smaller shuttle to Wiesbaden.

Robert had chosen to rent a car in Frankfurt and drive to Wiesbaden rather than wait three hours for another shuttle flight. Besides, considering how fast one could drive on the Autobahn, he could make the distance in no time.

His progress was hurt a little by a persistent cold drizzle that kept the road slick and wet. As he had not driven in a while, he knew to take it easy at first until his reflexes were more in tune to the task. Still the time passed quickly and before long he had left the open stretches of road for the curling inroads of the city.

Robert drove into the familiar streets, noting how little had changed in the seven years he had been away. He wondered if Hamm might still be the CIA's, or as it was more familiarly called, the Company's man in Wiesbaden. Hamm was the friendly sort. He ran a small bar in a less tourist-traveled section of the city.

For a second Robert thought about giving Hamm a call but he quickly dismissed the notion from his mind. Such a call could be misinterpreted and anyway, his cell phone was useless out of the States. Robert decided the first order of business was to find a phone, check out a few hotels, and see if his quarry had settled into one of them. He spotted a phone box at a corner and pulled over to park. Before stepping out into the cold, he fumbled in his pockets for the correct coinage. Pulling his coat tighter, he swung out into the wind for the phone.

No one at the first three hotels had ever heard of a Marya Dmitrievna or an Olga Holsted. The fourth hotel had an Olga Dreiden, but she was described as a rather obese, bleached-blonde in her sixties. The fifth call to a hotel brought good news. They had an Olga Holsted registered from earlier in the day. Robert quickly reserved a room of his own and headed back for the car out of the icy wind.

His mind raced with possible plans of action as he negotiated the city streets toward the hotel. He could simply confront Marya, or Olga, or whoever, or he could stay in the background and follow her while taking a little time to have her background checked through his Company connections. This was provided, of course, that anyone in the Company would have anything to do with him. Some agents considered leaving the service as onerous as defecting one's citizenship.

The hotel was one of the newly refurbished ones, for which Robert was thankful. The one thing he disliked about his stint in Europe was the lack of a decent shower. Most hung on the wall somewhere between his breastbone and his bellybutton and were designed as hand-held jobs anyway. The newer or rennovated hotels were installing more modern plumbing fixtures, mostly in response to tourist pressure.

Robert signed in at the front desk, all the while keeping an eye out for any sign of Marya. He had decided to watch her for a while and make a few inquiries of his own. He signaled to the desk clerk. "*Fräulein* Holsted's room number, please."

The clerk looked at him as if he were asking the combination to the safe.

"She is my secretary," he assured the clerk, at the same time presenting him his card. "I'm Dr. Robert Tate, McNaughton News Corporation."

"232," the clerk answered, handing him the key to his own room.

"*Danke*," Robert said. "Will you have the bellboy take my bag on up to my room and leave the key here at the desk? I have some business to attend to."

The desk clerk gave a sharp nod. "Very good, *Herr* Doctor Tate." He snapped his fingers at the bellboy who was propped up sleepily against the wall by the elevator.

Robert flipped up the collar of his overcoat and headed back out into the drizzle. He revved the small Volkswagen engine into the main business district and beyond. The architecture became decidedly less picturesque and the streets a little dirtier. He pulled into a parking space across the street from a heavy, square looking brownstone. A neon light flashed the name, *Die Bleu Angel*. Robert smiled, remembering Carl Hamm's near fetish about Marlene Dietrich.

He sprinted through the cold for the club's entrance. Robert pulled open the door and was nearly overcome by the cloud of smoke that billowed out. He wrinkled his nose and took in the last breath of fresh air he would get for a while and entered the dark, noisy beer hall. Robert immediately spotted Hamm standing behind the bar. Carl Hamm also noted Robert's arrival. A broad smile broke over the large, beefy man's face.

Robert nodded to him and headed for the bar. He looked about him, amazed, if you could call it that, at the changes that had taken place in the club. The whitewashed walls were now a black matte finish and the heavy wooden tables and chairs had been replaced with burgundy colored, vinyl-covered booths. The nature of the patrons had also changed. Gone were the lower working class brawlers and factory workers.

Robert eyed the leather suited crowd with dismay. Two men grappled in a passionate embrace in one of the dark booths near the small stage and another, possibly male/female, couple danced by the bar to some innate tune heard only by themselves.

The stage show was in full swing but the Dietrich impersonator's voice seemed a tad too throaty to Robert to be fully female. He glanced questioningly at Hamm, who only shrugged and wiped up a spill at the other end of the bar he kept polished to a high gloss. Robert took that as a signal and meandered through the crowd to the end of the bar and took a seat.

Hamm slapped a stein of dark lager down on the bar in front of Robert. "Hell, Tate! I never figured you to be a fag." His Tennessee twang was an almost welcome sound amid the guttural German surrounding them. "How long you been doin' gay bars, boy?"

Robert took a sip of his beer. "This is my first," he said, considering the truth of his statement. "I never figured you'd be tending bar at one, Hamm."

"It's a living. I go where The Man sends me."

"To hell and back, right?"

"I've been there, too," Hamm answered. "Anyway, this crowd looks like trouble, but they're really pretty harmless."

"Oh well," Robert said, hoisting Hamm a toast. "In your business you're used to watching your rear."

Hamm's laughter bellowed through the room momentarily overwhelming the piano player working with the performer. Even the juke box that blared heavy metal rock music by the door was no competition. No one in the room seemed to react to Hamm's howls of laughter, giving Robert the impression that they were used to periodic outbursts from behind the bar.

Hamm wiped his chin with the back of his hand. His eyes narrowed at Robert. "I heard tell you were out in the cold. Dumped the business and fled."

"If by that you mean I resigned, yes."

"Shit!" Hamm pulled a beer for himself. "I thought you were a career spook." Hamm studied Robert's face. "We heard it had something to do with that kid on your team—the one who caught a bullet in Estonia."

"Why would you think that?" Robert stared into his beer.

"It was around the same time," Hamm responded. "Losing an operative that way would be hard, I imagine."

Robert merely nodded.

"Anyway," Hamm continued, "it was probably a good time to get out. I heard that Russian colonel—what was his name? Hell, I can't remember. Anyway, he took out quite a few of our men up that way. We traced it to a fucking hemorrhage of classified documents from our embassy in Lithuania. You'll be happy to know we plugged that leak . . . the hard way."

Robert smiled. "You ought to retire yourself, Carl." He looked about the room. "This must be the pits for a man like you."

"It ain't so bad. I've worked worse places. Besides, it still makes a good contact point. I mean, really. Who'd suspect?"

Robert tried to laugh.

"If you're out, what the hell you doin' here?"

"I need a favor," Robert said flatly.

"Shit!" Hamm polished the bar. "What kind of favor?"

"I'd like to run a check on someone."

"Who?"

"A woman I've had some business dealings with."

"Business, huh? What kind of business?"

"We're competitors, so to speak, for the same product."

Hamm folded his massive arms onto the bar and leaned over. "The Company's not in the business of doin' favors. You know that."

Robert nodded. "For outsiders, yes. But you can't really consider me an outsider."

"You're out."

"Come on, Hamm. Is anyone ever really out?"

Hamm thought about that. "You sayin' you're still available?"

"I'm saying I worked this continent for 6 years. Most of the men working here I put here, including you. I did what I was told and then some. I figure I'm owed a few favors."

"Says who?"

"Don't be such an ass, Hamm." Robert finished off his beer. "Besides, I'm also in a position to return favor for favor."

Hamm eyed him with some skepticism. Robert extracted a packet about the size of a large wallet from the inside of his coat. He opened it on the bar and toggled the small switch on its side. The little black box lit up, chiming an innocuous tune.

Hamm's eyes lit up. "It's a chess board."

"A computerized chess board." Robert punched in a few moves by way of demonstration on the small game he had purchased at the duty free shop in anticipation of this moment. "It has eight levels of play. I could only get past three."

Hamm reached for the game but Robert covered it with his hand. "A favor for a favor?"

Hamm laughed. "Sold out for a few baubles and beads. All right, who's the mark?"

Robert handed him an envelope. "Information's inside. I'll give you a call tomorrow and see what you've dug up." He took his hand off the game.

Hamm snatched the game off the bar and studied it possessively. "Yeah, yeah. Call me tomorrow." He stuffed the envelope in his pocket. "Damn, those Japanese can do anything," he said, marveling at his new toy.

Robert slid off the bar stool. He pushed his way through the crowd by the door and felt a hand squeeze his buttock. "What the hell!" He turned quickly but could find no obvious culprit.

Several young men in tight, almost painted on leather pants stood about him in pairs and singles gyrating to the juke box noise. A bellow of laughter erupted again from behind the bar. He glared across the room at Hamm who only laughed louder. Robert spun out the door quickly allowing no one further opportunity for copping a feel.

He warmed up the Volkswagen and headed back for the hotel. He patted himself on the back for having had the foresight to purchase the small computer game. Along with his Dietrich compulsion, Hamm was an avid chess player and games man. He especially liked electronic gadgetry, and Robert knew the man would likely sell out his best friend for the right toy.

Robert parked at the back of the hotel, this time, and entered through the service door. He sent one of the houseboys round for his key, and then slipped up the back stairs. His room was on the fourth floor, which suited his purposes just fine, as it minimized the possibility of crossing Marya's path. He unpacked quickly and sat on the bed, taking a moment to collect himself. He tried to recall the sound and special nuances of Marya's voice. Hoping he would recognize her voice, Robert picked up the phone and dialed her room number.

The phone rang ten times before he finally hung up. Robert flipped his suitcase over on the bed and unzipped a side pocket, pulling out a small leather case. He opened it and eyed the slender, shiny, carbon-graphite lockpicks. "Let's see if we've still got the touch," he muttered to himself.

He knew he was taking a chance, not knowing how long she had been gone or when she would return, but he needed some answers quickly and decided to risk it. If Olga Holsted and Marya were one and the same he could take things easy. The thought that he might have been following the wrong person was not one he cared to face. He could not wait for Hamm's complete rundown. He needed immediate assurance that he was on the right trail.

The hall outside of Room 232 was heavily trafficked. Robert had to putter up and down the corridor for almost ten minutes before things quieted down. He worked quickly, pulling two of the picks from their leather case, and manipulating them in the lock. He fumbled from lack of practice but it was easier than he had anticipated. Within minutes he was safely in the room.

He went first to the dresser drawers, going through each one methodically, and taking the time to be sure none of their contents were badly disturbed. Finding nothing he moved on to the closet. In a coat pocket he found a credit card receipt made out to Olga Holsted. Robert considered the implications of such a well established alias. It took considerable financial backing to forge a passport and obtain credit cards.

He scanned the room for anything out of the ordinary. The phone book lay open on the bedside table, Robert settled into the chair beside it and flipped on the reading lamp. He studied the facing pages carefully and noted the faint pencil line under the name—Dieter, Carl.

On a hunch he turned over to the commercial listings under antique dealers. There were no obvious markings on the page except for a few dots where a pencil had been tapped on one of the larger advertisements. Robert noted the name with interest—The Schloss Gallery of Antiquities. He returned the phone book to its original state.

Robert reached for the phone and dialed the number. After a few rings a woman answered. He assumed his upper-crust Boston accent. "Yes, this is Dr. Robert Tate, Boston Museum of Art. Is *Herr* Schloss available?"

"He is not available at the moment," the secretary replied, unimpressed.

"I wonder if he might have some time available that I might have an appointment."

"May I ask what this would be in regard to?" The woman queried.

"The museum would like to engage *Herr* Schloss' help in locating certain objects d'art with which Herr Schloss is familiar." Robert added quickly, "We have a donor who is prepared to pay well for these services."

There was a moment of silence on the other end of the line. Finally the woman returned. "*Herr* Schloss can give you a few minutes Thursday morning at ten."

"That would be fine," Robert said. "Thursday at ten." He hung up the phone and sat studying the advertisement in the phone book.

The door lock rattled alarmingly. Robert spun around to the door in time to see the lock turning. He dove for the closet, sealing himself inside just as the door opened. The surge of adrenaline had driven his heartbeat up to the point that he could hear it pounding in his ears. He fought to suppress the accompanying acceleration of his breathing and pressed himself silently back against the closet wall, concealing himself as well as he could behind the clothing.

Robert shut out the sound of his heartbeat and focused his amplified hearing on the room beyond. He heard the jingle of keys as they were dropped on a table, and the sound of shoes dropping softly to the carpeted floor. Feet padded toward his hiding place, and he braced himself to lunge forward, in case he needed to take the intruder by surprise.

Robert relaxed only slightly as the footsteps passed him. The floor beneath him trembled slightly with the squeal and knocking of pipes as a faucet was turned on. Robert stepped forward carefully, resting his ear against the closet door. He strained for the slightest sounds, trying to make sense of each one. He heard the familiar scraping as a shower curtain was pulled over its metal rod. A few more seconds passed before he risked opening the closet door a crack. With painful slowness he eased the door ajar, allowing his eyes to readjust to the light.

The room beyond was empty and he heard the splashing of water in the tub through the open door of the bathroom directly to his right. He let out his breath, wondering if he might actually have held it for the duration. He eased himself out of the closet and closed its door with an almost imperceptible click.

"Don't move!" a woman's voice commanded.

Robert turned his head slightly. The shower curtain had been pulled back and a dark-haired woman stood naked, dripping wet, and sighting down a black luger pistol directly at his head.

"Ms. Dmitrievna," Robert acknowledged with a slight nod. "I'd know that pistol anywhere."

Chapter 14

Noah had tried to reconcile himself to the anonymous payphone call he had made to the police, but he was still racked with guilt. He knew there was nothing much the police could do but clean up the mess. The actual situation was too far reaching for one police jurisdiction to handle. He wrestled with the problem all the way from the airport, oblivious to the taxi driver's best efforts at non-stop small talk.

The taxi pulled to the curb across from the McNaughton Tower Building and Noah stepped out, pausing only to pay the driver. As he crossed the busy intersection he risked staring up at the thirty-plus floors of the steel and glass building, frowning at the lack of imagination. McNaughton News occupied the top three floors. Below that were the offices of various other splinter corporations in the McNaughton conglomerate.

On the long elevator ride up Noah reviewed his notes trying to formulate a condensed presentation for Madelyn. He only hoped that Madelyn would not opt to put more experienced field reporters on the job once she learned the extent of the story. They were on to something big—big enough for theft and multiple murders on an international scale.

He headed straight for his cubicle, hoping to find a message from Robert. His spindle was empty. "Rick," he called out across the room to the copy boy.

"Here I am," came the breathless reply as the boy rushed over. "Hi, Noah. When did you get back?"

"Just in, Ricky. Have I had any messages while I was gone?"

"No, sir. Not that I know of."

"Bobby hasn't called?"

"Bobby?"

"Dr. Tate."

The boy scratched his head. "Don't think so."

"Damn." Noah threw his bag down on the desk.

The boy stood by waiting.

"That's all, Ricky, thanks."

The boy started to leave.

"Oh, Rick, is Madelyn in her office?"

"Yes, sir," the boy said, rolling his eyes. "All day."

Noah grabbed his notebook and made a beeline for Madelyn's door. He went straight in.

"Madelyn?"

The older woman looked up from her desk. "Noah, you're back. Come in. We've been trying to get in touch with you and Robert. Is he in his office?"

"I wish," Noah said, falling into the chair in front of Madelyn's desk. "He's somewhere in Europe."

"Europe?"

"I thought he would have phoned in his location by now."

Madelyn sat back in her high-backed chair. "What the hell is Robert doing in Europe? I thought the two of you were in New Orleans."

Noah smiled. "That's old news. I just got back from Houston."

"Houston? What have the two of you been doing, for Christ's sake?"

"After the other egg was stolen from the New Orleans Museum, I went to Houston to follow up a lead on the egg's original owner."

"And Robert?"

"He was tailing the thief."

"Good grief! Now I am confused."

"There's a lot of filling in to do Madelyn. And another murder."

Madelyn sat forward sharply. "What? Another murder. This doesn't make sense."

Noah looked at his notes. "We traced the egg to its original owner . . . are you ready for this . . . one of the more famous alleged Grand Duchess Anastasias, living in Houston. You may not remember. She died somewhat destitute over thirty years ago."

"I vaguely remember something . . . but the murder?"

"Her husband, Alfred Gilroy. I was there when it happened."

"You were there? For Christ's sake, Noah! Why didn't you phone in?"

Noah took a deep breath and shook his head. "All I wanted was out of there. I phoned the police anonymously and caught the first plane back to New York. The police can't do anything anyway. It's too big. The FSB's involved."

"FSB!" Madelyn was beside herself. She reached for the decanter on the credenza behind her and poured herself a brandy. "FSB." She shook her head and looked hard at Noah. "This is starting to sound a bit wild, Noah."

"I know, I know, but it's true. Honest." Noah remembered the small, oddly-shaped cross hidden inside his shirt where it hung about his neck. Something made him keep silent about it.

"The Russians are out to find the Abdication Egg," Noah continued, "apparently at any cost. I guess it must have been a real embarrassment to them when it was stolen. But they're out for blood."

Madelyn still looked skeptical. "That might be true if it weren't for this." She slid a piece of teletype copy across the desk to Noah.

Noah picked it up and read.

"As you can see the egg has already been recovered."

Noah stared at the paper in disbelief. "How can this be? They say it never got out of Russia."

"Kind of washes out your story, doesn't it?"

Noah crumpled the paper in his hands. "It's a load of crap, that's what it is. They're just trying to save face."

Madelyn threw up her hands. "Oh, come on, Noah. It says right there the egg's back on display at the Kremlin Museum. People have seen it. There are wire photos. Now get real."

"I don't care what this says. Robert and I know for a fact that the egg is somewhere in West Germany and is being offered for sale in a private auction."

"That's not fact, dear, that's just your suppositions."

"Gilroy wasn't murdered because of a supposition and neither was Kozlovsky."

"You have no facts to show that those murders were connected in any way except in your mind."

"You know they're connected. This is all too much for coincidence."

"We're a news organization, Noah. We depend on facts. Provable facts. We can't publish hunches."

"Don't worry, Madelyn. Robert and I will have this story cracked in no time. He's probably made some major leads already."

"I doubt it, dear. I think we've spent enough money on this little race."

"Madelyn, you can't be serious."

"I know this was your first field assignment, Noah, and that it means a lot to you. I can sympathize. But we have to face facts. The egg has been recovered. It's over."

"I can't believe this. You're pulling us off the story?"

"I have no choice, Noah. Now where's Robert? I need to talk to him."

Noah sank into the chair sullenly. "Who knows? Probably laid out on the Riviera reading Dostoevsky."

Madelyn laughed. "Now don't be bitchy. Look at it this way. You got to do a little field work. It was fun, wasn't it? A little excitement! Life goes on."

They were interrupted by a knock on the door.

"Come in," Madelyn called out.

The door opened and the copy boy stuck his head in. "Sorry to bother you, Ms. Arnold, but Dr. Tate just phoned in."

"Is he still on the line?"

"No Ma'am. He's driving from Frankfurt to Wiesbaden, Germany."

"Well, let's have it." Madelyn took the slip of paper from him and shooed him out the door. "Wiesbaden! What's in Wiesbaden?" She punched the number into her phone with the end of a pencil.

While Madelyn concentrated on the phone, Noah checked his e-mail on his cell phone hoping for some communication from Robert. He could not understand how he and Robert could have been so wrong. Surely there was a connection, otherwise why all the murders? No matter what, the story was not finished as far as he was concerned. He wadded the paper up even harder.

"No answer on his cellphone," Madelyn said in annoyance. "I left a message for him to check in as soon as he lands."

"His cellphone probably doesn't work overseas," Noah muttered.

"He didn't say anything about where he might be staying?"

Noah shook his head. "Madelyn," his determination returned, "I think we're missing an opportunity here," Noah said. "You may think the story on the Abdication Egg is over but remember we still have these murders. If you just give Bobby and me a little time . . ."

Madelyn interrupted him with a raised hand. "We've wasted enough time and money on this. Personally, I had hoped you were right about the possible sale to private collectors. It would have made a great expose. But the fact is, the egg never made it out of Russia, it's been recovered, case closed."

"But the murders—"

"Can be explained in any number of ways. Look, Noah, we have plenty of stories to pursue with facts to go on. This is small potatoes."

"The FSB doesn't involve itself in small potatoes."

Madelyn couldn't help but laugh. "Oh, yes. The FSB. Let's try not to romanticize the facts, dear. The chances of this being a FSB operation are so remote—"

"They are not remote," Noah pressed, growing annoyed. "Robert pegged them almost immediately. And what about this Marya person who stole the other egg. She knew they were FSB as well. She—"

"Was a jewel thief, dear. That spells liar from the start." Madelyn stood with her hands on the desk. "Now

I have other work for you to do that's been backlogging while you've been off," she said, laughing, "chasing Russian spies."

"I have nothing pressing but those damn fashion shows."

"That's what we pay you for, dear."

Noah's face flushed with anger. "I'm tired of doing these busy-work, fluff stories, Madelyn. I didn't join this organization to do background research all my life. I thought you were moving me into the field with this assignment. It isn't fair to put me back at that desk."

"Life's a bitch, dear. That's how things are. I don't need another field reporter. I do need someone to do the background on these fashion angles."

Noah was so angry he couldn't speak anymore. He jumped out of the chair and stormed out of the office to his own. He flopped down onto the floor of his cubicle to sulk, tossing his notebook at the desk. "Damn, damn, damn, damn, damn, damn, damn!" he growled, stretching out his foot to give the file cabinet under his desk a kick.

"You all right, Noah?" The copy boy stuck his head cautiously through the waterfall of glass beads.

"Do I sound like I'm okay, Ricky?'

"No, sir," came the chastened reply.

"We had this story. Now she's pulled it out from under me."

"Yes, sir," replied the boy, sympathetically. "We could hear."

"Damn!" Noah spat again.

"The boss was all excited when you first phoned in about that other theft in New Orleans, but then after that call from the man at State all she wanted was to have you and Dr. Tate located and brought back."

Noah sat still for a moment, looking at him. "A man from State? What man from State? What are you talking about?"

"Some big shot at the State Department called. Then the Big Boss from the penthouse upstairs called. Boy, was her ass on fire after that!"

"Are you saying she was told to call us in?"

"Well, don't know for sure. But she sure changed after those calls. Maybe just coincidence, but—"

"Coincidence. There's that word again. I've had about one damn coincidence too many."

"Yes, sir."

"So, I've been pulled off a good story because of pressure from above. I knew I was on to something good."

"What about Dr. Tate," the boy asked, innocently.

"Who? Oh, yeah, him too."

Ricky played with a folded sheet of paper in his hands. "I guess Dr. Tate will be in a puddle of trouble if he doesn't call in soon, huh?"

Something in the way Ricky spoke caught Noah's attention. "Ricky?"

"Yes, sir?"

Noah studied the boy's face. Ricky wouldn't meet his gaze. Something was up. "Ricky, have you heard from Dr. Tate?"

Ricky looked at the ceiling. "If I did, you know I'd have to tell Madelyn," he said wistfully.

"Or . . ." Noah said. He stood sharply and faced Ricky squarely. "You could tell me and I will promise that I'll be sure and give the message to Madelyn."

"Yeah," Ricky said, shuffling his feet, "of course, you'd promise me that."

"Of course!"

Ricky held out the paper. "The travel office just sent down this expense report on Dr. Tate's corporate credit card."

"I see." Noah grabbed the paper and glanced it over.

"It shows a hold for a reservation at the *Das Kle* . . . *Das* something or other hotel in Wiesbaden."

"*Das Kleine*," Noah said quickly. He smiled at the paper. "Indeed." He folded the note neatly and pocketed it. "I owe you, Ricky."

Ricky laughed. "Yes, sir."

Noah scooted over to his computer keyboard. "Ricky, find me a cheap flight to Wiesbaden, please."

"Yes, sir."

"Now, Ricky!"

"Yes, sir." The boy dashed off.

Noah made a few furious pecks at the keyboard and then hit the printer button. While the page printed he fumbled in his messenger bag for his wallet and pulled out his credit cards. He looked at them for a minute, wistfully. "Well, boys," he said to them, "don't fail me now. You're all I've got." He returned them to the wallet as the copy boy returned.

"Here you go, Noah." He handed over the slip of paper. "Anything else?"

"Yes, Ricky." Noah grabbed the sheet from the printer, folded it and stuffed it in an envelope. "Would you please see to it that Madelyn gets this after I'm gone?"

"Sure, sir."

Noah grabbed a few personal belongings from his desk and stuffed a few photographs into his bag. "Ricky, it's been fun working with you. You've been a dear." He gave the boy a quick once over. "That shirt's from Armani Exchange, isn't it."

The boy blushed and shrugged.

"Aha! Gotcha!"

Ricky laughed.

"You like fashion, Ricky?"

"As much as the next guy, I guess," Ricky responded shyly.

"Right." Noah chuckled and pulled out his desk drawer. "Now what did I do . . . Ah!" He pulled out two brightly colored cards. "Here."

"What's this?" Ricky asked, puzzled.

"Take them." Noah pressed the cards into Ricky's hand. "They're passes to all the big Fashion Week events at the Waldorf. Enjoy!"

"Oh, my God!" Ricky stared at the tickets. "Oh, my God!"

"But you have to promise me something," Noah said.

"Anything," Ricky responded quickly.

"I'm supposed to write up my impressions for the news boys," Noah said. "You write it up! It's your chance to get your foot in the door of this News Agency."

"Madelyn will kill me!" Ricky said unable to suppress a big smile.

"At first," Noah said, "but then she'll be too relieved to get the story that she might actually promote you."

"To what?"

"My job."

"You quittin', Noah?"

"I'm quittin', Ricky," Noah answered, mimicking him. He laughed. "Take my advice . . .when you hand that note I just gave you to Madelyn, get the hell out fast."

The boy smiled. "Yes, sir. Good luck, Noah."

"Thanks, Ricky. I'm gonna need it."

Noah headed for the elevator wondering where in his apartment he might have misplaced his passport.

Chapter 15

Marya smiled in recognition. "Robert!" She lowered the gun and pulled a towel from the towel bar, daubing the moisture from her face. "I didn't expect to see you here. What a surprise."

"I'm sure," Robert replied. He had never seen skin so white. Her nipples stood out in the chilled air like onyx stones set in flawless alabaster.

"How did you find me?" Marya noted the direction of his gaze and began slowly to blot the moisture from her breasts with the towel.

"It wasn't difficult," Robert answered, suddenly conscious of his stare. "You left a good trail. My only trouble was keeping up with you."

Marya dropped the towel to the floor and sauntered past him. "Did you find anything interesting in the closet?"

"A little here, a little there." Robert watched her slip into an ill-fitting pair of long johns. "Your family must be celebrating Easter a little earlier this year."

Marya looked at him, puzzled. "What do you mean?"

"I usually don't find my Easter eggs until Easter morning."

Marya laughed, slipping into a ski jumpsuit. "Are you trying to imply something?"

"You tell me. You're the one who stole the egg from the New Orleans Museum. I'd just like to know why?"

Marya eyed him haughtily as she put on her boots. "I really don't know what you mean . . . but, even if what you say is true, who would have a better right? After all, it belonged to my family in the first place."

"Really?" Robert sat on the edge of the bed behind her. "There doesn't seem to be any record of that. As a matter of fact, it seems to have belonged to a little old lady in Texas."

Marya only smiled.

"We had a deal, Marya," Robert pressed on. "Information for information. I kept my end of the bargain. You skipped out on yours." He grabbed her arm. "And you left with a little more than information."

Marya shook free of him and began to stuff her hair into a ski cap. "You got what you wanted, Robert. You're here aren't you?"

"With no help from you. What the hell's going on?"

The corners of Marya's mouth peaked in an alluring smile. "Family business, Robert. Nothing that concerns the press."

"Oh, really. What family? Who are you working for? What did you want with that other egg?"

"So many questions."

"And I'd like a few answers."

"Robert, my dear." Marya sat down beside him. "In case you hadn't noticed, the people playing this game play for keeps. You'd be a lot better off returning to your office in New York before you end up like dear Vasily."

"Dear Vasily was murdered in New York. I have no intention of returning until I have some answers."

Marya got up from the bed and crossed to the window, peering out between the curtains. Robert was still conscious of the sweet scent she left behind—clean, exotic.

Marya turned her dark eyes on him. "I really had no information to trade you, Robert. You knew about as much as I did."

"Except the part about Wiesbaden."

Marya smiled seductively. "Well, I did hold that little bit back, but, enterprising as you are, you found me out anyway."

Robert was unimpressed. "That wasn't all you held back."

"Oh," Marya demurred.

"What about Carl Dieter?"

Marya's jaw tightened, and for a second Robert thought she would cut her hands with her fingernails.

"And let's not forget the Schloss Gallery," Robert continued, watching the tension in her face disappear as quickly as it came.

Marya came and sat beside him on the bed. "Robert, you are good." She turned her face up to him. "I underestimated you."

"Save it and put it to music," Robert said in disgust. He pulled away from her gaze and sat in the chair by the window facing her. "Yes, I am good." He looked at her hard. "And you might as well face the fact that by this afternoon I'll know who you are and who you work for. You could save us both a lot of trouble by telling me now."

Marya smiled. "But then you'd miss all the fun of finding it out all by yourself."

Robert tried to suppress his anger. "All right, we'll play hardball. I'm only after a story. You're after a lot more. I might remind you that there are other interested parties who would be very curious to know the information I've uncovered as well as anything I might tell them about you and your activities."

"What parties are you referring to?" Marya asked, narrowing her eyes at him.

"Well," Robert replied easily. "Just off the top of my head, say the Russian FSB for a starter."

Marya jumped off the bed. "You wouldn't dare. You're playing a very dangerous game threatening me, Dr. Tate."

"And why is that? Why should my talking to the Russian FSB worry you? Have you committed any crimes that you wish to admit to all of a sudden?" Robert stood up to face her. "Why should the FSB be a problem for you?"

"You don't understand a thing," Marya said, angrily.

"So, explain it to me. It was, after all, the Russians who were robbed. They're just trying to recover what is rightfully theirs."

"Rightfully theirs!" Marya's laughter was an ugly sound. "That's a matter of opinion."

Robert could not understand the sudden bitterness in her voice. "What's that supposed to mean? Of course the Abdication Egg belongs to them. It's one of their national treasures."

Marya stood silent.

"For God's sake, Marya, tell me. I'll just find out anyway."

"You do what you have to," Marya said, "and I'll do what I have to."

Robert sat back down, sighing with exasperation. "Marya, I'm just trying to get the story. I'm not in competition with you. You want the egg. Why, I don't know. The Russians want it because it belongs to them."

Marya sniffed her disagreement.

"Whatever!" Robert almost shouted. "Look, I don't particularly care who gets the damn thing. I'm just doing my job so I can continue to get paid. If you get the egg, fine. What am I gonna do, take it from you? I don't care. I just want the story."

Marya went back to the window for another look. Her expression softened. "What are you proposing?"

"What do you mean what am ... you know damn well what I'm proposing. I have sources that you don't have, and you apparently know what the hell this is all about in the first place." Robert lay back in the chair with his arms spread, pleading. "Let's put it all together, okay? We'll both be a lot farther ahead. You get what you want ... I get what I want."

Marya smoothed the material of her jumpsuit over the curve of her waist to her hips. "But that would mean I'd have to trust you."

"With a little more understanding of each other's position in this, that won't necessarily be so hard."

Marya thought a moment, pacing the floor in front of him. "All right, Robert. We'll play together." She sat on the edge of the bed facing him. "What do you know about Carl Dieter?"

"Whoa," Robert said, holding up his hand. "This part of the game we're not going to repeat. It's your turn to give. What do you know about Carl Dieter?"

Marya looked at him with a slight smile. She pursed her lips, moistening them. "Carl Dieter is a bastard. He stole the egg from the original thieves and sold it to Ivan Schloss." Her eyes became slits of light. "Carl Dieter is going to die very soon. I'm going to kill him."

"Why?"

"That's my business."

"Who were the original thieves?"

Marya smiled. "I don't know."

"Who are your sources of information?"

"Confidential."

Robert sat forward. "Well, at least that's something."

Marya laughed. "We're going to get along wonderfully, Robert."

"What is the next move you're planning?"

"I was on my way out to have breakfast."

"It's the middle of the night, for Christ's sake."

"Check your watch again, Doctor," Marya said, feigning offense.

Robert did. It was almost eight. The fact that it was growing light outside had completely eluded him.

"My God!" Robert said in exasperation. "I haven't even been to bed yet."

"We can do that first, if you like," Marya purred, stretching out on the bed.

Robert stood up. "Let's eat."

"But Robert," Marya teased. "We need more understanding, more closeness, more trust."

"We'll talk about it over coffee," he responded, heading for the door.

Marya made a disappointed sound and got up to follow him, grabbing her purse off the bed. "It was just a thought, but perhaps I'm not your cup of tea."

"Where are we headed?" Robert asked, opening the door and ignoring her.

"I know a marvelous little café in the business district," Marya said, brightening. "It's on Weimarstrasse."

The name sounded familiar to Robert. He searched his recent memory. "*Weimarstrasse*." He recalled the phone listing. "That's the street Dieter lives on."

"Yes," Marya said, brushing past him out the door. "He's just across the street from the café."

The drive was a short one, but parking was at a premium and Robert had to make the block several times before finding an empty spot at the curb.

Marya sprang out of the car, energized by the morning air. "Looks like we're going to end up walking a bit anyway," she said, taking in a good portion of the crisp atmosphere. She jogged in place beside the car, her breath building up a cloud of condensation around her. She laughed. "Let's race."

Robert looked at her wearily, rubbing his face. "I wish I had taken time to shave."

"It looks sexy," Marya called out, starting down the sidewalk at a slow pace. "Leave it like that."

Robert followed after her, making no effort to keep up.

Marya ran a few tight circles around him and then slowed to a walk beside him. "You Americans," she said in mock derision. "You can do nothing before your morning coffee."

"I'm not insulted," Robert said, opening the door to the small café. "But this place had better make a good cup of it."

Marya led him over to a table by the front window. "They have the most wonderful sausage here," she said hungrily, taking a seat. "Let's have that, and some eggs, and potatoes, and . . ."

"Hold it, hold it," Robert groaned, feeling the return of his indigestion. "All I want is a cup of coffee, maybe some toast."

Marya frowned at him. "How can you get through the day on that?"

"My God, you're like a female version of . . ." Robert stopped short. "This isn't the only meal I plan to have today, for Christ's sake!"

"You never know," Marya cautioned, happily scrutinizing the strudel on the table next to them.

Robert caught the waitress's eye and motioned for some coffee. She brought the steaming pot over immediately and filled their cups.

She took out her pad. "*Bitte?*"

"*Anglais?*" Robert asked.

"*Ja*, I speak English," the waitress said with a gap-toothed smile.

Marya smacked her lips. "Sausage, eggs, potatoes . . . oh, and a little of the strudel please."

Robert rolled his eyes. "Just toast for me please and a little marmalade."

"*Danke*, thank you," the waitress said, eyeing him sadly.

"She's probably wondering why you even bothered coming in," Marya chastised.

Robert decided to changed the subject. "Any activity across the street?"

"Nothing since we've been here. But you have to know Dieter. He's just come into a lot of money. That means he doesn't bother to go into work anymore." Marya sipped her coffee. "Dieter sleeps late these days." She stared out the window.

"Exactly which building is it?" Robert asked, trying to follow her gaze.

"Just there, across the street," Marya said with a nod in the direction. "Above the tobacco shop."

"Got it. Dieter's shop?"

"Yes," Marya replied wistfully. "Though he's hired someone to run it for him now."

The waitress came over with their food. Robert pulled the saucer of toast over to his corner of the table to make room for the plates bearing Marya's breakfast.

"What is your plan?" he asked, reaching across for the marmalade.

"Just to watch . . . and wait." Marya attacked the sausage. "I want to speak to him alone."

"He has a wife?"

"No, nothing so steady," Marya managed through a mouthful of potatoes.

"Ah. He can afford to buy companionship now." Robert watched in awe as she inhaled the plates of food. "You're going to make yourself sick."

"Hmmm?"

"All this spicy food so early in the morning."

Marya swallowed. "Americans. Such weak stomachs."

Robert caught a glimpse of movement out of the corner of his eye. "Someone's leaving." He squinted through the glass at the figure coming out of the tobacco shop. "A woman."

Marya glanced up briefly and then returned to the last of her sausage. "Yes, that would be Brilda."

"Brilda?"

"Dieter's current whore."

Robert watched as the scantily clad woman teeter-tottered on spiked heels away from the tobacco shop, trying to keep her wig in place in the stiff breeze. "Charming."

Marya laughed and drained her coffee cup. "That was wonderful, Robert," she said, stretching and giving his hand a pat. "I want a breath of fresh air while you take care of the bill." She shouldered her purse and stood up.

"While I take care of the bill?" Robert's eyebrows went up. He surveyed the empty plates in front of her. "Right."

Marya sauntered out the door and stood stretching in the crisp air. Robert pulled out his wallet and extracted a credit card for the waitress. He followed her to the register and waited as she fumbled with the embosser, trying to figure out its mechanism. Finally giving up, she printed the information from the card to the charge slip and handed it to him for his signature. Robert quickly totaled the bill, tore his copy off and headed for the door.

"Marya?" He looked around. She was nowhere to be seen. "Damn it to hell!" He sprinted across the street to the tobacco shop.

A thin, arthritic old man behind the counter looked up as Robert entered the shop. Robert gave a quick glance around the shelves of magazines and cigar boxes but saw no sign of Marya.

He walked casually over to the counter and the old man. "Excuse me. *Anglais?*"

The old man shook his head.

"Damn," Robert muttered under his breath. His German was a little rusty. "My friend . . . *meine freund, Bitte? Eine Fräulein?*"

"*Fräulein Holsted?*" the old man piped, trying to be helpful.

"*Ja, ja.* Where . . . uh . . . *wo ist Fräulein Holsted, Bitte?*"

The old man pointed to the stairs at the back of the shop. "*Dort.*"

Robert smiled at him. "*Danke, Mein Herr, Danke.*" He gestured to the stairs with a questioning look. The old man only shrugged his shoulders and returned to the magazine he was reading.

Robert bounded up the stairs. He tried the door at the top but it was locked. He stood for a moment listening to the unmistakable sound of a man whimpering and crying behind the door. He debated breaking the door down but decided not to risk making such a row. He rapped lightly on the door. The whimpering ceased immediately but no one opened the door.

Robert called out through the door, "Marya, you open this door now or I'll break it down. Now!" He knocked again, louder. "Marya!"

The dead-bolt slid back with a soft thump and then silence. Robert tried the knob again and the door opened. He entered cautiously. Marya sat on the edge of a mammoth four-poster bed, impatiently rocking her pistol, now equipped with a sleek, black silencer, in her hand. On the floor at her feet lay a squat, hairy, heavy-set man in his underwear, clenching his right knee, or at least what was left of it.

Robert quickly shut the door. "What the hell . . ."

"Come in, Robert, dear. Carl was just telling me what he did with our missing egg." The ice in her smile sent a shiver through Robert.

"What the hell do you think you're doing?" Robert demanded. "This is not necessary."

"I say it is," she replied evenly. "At any rate it's too late to worry about. What's done is done."

"She's mad!" Dieter cried from the floor, moaning. "You must do something!"

"Shut up, you filthy bastard!" Marya snapped, turning her pistol on him again.

"You should be dead!" Dieter said with a whimper. "I killed you." He looked up to Robert pleading. "She's a demon from hell!"

Marya laughed. "You stupid, fat pig!" She aimed the gun at his other knee.

"Stop it!" Robert started for her.

"Not another step, Robert," Marya warned.

Robert froze in his tracks.

"This is my problem," Marya said evenly, "and I won't have you interfering with it. As soon as this pig tells me what I want, we'll leave. Until then, my family will not tolerate anymore of his treachery."

She lowered the pistol level with Dieter's other knee. "Get on with it, traitor. Stop wasting my time."

Dieter cowered against the wall, trying to stem the flow of blood from his splintered knee-cap. "You are dead! I know I killed you!"

"Obviously you didn't!" Marya put a hand to her chest, remembering the pain he had caused her. "Bad luck for you," she said, spitting on Dieter. She looked at Robert. "I had a pistol in the breast pocket of my jacket when this swine shot me. It deflected the bullet, but not completely." She looked down at Dieter. "And you will tell me what I want to know because there will be nothing to deflect my bullets, traitor!"

"I told you, Schloss has it!" Dieter groaned as a tremor of pain racked his body. "I needed the money. I don't know where he's got it."

Marya squeezed on the trigger.

"I'm telling you the truth," Dieter whimpered. "If I knew where it was I would tell you."

"He's telling the truth," Robert argued hotly. "We know for a fact who has the egg now. Let's get out of here."

Marya pursed her lips. "You disappoint me, Carl. You've been much too cooperative." She stood and started for the door. "You betray your family. Now you betray Schloss."

"I needed money," Dieter spat through teeth clenched in pain. "The family did nothing for me! If they want the egg then let them buy it from Schloss. It means nothing to me. Russia will never be returned to us. You can tell . . ."

Marya spun on him in an instant. Her pistol made a spitting sound and Dieter's head slammed against the wall in pieces.

"Goddamn it!" Robert sputtered, grabbing for Marya's gun.

She turned it on him just as quickly. "Don't be foolish, Robert."

Robert froze again. "That was murder!"

Marya smiled at him and returned the pistol to her purse. "That was an execution." She brushed past him out the door.

Chapter 16

Robert cursed silently and spun the car out of the business district. He had not anticipated Marya's disappearing again, or he would have never taken the time to search Dieter's room before leaving. He hammered the steering wheel with his fist, chastising himself for having been fool enough to trust her again. He decided it was time to pay Hamm another visit and see what he had come up with.

He skidded to a stop outside *Die Bleu Angel*. Now that it was daylight, parking around the club was vacant and the building looked deserted. He tried the front door but it was locked, so he walked around the side looking for another entrance. He spotted another door near the back next to a pile of plastic garbage sacks filled to overflowing. He tried this door and, finding it locked as well, pounded loudly on it with his fist.

He hammered several more times until he finally heard the locks inside being released. He stepped back, and the door opened as far as the inside safety chain would allow. Robert could make out the sheen of bleached hair and the smell of a cigarette through the crack.

"*Geschlossen!*" A woman's smoke-deepened voice shouted out at him.

"I'm here to see Hamm," Robert told her, pressing against the door to keep her from closing it.

"Closed!" she reiterated in English.

"My name is Robert Tate. I'm here to see Hamm. Tell him I'm here. He'll see me."

She tried vainly to push the door closed but he kept his weight solidly against it. Finally she left the door cursing. Robert waited patiently and within a few moments she was back, releasing the safety chain.

"*Kommen Sie,*" the woman said, pulling open the door. She stood clenching her bathrobe closed at the neck.

Robert stepped in quickly out of the cold and the woman slammed the door to behind him. She padded heavily ahead of him in her house slippers, leaving a trail of acrid smoke and guttural profanity. Robert followed her to the bottom of a stairwell.

"Up here, Tate!" he heard Hamm call down to him. "You're a little earlier than I expected."

Robert started up the stairs. "My need for that information is a little more pressing now. I'll take whatever you've got." The stairs ended in a small loft.

Hamm sat at a desk under a gabled window ahead of him, pecking at a computer keyboard. "Come in. Have a seat."

"Rather an impressive set-up, Carl," Robert said, greeting Hamm with a smile. "You always had a knack for mastering the latest technology."

Hamm's laugh bellowed through the loft. "If by that you mean I like to tinker with the newest gadgets, yes. Since you were control agent in these parts we've made a few improvements. Everyone's linked by satellite now. The latest intelligence at your fingertips."

"Considering how easy it is to acquire a satellite transmission," Robert commented, "I assume it's at the Russian's fingertips as well . . . and the Chinese, the Saudis . . ." He sat in a large, overstuffed chair beside Hamm.

"Only if they can break the encryption and there's the rub. Company technology is far ahead of anything anyone else may have."

"What have you got for me?"

Hamm threw him a folder with several pages of computer printout and faxed documents stapled inside. "There's information on the girl. By the way, her real name *is* Marya . . . but Marya Alexandrovna . . . not Dmitrievna."

Robert studied the printouts. "Hmmm, which means Marya, daughter of Alexander in Russian. All Russians have three names. All you have here is the Christian name and the name of the father. Where is the family name?"

"I've got stuff coming up on the family now. Give it a few seconds."

Robert returned to the folder. "I see she attended a preparatory school in Connecticut. She would have needed a visa. The State Department should have a dossier on her."

"It's all coming up," Hamm grunted. "Don't be so impatient."

Robert watched the printer spewing out pages of documents. "The Company has access to State Department computer files now?"

Hamm smiled mischievously. "Well, we're not supposed to. But, if you'll pardon the expression, we have ways."

Robert nodded. As long as they maintained discretion the Company was literally allowed to get away with murder.

Hamm pulled some of the pages off the printer and handed them to Robert. "There, start on these. Ought to keep you busy awhile."

Robert scanned the pages. "This is all censored. What's the deal?"

Hamm took a look. "That's strange. Usually only information dealing with nuclear stockpiling and other strategic defense matters is censored like this."

"I'm just asking for information on this woman and her family. What the hell's going on?"

"Let me check the computer again," Hamm said, turning back to the keyboard. He input a few coded messages. "These are sealed files. You have to have special authorization to open them."

"Well, let's see what we do have." Robert flipped through the censored documents. "Maybe we can surmise the rest."

"Oh sure. Right!" Hamm almost laughed.

"The grandfather . . . name deleted . . . and a family member, a sister, given political asylum by Norway in October of 1918." Robert looked puzzled. "Why in the world would they be given political asylum? 1918. That would be the time of World War I."

"Armistice Day was November 12, 1918," Hamm offered.

"They joined an already large community of White Russian exiles there. Those would be exiles from the Revolution in 1917."

"Ah, Lenin," Hamm said mockingly. "My hero."

"This is interesting. They arrived to Norway via Germany. I'll be damned!" Robert looked at Hamm in surprise. "They had diplomatic papers giving them safe travel under the Kaiser's personal protection. Who the hell were they?"

"Traitors?"

Robert shook his head. "No, I don't think so. They wouldn't have been welcomed by the Russian exiles if that were the case."

"Beats me then."

Robert leafed through the photocopied documents that had been faxed from the Company archives.

"Here's something." He pulled out one of the documents. "It's a copy of a diplomatic telex. 'The hostages are safely across the border.'" Robert stared at it. "The hostages. What does it mean *the hostages*?"

"Got to be the grandfather and his sister," Hamm said, glancing at the communiqué."

"Make that great-grandfather . . . but hostages? What kind? Why?" Robert pointed to the printer which had grown silent. "I need some recent history. Let's have the rest."

Hamm pulled the pages from the printer and handed them to Robert.

Robert scanned them quickly. "The family's certainly got money. Father's heavy into investments, commodities, industry. There it is again. Only the first two names, Alexander Nikoleivich. No family name."

He flipped through the papers. "Here's a record of a marriage to a granddaughter of the Grand Duchess Xenia. One daughter, Marya Alexandrovna. Mother died shortly after birth." He looked up at Hamm. "That's it?"

Hamm shrugged. "That's all the archives have and all the computer will cough up."

"Bullshit!" Robert went over to the computer. "There is no security reason why these files should be censored. There must be some mistake."

"Tell it to Washington."

"Have the Level IV access codes been changed since I was here?" Robert asked, thoughtfully.

"That was over seven years ago. I'm sure they have been."

"Carl, know thy enemy. Let's bet on the consistent nature of even the Company bureaucrats."

"What do you mean?"

Robert typed in his former call codes. "I'll lay you odds my codes are still good."

"Ain't no way, brother."

The computer screen flashed.

"What's it say?" Robert asked with a smile.

Hamm stared in disbelief. "No way. I ain't believin' this."

"I told you. Look, it still identifies me." Robert nudged Hamm out of the chair and sat down. He typed a few more numbers. "Ha!" He pointed to the screen. "It clears me for computer access."

Hamm shook his head. "We live in a scary world."

"I had Level IV clearance before I left. Let's see." He pecked away at the keyboard. "I'm in!"

Hamm eyed the acceptance message on the screen. "You know you could make a fortune as a foreign agent."

"Right now I'd rather know who this family is and what makes them so important and internationally sensitive."

"There's your call prompt." Hamm nodded to the computer screen. "Go for it."

Robert grabbed up the sheaf of printouts and checked the headers for the file code. He entered it and watched the computer screen. "Come on, come on! What's taking so long?"

"Give it a break, Tate. Even a computer takes a few seconds to sift through a million-plus files for your one." Hamm leaned in next to Robert to read the next line of text that scrolled across the screen. "That's just a prompt for you to clear the room before accessing the actual file. Just a security precaution."

"Are you going to leave?" Robert asked with a raised eyebrow.

"Hell no," Hamm answered flatly.

Robert laughed. He hit the return key to access the file. The screen blinked off and the printer started up again. It stopped within seconds.

"One page?" Robert stood up to retrieve the document. "All that trouble for one page?"

"Must be one hell of a page?" Hamm quipped.

Before he could retrieve it from the printer Robert's eye caught the file name at the top. "What the hell!" He grabbed the paper off the printer and stood staring at its contents.

"Well?" Hamm pressed.

"I'll be goddamned!" Robert said, clearing his accesses off the computer screen.

"What?"

"Thanks a lot, Hamm, I owe you one," Robert answered, stuffing the paper in his pocket and grabbing for his coat.

"Wait just a damn minute, partner. What's it say?"

Robert made a dash for the stairs, struggling into his coat. "I'll give you a call later, Carl. This is too hot to wait." He ran down the stairs with Hamm in pursuit.

"At least tell me I didn't give you any defense secrets!" Hamm called after him.

"You're clear!" Robert hollered back to him. "Just a little rewrite of history." He fled out the door and around the building to his car.

Chapter 17

Robert stood out in the cold pacing beside his car. He was excited by the historical significance of his find, and at the same time, anxious that the job had suddenly taken on a new dimension of danger. His thoughts went to Noah.

"Fuck it!" Robert said aloud, clearing his thoughts. Noah was safe back in the States. Robert pulled open the car door. He'd have to find a way to clean up these matters quickly before Noah's involvement got any deeper.

Robert revved up the cold engine and threw it into gear without waiting for it to warm up. He patted the paper in his pocket and felt his heart pounding. He sped through the streets as fast as he could safely guide the car, finally screeching to a stop in front of the hotel. He raced across the street, through the door, and up to the desk without breaking stride.

"*Fräulein* Holsted," Robert called to the desk clerk. "Has she returned?"

"Yes, *Herr* Tate," the clerk replied.

"Is she in her room?"

"No, *Herr* Tate." The clerk raised his eyebrows. "Madam checked out of her room and asked to be put in yours . . . with you. I hope that was all right, *Herr* Tate, you did say that . . ."

"Yes, yes," Robert said running for the stairs. He bounded up them two at a time. He tried his key but the safety chain was on. He pounded on the door mercilessly until Marya, rubbing the sleep from her eyes, came to open it.

"Robert, darling, what's all the banging about?"

Robert slammed the door behind him and followed her back to the bed. He turned on Marya. "What the hell did you think you were doing? You give me one good reason why I shouldn't be on the phone to the police."

Marya stretched out on the bed. "Robert, dear, don't be so excitable."

"Excitable! You just killed a man in cold blood!"

"It was a killing well-deserved. He tried to kill me and he betrayed my family."

"How? And what gives you the right to go around killing people?"

Marya smiled up at him. "You know as well as I do that all justice is not meted out by the courts. Family justice is an age-old remedy."

"Not in this day and age it isn't.

"You can't be that naive, Robert."

Robert stood fuming by the window, clenched fists on his hips. "You didn't even wait for me. You just left me there holding the bag."

"I had some other business to attend to," Marya answered. "You're a big boy. I figured you could take care of yourself."

Robert looked back at her. He hadn't noticed the thin, silk pajama top barely covering her thighs. Stretched out on the bed as she was, it was hiked even higher. When she rolled over to face him he thought, for an instant, that she had nothing on underneath.

"Marya Alexandrovna," Robert said, trying to achieve a look of disdain.

"So," Marya said, unconcerned. "You know my real name."

"Oh, you'd like me to think that was it, wouldn't you?"

Marya sat up. "What do you mean?"

"I mean I've run a full check on you, including secret archive files from the State Department."

Marya jumped from the bed like a cat. "Impossible. How could you?" She stood facing him. "You're lying."

"First rule of warfare, my dear. Know your enemy."

"You're a private investigator for a news service. Now you would have me believe you're sifting through secret government files." Marya laughed haughtily. "Why are all men so over impressed with themselves?"

Robert took the printout from his pocket and held it up to her. "Take a look at the code name at the top."

She reached for the paper, but he held it out of her reach. She squinted across the distance and read the line. "How?" Her face paled even whiter. "That is a fake!"

"No, no. It's the real thing," Robert said. "And so, apparently, are you."

"It is not possible." Marya paced the room around him. "How did you get that? Who has broken our promise of secrecy?"

"Quite simple really," Robert said, grabbing her arm and pulling her around to him. "I used to be part of the U.S. Intelligence team in Western Europe. I still have many friends in the service. One did me a favor."

Marya looked at him with renewed interest. "You are CIA?"

"Was."

Marya leaned back on the bureau. "So . . . you know my little secret."

"Hardly a *little* secret," Robert parried. "I assume the Russian government is aware that their former Royal Family is still intact?"

"Of course." Marya took in a deep breath, causing her ample breasts to expand against the thin, cashmere sweater she wore. "They were, after all, the ones who traded the heir and his sister to the Germans in the first place."

"Can I also assume that they know you're involved in the theft of both the Abdication Egg and the egg at the New Orlean's Museum of Art?"

"No you may not." Marya leaned forward seductively. "But FSB has been following you and your . . . companion to see if you can lead them to the ones who are involved."

"Of course." Robert shook his head. "Should I call you, Princess?"

"I have no interest in titles," Marya said. "My father and grandfather have a greater claim than I."

"And the Tsesarevich?"

"He died before I was born, some forty years ago."

Robert considered this. "He lived surprisingly long considering his condition."

"Medicine made some significant strides in the west," Marya said with a shrug. "He was severely crippled by his disease, but like all of us, he was a survivor."

"So," Robert leaned into her, "Your Royal Highness, the Princess Marya Alexandrovna *Romanoff*."

Marya smiled. "Very impressive. Not many men can make a fool out of me."

"Save it," Robert snapped, tightening his grip on her. "I want to know what the hell is going on. I know who you are. I know who your family is. But what is the deal about this damn egg?"

Marya jerked free of him. "It belongs to us."

"That's a load of crap. It belongs to the Russian people now."

"That's a matter of opinion," Marya said through clenched teeth. "It's ours. We want it!"

Robert took in her reaction, suddenly realizing the point. "You stole the damn thing in the first place, didn't you?"

She rolled her head back to him with an alluring half-smile.

"Didn't you?" Robert grabbed her arm again and pulled her back to him.

"What if I did?"

"Jesus, God-awful Christ!" Robert seized her by both shoulders. "What kind of game are you playing? Do you think for one minute the FSB will let you live when they find this out."

Marya smiled up at him. She wrapped her arms around his neck and pulled him closer to the bed. "I'm a big girl too, Robert. I can take care of myself."

"You're a fool!"

"You will take care of me then," Marya said.

"Then I would be a fool. You'll end up getting both of us killed."

"Let's not fight, Robert."

"Damn right!" Robert snapped, sarcastically. "Why don't we just go out and see who you'll murder next?"

"I don't feel like killing," Marya purred, pressing close to him.

"Forget about it!" Robert said in a low voice, stepping back from her.

"Robert . . . sweet Robert," Marya said as she pulled the pajama top off over her head. "There's nothing more one can do until morning, except . . ."

"I'll sleep on the floor," Robert said quickly.

"Don't be silly." Marya unsnapped her black silk bra. "Let's not waste this opportunity to get to know each other better."

"I think I know you very well, as it is," Robert said, turning his back to her.

"Robert." Marya encircled Robert's chest with her arms, pressing into his back. "Don't you find me desirable."

"I'm not interested," Robert said, peeling Marya's hands from his chest.

"I see." Marya smiled and leaned in, breathing heavily into Robert's ear. "If you like, you can take me from behind—fantasize that I'm anyone else you may desire."

"Don't be ridiculous!" Robert turned to face her. "This isn't going to happen, Marya, so—"

"If you like," Marya said, wrapping her arms about Robert's neck, "you can even call me . . . what's his name . . . Nora?"

"It's Noah," Robert said evenly, "and if your know that, then you know good and well that *this* is not going to happen."

"Robert," Marya purred, "you must trust me to be sensitive to your needs?"

"I don't trust you farther than I can spit a brick."

"Then kiss me," she pulled his face toward hers.

"What? Wait just a damn . . ."

Marya fell back onto the bed pulling him down on top of her. She pressed her lips hungrily to his and held him struggling on top of her.

The door flew open.

"Bobby, it's me. I thought I'd never find this . . ." Noah froze in the door, dropping his suitcases to the floor. "What the hell's going on here?"

Chapter 18

"Noah!" Robert managed to extract himself from Marya's hold. He stood up straightening his jacket. "What are you doing here?"

"What am I doing here? What am I doing here!" Noah's face was flashing shades of red. "Don't you know? I'm a voyeur. This is how I get my kicks!"

"We . . . We were just discussing some information I uncovered about Marya's family," Robert stammered. "I . . ."

"Put it to music and whistle Dixie, Bucko!" Noah fumed. "What do you think, I was born yesterday? Discussing some information, my Aunt Fanny!"

"Now don't go off half-cocked," Robert said, trying to pull Noah's suitcases in so he could shut the door. "How did you get in?"

"They gave me a key at the desk. I guess they figured what's one more occupant in the room with you."

"Don't be childish," Robert said reprovingly.

Marya remained stretched out on the bed chuckling. "Robert, there's no use pretending. We were fooling around."

"We were not!" Robert snapped. He turned back to Noah. "She was trying to change the subject . . ."

"Some change of subject!"

"Noah, if you're not going to be reasonable about this . . ."

"Look," Noah said. "I'm a grown man. You're a grown . . . old man. You don't have to make explanations to me. What you do is your business." He sniffed. "Business! Well, now, there's an interesting word these days."

"Let's try getting down to it then, shall we?" Robert hoisted Noah's suitcases up onto the bed beside Marya. "What did you find out in Houston?"

Noah looked at him self-righteously and then glared at Marya.

"It's okay," Robert assured him. "Marya is going to work with us this time." He continued before Marya could speak. "If we don't get this story, she knows we'll have to write about another one I've uncovered."

Marya lay back on the bed silently under Robert's meaningful gaze.

"Now. What do you have?" Robert asked, turning back to Noah.

"Gilroy's dead."

Robert raised an eyebrow and Marya sat up sharply.

"While I was interviewing him, two men," Noah said still peeved, "FSB guys I'll bet—it's getting where you can smell them—came to the house. I was in the kitchen when Mr. Gilroy answered the door. They murdered him."

"Why him, for God's sake?" Robert asked.

"There was supposed to be a small crucifix in the egg she stole," Noah glared at Marya again, "which Mrs. Gilroy apparently kept when the egg was originally sold. The two men knew about it and tried to force Mr. Gilroy to give it up."

Marya jumped from the bed. "Did they get it?"

"They must have," Noah hedged.

"Did you see it?"

"Oh, yes," Noah replied with a Cheshire smile. "He showed it to me. Quite an unusual piece. Very ornate and oddly shaped."

Marya sat back down, crestfallen.

"What's the deal with this, Marya?" Robert asked. "What's the significance of this other egg? Why did you really steal it? What about this crucifix?"

Marya closed her eyes and took in a deep breath. "I told you. It belongs to my family. It is a precious heirloom we want returned."

"Bullshit!"

"Believe what you want. I'm telling you the truth." Marya turned away from him, refusing to argue further.

Robert grabbed Noah by the shoulders. "You got out okay?" Robert looked at Noah, his face clouded with concern.

"Like a bat out of hell," Noah responded. "I was lucky." He shook free of Robert's hands and plopped like an angry child onto an over-stuffed chair beside the window.

"All right then," Robert said, pacing in front of the bed. "We need to get some copy together for the office. Can't sit around looking like we're spinning our wheels."

"Oh, yeah." Noah fidgeted in the chair. "There's one more thing."

"More?"

"Madelyn took us off the story."

Robert stood dumfounded. He finally found his voice. "What? She did what?"

"We're off the story. That is, you're off the story. I quit."

"Why the hell did Madelyn do that—and why did you do *that*?"

Noah smirked. "First answer, the law came down from on high, and second answer . . . why do you think?"

"Goddamn, Madelyn!" Robert began to pace again. "She'll do anything to keep from rocking the boat. Damn!"

Noah pulled his knees up and wrapped his arms around them, rocking silently in the chair.

"Wait a minute." Robert's brow puckered. "If we're off the case and you quit, what the hell are you doing here?"

Noah cocked his chin in a defiant pose. "I'm not quitting this story, just the job."

Robert threw his hands up. "Look, if we're off the story, we're off the story. It's as simple as that. Neither of us have the financial resources to keep this up."

Noah came up out of the chair to face him. "You can't be serious. You're quitting? What kind of reporter are you? You can't quit this when we're so close to breaking it open."

"Noah you're not being practical, and you're also not seeing . . . or you're refusing to see how dangerous this assignment is. You barely escaped being killed, not to mention what's been going on around here." Robert threw a glare in Marya's direction.

Marya merely shrugged and reached for her cell phone on the nightstand, though keeping an ear tuned to the argument going on around her.

"We might as well pack up and go home." Robert added.

"I will not!" Noah exclaimed. "You go right on back to your stuffy old house. I'm staying here."

"You cannot stay here. You don't know anything about this country or the people. You don't know how things work here."

"I'll learn." Noah's eyes flashed up at Robert.

"You'll learn, my ass." Robert massaged the beginnings of a headache at his temples. "I need my job and you need your job, Noah. Now face it and quit trying to be Anderson Cooper or whatever hero you're fantasizing about."

Noah drew his fists up to his chest, fuming. "How dare you talk to me like that? At least I'm not a wishy-washy, corporate puppet. What's wrong with a little heroism anyway? God! You're such a damn know-it-all! At least I'm willing to take a chance and do something that's right . . . that's important. At least it won't be said of me that all I did was sit in some historical pile of bricks all my life reading and writing drivel that didn't amount to a hill of beans or do diddly-squat for anyone else."

"Look, Noah," Robert said, feeling the sting of his own conscience as well as the boy's words. "I've played my part in that game already." He was almost screaming at Noah. "I've already done that, okay? I've already given my pound of flesh for truth, justice, and the American way. I don't need some Pollyanna from the sticks preaching to me about shit!"

Marya snapped her cell phone closed and kicked a pillow up at Robert to get his attention. "So, Dr. Robert Tate of McNaughton News Corporation. You *are* ex-CIA."

"CIA?" stuttered Noah, jerking his head from Marya to Robert.

"So fucking what?" Robert snapped. He turned away from Noah and headed for the closet to retrieve his own suitcase. "If you want to hang around here and make a fool of yourself, or get yourself killed, that's your business. I'm going back to New York."

"You were in the CIA?" Noah pursued him to the closet. "You were in the CIA, and you didn't tell me?"

"Not just in the CIA, Mr. Taylor," Marya said from the bed. "It seems that, at one time, Robert controlled the entire Eastern European operation."

"What!" Noah grabbed Robert's arm and tried to jerk him around. "You?"

"Like I said, kid, I've already played my part in the big picture. And though I doubt it'll do any good, here's a little advice for you from someone who's been there. It ain't worth it." Robert returned to his packing.

Noah darted about the room in a burst of nervous energy. He ignored Marya, who lay on the bed watching him and Robert.

"All right, Bobby, all right," Noah said finally. "Your reasons for pursuing this case are different from mine. Granted. You're in it for the money, I understand that. You have things that are important to you that you don't want to lose."

Robert emptied the contents of the chest of drawers into his suitcase with methodical precision, refusing to even look at Noah.

"There's still a way to make money with this," Noah continued to press. "Don't you see? We can sell this story to any of the wire services."

Robert had heard enough. "And then what? Provided we're still alive to collect this little pittance, then what? We'll both still be out of a job."

"Dammit, Bobby, innocent people have been killed, and like it or not we're in the middle of it all."

"You really are naive if you think for one minute that there is anyone innocent connected with all this crap."

"Bobby, you can't quit! We're so close! Look, we can get the egg ourselves. Just imagine the money you could sell it for."

"Good God!" Robert laughed harshly. "When will you stop day-dreaming?"

"It is a shame," Marya said, interrupting. "With your connections and expertise, you, more than anyone else, could probably recover the Abdication Egg."

Robert looked at Marya in disbelief. "You, I didn't expect to be as crazy as this one."

"Just because you quit the story, what makes you think the FSB will stop pursuing you?" Marya asked.

"Oh, my God!" Noah's hands went to his face. "She's right!"

Robert leaned back against the door, defeated.

Marya rolled to the side of the bed and kicked his suitcase shut with her foot. "My family would be willing to pay a great deal of money to anyone who would recover that egg for us." She sat up smiling at him. "You did want to work together, Robert. Here's your chance. I can trust you a lot easier if you're working for us rather than for someone else."

"You can't be serious."

"I am. I have full authority from my grandfather to do whatever is necessary to recover that egg, including hiring agents outside the family."

Noah pushed himself in between Robert and Marya. He stood, facing the woman, hands on hips. "What kind of deal are you offering?"

Robert pushed back at him. "I'm not interested in making any deals."

"No, no, Robert. Be reasonable. Noah is right," Marya said giving a wave in Noah's direction. "You should listen. We will pay all your expenses and a thousand dollars a day."

Noah's eyebrows went up. "A thousand dollars?" he stammered.

"All right, fifteen-hundred."

"Fifteen-hundred, Bobby!"

Robert shook his head. "It's all still too temporary. I like my job and the security it offers. I'm not interested."

"If you succeed in recovering the egg for us, my family will pay you a substantial bonus."

"How substantial?" Noah questioned.

"A hundred thousand dollars."

Noah's voice caught in his throat. All he could do was grab Robert's sleeve and shake him, wide eyes pleading with him.

"That's a lot of money," Robert said.

"Is it enough?" Marya asked, stretching back out on the bed.

"It really doesn't matter if we both get killed, does it?" Robert closed the latch on his suitcase. "Personally, my life is worth more to me than a hundred thousand dollars."

"Dammit, Bobby…" Noah began.

"Of course," Marya interrupted. "What was I thinking? Two-hundred fifty thousand."

Noah looked like he might faint. "Two hu… Bobby … dude!"

Robert silenced him with a look. "We could be killed."

"But, Robert, you're a professional," Marya stretched out on the bed. "You're dealing with amateurs, common thieves. You have more than an edge."

"Common thieves don't steal priceless works of art from the Kremlin."

Marya smiled. "I did that, Robert dear. We're looking for the swine . . . other than poor Dieter . . . who stole the egg from me before I could get it home."

Robert's face flushed with anger again. "Someone tell me why I'm not surprised at this."

"Who's *poor Dieter?*" Noah asked.

"Never mind!" Robert pointed at Marya. "You stole the egg from the Kremlin?"

"Well, they wouldn't give it to me."

"Shit!" Robert slapped himself on the head. "I knew it!"

Marya laughed. "It's water under the bridge at this point, Robert."

"Somehow I doubt that the FSB and the Russian State will feel the same way."

Marya shrugged her shoulders again.

"And," Robert continued, "I don't need to remind you that the FSB are not amateurs."

"You can handle them, Bobby," Noah said excitedly. "But you're right about the danger factor." He looked haughtily at Marya. "Two hundred and fifty thousand dollars is not enough."

"What!" Robert exclaimed.

"All right, Mr. Taylor," Marya nodded in agreement. "Perhaps I underestimated that aspect. I'll raise the ante to two thousand dollars a day plus expenses."

"And the bonus?" Noah asked, trying to keep from dancing.

"A half million dollars," Marya replied, without batting an eye.

"Stop trying to buy me!" Robert demanded before Noah could react.

"Robert, darling, you are driving a hard bargain," Marya said, shaking a finger at him. "All right. Five thousand a day plus expenses and a million dollars upon delivery."

"Sold!" Noah shouted, slamming his fists into Robert's back excitedly.

"Just a damn minute!" Robert interrupted.

"A million dollars, Bobby!" Noah threw his arms about Robert and hugged him tightly. "Dude, you can't afford to turn this down. When we recover the egg . . ."

"If we recover it."

"When . . . If . . . Whatever! The point is you can put a new roof on that monstrosity of yours and have enough to keep it up in style until doomsday."

"Listen to him, Robert," Marya interjected.

"Both of you just back off!" Robert pushed Noah off him and fled to the window and stood nervously tapping his fingers against the glass, staring down at the people in the street below.

The offer was more than tempting, but the thought of returning to a lifestyle he thought he had left behind weighed heavily against any amount of money. He thought of his house back in New York, realizing for the first time that he really could not afford it. He had been fighting unsuccessfully, ever since inheriting it, to keep the house from crumbling into disrepair. Still, he couldn't lose it. The house was all he had left of his family. He turned back to face Noah and Marya, his mind made up.

Robert looked at Marya with poker-faced detachment. "A million and five thousand a day plus expenses. Okay, but we'll need some money up front."

Noah almost jumped across the room to Robert, but Robert raised a hand to stop him.

Marya raised an eyebrow at him. "How much?"

"We'll need at least fifty thousand up front. If you want me to use these connections, as you call them, I have to be prepared to pay them."

"Fifty thousand dollars would do it?" she asked.

"It would be a start."

Marya reached for her cell phone again. She punched in a number and while she waited asked, "What bank do you want the funds transferred to?"

Robert pulled his wallet from inside his jacket and extracted a card. He handed it to Marya. "This is my bank in Frankfurt. That's my account number."

"He has a Frankfurt bank account." Noah danced about the room.

Marya took the card. "I'll take care of it." She spoke Russian into the phone.

Noah threw his arms around Robert's neck before his mentor knew what hit him. and hopped excitedly from foot to foot. "I knew it, I knew it, I knew it! This is so fantastic!" He peppered Robert's face with kisses.

Robert tried to pry the boy's hands apart behind his neck. "Calm down, Noah."

"How can I calm down? We just made fifty thousand dollars."

"We just spent fifty thousand dollars."

"What?"

"That money is for up front expenses so don't get too excited."

"Oh, to hell with it!" Noah said, suppressing the urge to laugh hysterically. "I've never spent fifty thousand dollars before, either. My God! A million dollars!"

"Don't spend that yet. We haven't earned it."

"We will," Noah said, continuing to dance about Robert.

"Not if we're killed first."

"We won't be."

"We might."

"No we won't."

"What makes you so sure? I'd like a little assurance of that myself."

"Because you won't let us."

"I won't let us?"

Noah looked at him with a sudden hurt expression. "Why didn't you tell me you were a CIA agent?"

"Was."

"Whatever. Still, it's something you could have told me."

"Now you know."

"Is there anything else I should know?"

"Nothing that you won't find out sooner or later, I'm sure."

"It's done," Marya said, closing her cell phone. "The funds have been transferred. You can call and confirm it with your bank."

"There's plenty of time for that," Robert said. "We have to decide on our next move."

"Oh, this is too much for one day," Noah said, holding his stomach. "I'm famished."

"So am I," Marya agreed. "There's a wonderful beer garden not far from here with even more wonderful bratwurst!"

"Dear God!" Robert moaned.

Chapter 19

Robert stretched back into the reclining seat and reached up to close the sliding shade over the small window that magnified the glare of sunlight at the jet's thirty thousand feet cruising altitude. He hadn't wanted to purchase first class tickets, but it was the only thing that would shut Noah up. He glared at the empty seat next to him and hoped he could fall asleep before its occupant returned.

"Miss me?" Noah's voice gave Robert something of a start, snapping him out of his much desired relaxation.

"Are you through stalking about the cabin?" Robert asked wearily.

"I wasn't stalking." Noah plopped down into his seat. "I was talking to the stewardess."

"The stewardess?" Robert couldn't help smirking. "Or do you mean that young steward?"

Noah smiled and batted his lashes. "I have no idea what you're talking about."

"Right." Robert folded his arms across his chest. "I need to get some sleep."

"Sleep?" Noah slapped Robert's forearm. "I'm too excited to sleep!"

"I'm not," Robert said with finality, closing his eyes.

Noah stared at Robert for a moment. "Fine!" he said, crossing his own arms angrily. "I get it!" He stood the silence until he could stand it no more. "No, I don't get it!"

Robert stirred and tried to turn toward the window.

"You haven't said a civil word to me since New Orleans," Noah complained, "ever since we . . ." Suddenly things were clear. "Okay, okay." He turned to Robert. "Obviously we need to talk this out."

Robert ignored him.

"I said," Noah grew louder, "we need to talk this out."

"Noah," Robert muttered, "I'm trying to sleep here."

"Sleep?" Noah looked around at the other passengers. "You sure weren't interested in sleep that last night in New Orleans!"

Robert shushed him. "I don't want to talk about this right now—let me sleep," he whispered.

"Well, I do want to talk about it."

"Shut up, Noah."

"And you certainly didn't say that in New Or—"

"I'm done with this!" Robert turned away to the window again and closed his eyes.

"Oh, well," Noah said, winking at the older woman across the aisle, "he should've thought about that before sleeping with a sixteen-year-old."

"What?" Robert sat up quickly. "You are not sixteen!" He noticed the older woman's scowl. "He is *not* sixteen—he's twenty-six if he's a day."

"I am not!" Noah glared at Robert again. "Are you

ready to talk yet? Otherwise, I have so many stories left to tell our fellow passengers."

"Goddamnit!" Robert jerked Noah around to face him. "What are you doing?"

"You made love to me," Noah said accusingly, "and you've obviously got some issues with that."

"You don't know anything—"

"I know that ever since, you've treated me like I've got herpes or something."

"I have not!"

"Have too!" Noah's eyes misted over. "What did I do? Did I make you mad? "I . . . was I . . . not good enough?"

"Noah—"

"Can't handle the poor, white trash from Texas, is that it?" Noah persisted. "Good enough for a fuck, but too stupid—"

"Now stop it!" Robert put a hand over Noah's mouth. "Stop it! Quit putting words in my mouth."

Noah plopped back into his seat, arms still crossed like a barricade—his eyes a mixture of fire and water. "I should've known," he said, finally.

Robert relaxed back into his own seat, exhausted.

"You had your fun." Noah teared up. "Guess I was pretty easy." He began to sob. "You bastard!" The flood gates opened.

Robert squeezed his eyes shut, trying to keep an emotional distance. His resolve was shaken by a black, leather purse that circled over his headrest and struck him in the crown. "Shit!" he cried out, sitting up quickly. He turned to face a middle-aged woman with big, brown-dyed hair, and the expression of a valkyrie coming in for the kill.

"Shame!" the woman's voice shot at him. "You're old enough to know better! Shame!" she reiterated, shaking her purse at him. She reached over to pat Noah's shoulder. "Poor dear," she cooed. "You're too good for this . . . this . . . Her eyes sighted down over her eyeglasses at Robert. "Pedophile!"

Robert covered his head with his hands. "I am not a pedophile, madam, thank you very much—now mind your own goddamn business."

"Don't be mean to her because of me," Noah sobbed, wiping his eyes. "She's just trying to help."

"Help?" Robert's voice rose. "By hitting me on the head?"

"You deserved it!"

"Sir?" The young steward had descended on the scene. "Sir?" He leaned into the seats, eye to eye with Robert. "Sir, you need to settle down. You're disturbing the other passengers."

Robert's jaw dropped. "But—"

"This is the only warning I'm going to give you, sir," the steward cautioned. He put a hand on Noah's shoulder. "Are you all right?" he asked, pressing a tissue into Noah's hand. "Can I get you something to drink?"

Noah nodded, trying to regain his composure. "Thank you," he said, his voice shaking. "Could I have a vodka martini?" He wiped his eyes again. "Do you have Grey Goose?"

The steward smiled, nodded, and headed down the aisle.

Robert thought about ordering his own drink of choice, but the look the steward gave him, made him rethink that plan. He sighed. "Okay, Noah," he said, resigned to his fate. "I'm sorry you're upset. I'm sorry I didn't want to discuss this. I'm sorry I'm so tired I can't see straight." He turned to face Noah. 'Let's talk about it."

Noah looked away and blew his nose into the tissue.

"You were right," Robert said, "we should talk about all this."

"I'm not talking to you," Noah said with a sniff.

"Oh, for God's sake!" Robert poked Noah on the shoulder. "You turn around right now and talk to me or I promise you, I'll end this little partnership and your little soap opera before the plane lands."

Noah folded his arms and plopped back into his seat angrily, pouting.

"Well?"

"Well, what?" Noah huffed and puffed for a moment.

"Okay, look." Robert searched for the right words. "I do *not* think you're stupid. I don't think you're . . . not good enough."

"What, then?" Noah wouldn't meet Robert's gaze.

"Noah . . ." Robert shook his head at the petulant boy. "What we're doing is dangerous. I realized early on that getting close to you was going to be too easy. If we weren't working together, this would be very easy, but . . . I can't let my feelings for you develop any further."

Noah's head jerked around. "That doesn't make any sense," he said, finally looking Robert in the eye. "The fact that this mess is dangerous is all the more reason for us to be close—to need each other—to care about each other."

"No," Robert responded, "you don't understand. You're too much of an optimist to see the possibilities we face."

"I think we would be so good together. We are good together. I want to be close to you. It makes the danger bearable."

Robert shook his head again. "We are too different."

"Opposites attract."

"Jesus!" Robert laughed out of exasperation. "And while we're deep in this little love affair you're idealizing, what happens if I get killed?"

Noah blinked. This was not a possibility he wanted to consider. "That's not going to happen."

"Yes, it could," Robert insisted. "I've dealt with people and situations like this many times before and people most certainly get killed. Good God, Noah, you've already experienced that!"

"Yes, but," Noah hesitated, "but not to you. You're too good at the game. You know how to deal with all this—"

"This is not a game, and I don't know shit!" Robert's emotions clouded his usual reserve. "And if not me, then what if you get killed?"

Noah sat stunned. "Me?"

"Yes, you!" Robert put a hand on Noah's arm. "You could get killed."

Noah thought about this. "I could get hit by a taxi crossing the street to Starbucks, too, but there's no since living my life under that kind of paranoia."

"Have you considered that maybe I do live my life with that kind of fear—and it's not paranoia, it's reality. I'm not talking about accidents with taxis. I'm talking about our walking willingly into situations that could get either one of us killed!"

"But—"

"But nothing!" Robert closed his eyes, trying to keep the memories at bay. "I have lost someone that way. I have had to wake up and realize that someone I love isn't there anymore. I have had to try and pick up the pieces and move on, and it's *not* possible. The pieces stay in pieces, Noah. I'm not . . . enduring that again!"

Noah stared at Robert. "You lost someone? I . . . Oh, Bobby . . . I . . . didn't know. I'm so sorry."

"Stop!" Robert held up a hand. "I really don't want to talk about that anymore. I just want to forget about it." He sat back in his seat. "It's just best that you and I try to keep things on a business basis. We have a job to do, that's all."

Noah couldn't believe his ears. "I can't do that, Bobby."

"Noah—"

"No. You have not been listening." Noah reached out to turn Robert's face to his own. "I can't just be your business partner. I can't be just a neutral, third party in all this. My . . . feelings for you are way past that, and I think you feel the same way."

"You don't know me or my feelings," Robert protested, trying to pull away.

"Bullshit!" Noah's smile was ablaze. "You're not that complicated, boyfriend, and neither is love."

"Shit!" Robert sat up. "I think this thing between us is more about lust than love."

Noah giggled. "Well, yes, there is that, but you're not one to succumb to . . . animal passions without good reason."

"And what good reason might that be?" Robert couldn't pull his eyes away from Noah's beaming face.

"You said it yourself," Noah reminded him. "You have feelings for me—and not just lust." His eyes moistened once more. "That's so sweet."

"God!" Robert sat back again. "All right! I have . . . feelings for you . . . but I can't live through losing someone again, I—"

"That's bullshit! You're already proven that you can."

"Are you kid—"

"That's not what I meant," Noah added, quickly. It's just that life goes on. If we try to avoid the deeper, wonderful parts of living, what are we left with?"

"Noah . . ."

"I mean it, Bobby. Is that townhouse really enough?"

"You don't understand."

"If something happens to me, you'll remember me forever and nothing can take away any of the beautiful memories we're going to create together. Better to have loved and lost—"

"Please don't be trite." Robert rubbed his temples.

It's better to live right here . . . right now, Bobby," Noah smiled, "than wallow in the past or fret about the future."

"Easy to say."

"That doesn't make it any less true," Noah said, taking Robert's hand.

"Noah—"

A familiar black purse descended from behind, once more striking Robert off guard. He turned sharply to face the purse's mistress, glaring at him through the space between the seats.

"Grow up!" the woman hissed at Robert. "You're being a god . . . damned . . . asshole! I've buried two husbands—two loves, and I don't regret one minute of it!"

"Really?" Robert rubbed the pate of his head. "You don't regret burying them?"

The purse raised ominously into the air.

"Okay, okay!" Robert reached up to push the purse back at its owner. "You've made your point! Now would you mind minding your own business for a while. I'm trying to have a discussion with my boyfriend!"

"He's winning!" the woman said with a smirk.

"I know he's winning, madam, but you're not helping the situation." Robert turned back into his seat and closed his eyes again, praying he would pass out from sleeplessness. He felt Noah's head settle against his shoulder. "Shut up and go away," he said, quietly.

Instead, Noah encircled his arm into Robert's and snuggled closer. Robert looked at him and found the younger man staring up at his face. Robert had seen that look before, in another time and place, and the effect it had on him was just as quickening. He sighed into the boy's face. "Goddamn it."

Noah smiled up at him. "Gotcha." He pulled Robert's face down and kissed him.

Robert cursed the smile that broke over his own face. He leaned back against the head rest. At least now, maybe he could get some sleep.

"You're really tired, huh?" Noah asked.

"Shut up."

"Too tired."

"Shut up."

Noah looked about for a moment. "Oh, the bathroom's finally free." He leaned his head against Robert's ear. "I'm going to the bathroom," he whispered.

"Send me a postcard," Robert responded, still trying to doze.

"I want to do something dangerous."

"Jump out of the plane without a parachute." Robert could feel Noah's eyes narrowing at him.

"Listen here, old man, we're gonna make a memory . . . right now . . . whether you want to or not."

Robert dropped his chin to his chest. "What are you talking about now, Noah?"

"We're at least a *mile high* right now, right?"

"So?"

Noah turned back to the woman behind them. "Ma'am, he needs another smack with that purse."

The woman sat forward. "I got this, hon." The purse rose.

Robert jerked up. "Don't even think about it!" he

said, glaring at the woman.

"Boy," she said, "you need to start using something other than your brain before it falls off for lack of use."

Robert stared wide-eyed through the seats at her. "What are you—"

"Come on." Noah stood laughing. "You'll be a lot safer with me," he motioned to Robert to follow, "in the bathroom," and headed out into the aisle.

"What?"

"Dumbass!" came the woman's voice from behind him.

"Oh . . ." Robert's sleep deprived brain caught on. "God . . . dammit!" he said, surrendering, and got up to follow, but not before flipping off the purse lady from behind his back.

Chapter 20

Noah's first view of Moscow was a disappointment—not at all what he had expected. The buildings about the international airport were not particularly esthetic, especially since Noah was expecting Byzantine spires and a Kremlin-like, overall design. Instead, what greeted him as he exited the plane onto the runway was an odd assortment of low, utilitarian structures, sunk in drifts of snow and ice. The wind was gale-like, cutting right through his favorite Hugo Boss wool blazer. He shivered uncontrollably.

"I told you to put on your overcoat," Robert scolded, reaching from behind Noah to take his messenger bag and overnight bag so that the shivering boy could maneuver into his black, Burberry wool coat.

"I didn't think any place could be colder than New York," Noah said, accepting his help.

Robert shook his head and escorted his protégée down the wobbly ramp onto the runway. "Customs check is this way." He pulled Noah into the direction of one of the low, grey buildings ahead of the other passengers.

Noah glanced down at his feet, tingling towards numbness in his Bruno Magli oxfords as he tip-toed through the slush. "You've been here before?"

"Once or twice," Robert said. "You know, you'd have been a lot more comfortable if you had worn something more practical like I told you. This isn't the runway at Nordstrom's."

Noah came to a sudden, sliding stop. "Oh, my God!"

"What's wrong now?" Robert caught him before he went face down in the icy mud.

"What if they recognize you?" Noah's voice dropped to a tense whisper. "You're CIA, remember?"

"Was." Robert grabbed the boy's arm and pulled him into the relative warmth of the building.

"Was! Is? What's the difference?"

"If you'll stop acting like we're trying to smuggle in heroin, we'll be just fine."

"But they probably have your name, maybe even your picture on a computer. They'll run a check and . . ."

Robert put his hand to Noah's mouth and smiled at the other passengers who were beginning to stare. "This, kid, is one of the world's largest bureaucracies. Officials have to fill out forms in triplicate just to take a piss."

Noah smiled up at him through the tips of the fingers covering his mouth. He could smell the light, spicy, scent of Robert's cologne still clinging to his hands.

"Besides," Robert continued. "Anything *thorough* is the exception, not the rule here." Noah followed at his heels as Robert got into line for the passport and visa check.

A stocky woman with the face of a bulldog scanned his passport and then his face. "*Gaspadin* Tate," she managed through a thick-tongued accent. "Your reason for visiting Russia—business or pleasure?" Her voice had an accusing edge.

"A little of both," Robert replied in his most cultured tones. He gave her a warm smile. "My colleague and I," he nodded at Noah whose face froze in a frightened smile, "will be spending most of our time at the State Museum researching a book."

The woman drew her massive chest up, flashing a row of medals and ribbons. "Pleasure!" she announced emphatically and pounded the passports with a large stamp. "Enjoy stay!" She returned the passports to Robert.

"What did she call you," Noah whispered, "Gaspar or something?"

"It means the equivalent of *mister*," Robert said returning Noah's passport to him.

"Not *comrade*?"

Robert grabbed for Noah's hand, rescuing the fingernail the boy had been chewing on, and pulled him along to the front of the terminal. "Let's go."

"What's the hurry?" Noah complained, stumbling along behind him.

"If we don't hurry, all the cabs will be gone. We could be stuck here for hours waiting for transportation."

The weight of his overnight bag wrenched at Noah's arm as he struggled to keep pace. "Let's just call for the hotel limo, for crying out loud."

Robert threw him a patronizing glance. "This is Moscow, young Valentino, not New York." He held the heavy glass door open for him impatiently. "There's a cab over there." He pointed toward a small, rusty-white hatchback. "Go for it!"

Noah started for the car but his feet were too wet and cold to risk walking fast, much less running. Robert dashed ahead of him. He had already given instructions to the driver and tossed his carry-on into the back by the time Noah waded up beside him.

"I'm not having any fun, Bobby," Noah said, panting.

"Good." He took the boy's bag tossed it in with his own. "This is business."

"This is Russia," Noah moaned, falling into the back beside his bag. "Land of Dr. Zhivago, Catherine the Great, the Bolshoi."

"No, this is what's left of the once evil empire, the Soviet Union," Robert corrected, climbing in the opposite side. "Land of Stalin, the archipelago, the former KGB . . . now FSB." He nodded to the driver who spun the small car out of the slush and into the street.

They rode in silence. Robert stared ahead while Noah watched the dreary skyline morph into more exotic visions.

"Where are we going first?" Noah asked. "A hotel I hope. My feet are soaking."

"Sorry, but I warned you," Robert said, shaking his head again at Noah's thin, leather oxfords. "We're going straight to the Armoury Museum."

Noah's brow furrowed with disappointment. He started to protest but Robert interrupted with a wave of his hands. "We don't have time to sightsee. We're here for a specific purpose, and I don't want to be here any longer than I have to be."

Noah sat stiffly back into the car seat, his arms wrapped tightly about himself, sulking. "You ought to learn how to enjoy life a little more."

Robert raised an eyebrow at him. "I'll enjoy life plenty after we've been paid."

The twinkle came back into Noah's eye. "Paid? I almost forgot." He sighed and looked out the window. "Well, you sure know how to make a boy feel better."

The automobile's wheels skidded slightly in the slush as the cab driver pulled to a stop beside an imposing red brick wall that stretched into the distance broken only by an occasional tower.

"Why are we stopping?" Noah asked, searching the street around them.

Robert exchanged a few terse words in Russian with the driver before throwing open his door. "Come on," he said, stepping out into the cold. "We have to walk the rest of the way."

"Walk? How far?" Noah hopped out his side of the car and pulled his heavy suitcase out. "I thought we were going to the Kremlin."

Robert was ahead of him, moving toward an open gateway that seemed a mile away through the vaulting red brick. "This is the Kremlin."

Noah was attempting to tip-toe through the dirty slush. "This is a brick wall," he complained after Robert. "The Kremlin is a beautiful palace. I've seen pictures, so find yourself another sucker."

"Kremlin is the Russian word for fortress," Robert said with professorial boredom. "The Kremlin is a series of palaces and structures surrounded by this wall. It isn't just one building."

Noah dropped the hard-shell suitcase into the slush. "I knew that." He stood panting. "How much farther?"

"We've a good distance to go. The Kremlin's a big place."

Noah called after him, "Can't we take the cab?"

"Only official cars are allowed into the Kremlin. Everyone else is on foot."

"My feet are frozen!"

"That's your fault."

"Damn you, Bobby Tate!" Noah scooped up a handful of dirty ice and threw it at him. "You come back here and help me!"

Robert turned, but stood his ground. "I told you not to bring all that crap."

Noah stomped his foot, sending a spray of ice and water over his already leaking oxfords. "Stop being so mean! I didn't bring anything I didn't need."

"It seems to me you didn't bring anything you could use," Robert said, pointing at Noah's poor choice of shoes. "Besides, I seemed to have done quite nicely with a briefcase."

"In case you haven't noticed recently, I have very specific skin-care needs, besides which I am not used to traveling great distances for short periods."

Robert stood, hands on hips, not budging. "This is what fieldwork is all about. Far be it from me to spoil your *fun*."

"I can't lug this thing all over Moscow."

"We'll check it at the Museum, and pick it up when we're done."

"How much farther?"

Robert pointed ahead. "Across the square."

Noah followed the direction of his finger. "Across the square! It's as big as five football fields."

Robert shrugged and started out across the slush once more.

Noah's glare bore into Robert's back. He threw his head back and let out an ear-piercing scream.

Robert almost slipped to the ice and mud pavement. He spun around and sprinted back to Noah, sputtering.

"Are you completely insane? Do you want to get us arrested?" Robert stood over his young nemesis menacingly.

Noah was not impressed. "Help me with this bag," he said between clenched teeth, glaring up with satisfaction at Robert's red face.

"All right, all right." Robert grabbed up the heavy suitcase. "Stop making such a fool of yourself." He thrust his own briefcase at Noah. "Think you can manage this?"

Noah batted his lashes at him. "My knight, to the rescue again." He smiled thinly, grabbing the briefcase.

Robert hauled the suitcase across the square, grunting. Noah hopped along from paving stone to paving stone behind him, trying to keep as far above the muck as possible. He could barely feel his toes through his thin, wet, frozen socks.

"This is the Armoury Tower," Robert said, at last arriving at the gate. "The Museum is just inside."

"Thank God," Noah moaned. He looked down picturing his blue toes.

Together, they climbed the marble steps and pushed through the heavy doors into a decaying foyer. Large cracks spider-webbed the grey walls, broken only by the occasional white circlets of water damage. A desk with peeling veneer sat next to the only other door and was manned by a young woman in military woolens.

Noah shivered and stomped the slush from his feet. "Geez, it's not much warmer in here."

"Hush!" Robert hauled the heavy suitcase over to the desk. "Good afternoon," he said in his most American voice.

"Closed," the young woman said quickly, rising to her feet.

Robert pulled out his PI identification. "American Press."

She studied his credentials for a moment and smiled nervously. She motioned to them to wait and hurried off through the doorway.

"What does she mean, *closed?*" Noah's set the briefcase on the floor and massaged his arm. "What kind of hours do these people keep, anyway?"

"Budget cuts," Robert answered. "This economy is almost bankrupt so you can bet museums are at the bottom of appropriations lists."

"So what else is new?" Noah sighed impatiently. "How long do you think it'll be, Bobby? That little snack on the plane is wearing thin."

Robert threw his hands up. "How, the hell, do you keep from weighing five hundred pounds? I swear all you do . . ."

He was interrupted by the arrival of the guard followed by an older man, bundled up in a heavy coat, and thin white hair jutting from under a beaver cap.

Robert offered up his identification again. "American Press about the Fabergé egg," he said with a broad smile.

The older man waved his ID away. "I am Dr. Anatole Gatenyan, State Curator. We are closed." He started to turn to leave.

"We are here to verify the fact that the stolen Abdication egg has, indeed, been recovered."

The old man turned back. "It has been." Gatenyan did not attempt to hide his annoyance. "Statements have already been released to the foreign press corps."

Robert stepped forward. "Yes, well, you must understand that there is a considerable amount of skepticism on that issue. Our instructions are to see it for ourselves, and if possible, photograph the egg."

"Impossible."

"Then I will have to write that the egg's recovery cannot be confirmed."

The old man's eyes narrowed.

Robert continued, "And that the previous statements alleging the egg's recovery were, more than likely, merely a face-saving ploy to silence criticism that recent budget cuts have compromised Kremlin security."

Gatenyan paled angrily. "Western reporters think we have nothing better to do than escort them around on free tours. I have work to do."

Robert pulled out an American one hundred dollar bill folded and clutched it between his finger. He tapped the numbered edge of the bill against his chin where only the old man could see it.

"I know it's a bother, Dr. Gatenyan, but surely you can see how you would benefit by having as many international news agencies as possible see the recovered egg for themselves."

Gatenyan's eyes widened at the sight of such a small fortune. "It is still a bother," the man said, extending his hand for the reward, "but I cannot argue with your reasoning. Come this way." He started through the door.

"Hold it" Noah commanded, grabbing Robert's sleeve before he could follow the old man. He stood pointing to his suitcase.

Robert snorted with annoyance. "You and that damn case."

Noah took a deep breath, portending a loud scream.

"I'll take care of it," Robert said quickly, "I'll take care of it."

Noah smiled and sat down Robert's briefcase as well. He stroked Robert's cheek with his fingers as he passed by to follow Gatenyan through the door. "Such an *old* world gentleman," he purred.

"Watch this for me," Robert said to the young woman behind the desk.

She stiffened and frowned at the imposition.

Robert hauled the suitcase up on the desk and flipped its release catches. He rummaged about through its contents before pulling out a couple of unopened packages of expensive skin-care product. "I'm sure my assistant would want you to have these for your trouble," he said, closing the case with a snap.

The woman guard picked up the packages and fingered them with undisguised excitement. "Shall I watch your bag as well?" she asked, as if hoping for further reward.

"Thank you, no," Robert answered with some regret. He wondered what else of Noah's he could give away, but grabbed up his briefcase instead, and headed after Noah and Gatenyan.

Gatenyan led them down a vaulting corridor, lit only by the judicious spacing of wide, narrow windows set close to the ceiling. Robert took Noah by the elbow and pulled him along to prevent his absent-minded pauses to study the renderings of various imperial portraits that adorned the walls. The current thriftiness of the State apparently made the use of artificial lighting an unnecessary extravagance in the once famed museum. They passed through several darkened galleries, occasionally encountering a low wattage bulb burning just above the doors into those exhibition rooms lit only on an as needed basis.

Noah was too enthralled with trying to absorb as much as possible from the innumerable paintings along the way to engage Robert in conversation. Robert welcomed the momentary cease-fire and did his best to keep the boy aimed in the right direction. They followed Gatenyan into what seemed to be one of the innermost galleries. Robert and Noah stood at the door trying to focus what little available light there was.

Gatenyan fumbled in a corner for a moment before finding the toggle switch he was looking for. The rows of glass display cases encircling the room erupted in a blaze of light, amplified and prismed by their jewel-encrusted contents. Noah could only gasp as he stood steadying himself against the doorjamb.

Robert scanned the veritable fortune in useless, whimsical, yet priceless artifacts that rested on crushed velvet behind the faceted glass. He raised an eyebrow at Noah's open mouth. "So this is the Imperial Russian toy box."

Noah swallowed. "Beats my hat pin collection, that's for sure."

"You have a hat pin collection?"

Noah refused to be baited. "What an exquisite display," he said to the curator.

Gatenyan puffed with pride. "It was the nature of the Tsars to be wasteful." He bent over to examine a favorite collection of various bejeweled and enameled animal miniatures. "Still, even their waste has survived the centuries. If you wish to call art, waste!" The edge in his voice emphasized what was obviously a commentary on the current state of Russian politics.

Noah headed toward an impressively tall display case across the room. "These are the Easter eggs?"

Gatenyan waved a hand. "Some of the best examples of the Fabergé art in the world. The Abdication Egg is on the third shelf, center."

Robert followed Noah to the case. While he stood, nose to the glass, studying the delicate, egg-size object, Robert took note of the fresh putty around the display glass borders.

"I don't suppose there's any way we could take it out of the case to examine it, is there?" Noah did not take his eyes off the Abdication Egg.

Gatenyan looked horrified. "Absolutely not! These art objects are sealed into a purified air environment. They may not be handled in any way."

Robert tapped Noah's shoulder. "I assume there's not much more we can do."

Noah shrugged him off. He turned to Gatenyan. "I'm sure new study photos were taken of the egg to document its condition after recovery."

Gatenyan raised an eyebrow. "Of course."

"May we see those?" Noah asked.

"I can assure you the Abdication Egg was recovered in perfect condition."

"And we have every confidence that is true," Robert interjected. "But the McNaughton News Corporation requires a little more."

Gatenyan huffed. "They're in the files in my office."

"That would be the final proof we'd need," Robert said, taking Gatenyan's arm. "Come along, assistant!" He pulled Noah away from the display.

They walked the length of the marbled corridor to the suite of offices at the end. Gatenyan pulled the ring of keys from his belt and unlocked the office door. He allowed then entry reluctantly. The office, itself, was sparsely furnished, but what furniture was there was heavily laden with a menagerie of papers, files, massive journal volumes, and boxes of the same.

"Please do not touch anything," Gatenyan warned.

Robert gave Noah a knifing glance to further stress that warning. Noah resisted the urge to raise his middle finger.

Gatenyan went straight to the row of file cabinets behind the mound of paper that was his desk. He pulled open a drawer and rummaged through it hurriedly. With a satisfied grunt he pulled out a tattered bundle which he took with him to his chair. He sat heavily and pulled the rubber bands from around the file. After another moments search, he extracted two letter-sized, clear plastic folders containing negatives and held them out to Robert.

"Don't you have any developed shots?" Robert asked, frowning at the folder.

"These are better," Noah said, snapping the folder from Gatenyan before Robert could take them. He dashed to a table by the door and reached out to move a stack of portfolios. He paused, turning to Gatenyan. "May I?"

The curator nodded, though scowling his annoyance.

Robert moved to Noah's side and helped move the heavy portfolios from the table to reveal a small light box. Noah pulled several strips of negatives form the folder and held them up to the light while Robert felt about the box for an on switch.

Noah slapped one of the negative strips down onto the light board as it flickered on. "These are very good quality," he said, glancing back at Gatenyan.

Gatenyan shrugged. "We manage," he said, acidly.

Ignoring him, Noah turned his attention back to the negatives glowing atop the light board.

"Can't see much," Robert said. He squinted harder trying to make out some detail in the credit card size negatives.

Noah pulled at one of the chains about his neck and extracted a jeweler's loop from inside his shirt. "The right tools for the job, my daddy used to say."

Robert stepped back from the board to allow Noah a better vantage. Noah bent over the strip of negatives, examining them like so many diamonds.

"Ha! There we are," Noah trumpeted. He stabbed a finger at one of the negatives. "Just as I suspected."

Robert leaned into the boy with his back to Gatenyan. "Keep quiet," he whispered close to Noah's ear. He straightened. "Let me have a look," he said, louder. "Two witnesses for their authentication will carry more weight."

Noah looked at him puzzled.

Robert smiled thinly. "So you're absolutely sure this is the Abdication Egg?" His look was pleading.

Noah shrugged, playing along. "Yes, absolutely." He pointed to one of the negatives and offered Robert the magnifying lens. "Take a look at the detail in this one."

Robert let out his breath and took the jeweler's loop from Noah and bent over the negative. He recognized the image as a shot of the bottom of the egg. He focused the lens over the small monogram stamped into the egg's base. He recognized it instantly. "That confirms it," he said, straightening. He returned the loop to Noah. "Thank you very much for your time and patience, Doctor." He slipped the negatives back into their protective folder and carried them back to Gatenyan's desk.

Gatenyan took the folder from him. "Will that be all?"

"If you wouldn't mind answering a question or two more, Doctor? We could use a little more background on the Abdication Egg to round out our story."

Gatenyan consulted his pocket watch. "This has put me far behind in my work, as it is."

"I appreciate that, Doctor, but we will only take a minute or two more," Robert assured him.

"Very well," Gatenyan said, straightening in his chair. "A few more questions, but then I must return to my work."

"Thank you, Doctor." Robert motioned Noah to his side. "Doctor Gatenyan, we have found nothing in the printed history of this egg to give us an idea of what it contained."

"Nothing at all," Noah affirmed, nodding.

Gatenyan shrugged. "That is because the Abdication Egg has never been opened."

"Never?" Noah frowned.

"The egg was designed with a rather complicated locking mechanism and no key or any design specifications for a key have ever been located," Gatenyan said.

"But surely your experts could get it open," Noah prodded.

"Not without damaging a priceless objet d'art," Gatenyan said with a frown. "The egg was thoroughly x-rayed and found to be empty in any event."

"Empty," Noah and Robert said simultaneously.

"Confirmed by x-ray," Gatenyan continued. "The opinion of experts is that the egg was not designed to contain anything of importance in the first place." He sat back in his chair. "You see, tied into that complicated lock mechanism I mentioned was what appears to be an ingeniously designed explosive device. We believe it was a devious design of the Tsar's to get even in some small way with the revolutionary forces that were moving to overthrow him."

"I see," Robert said.

"I don't," Noah chimed in.

Robert sighed at him. "Consider the old saying, curiosity killed the cat."

"Ah," Noah said, still looking confused.

Robert turned back to Gatenyan. "May we see the x-rays?"

Gatenyan looked back at the imposing row of massive file cabinets with undisguised displeasure.

"It will be the last thing we'll bother you for," Robert assured him.

The unhappy curator shuffled over to the row of over-stuffed filing drawers and pulled one out hastily, dislodging a waterfall of papers from the stack on top of the cabinet. He muttered some obscenity in Russian and extracted one of the yellowed folders. "I hope this will not take long," he said, holding out the folder to Robert.

"This should only take a moment," Robert said with an apologetic look. He handed the folder to Noah.

"Let's have a look." Noah pulled his jeweler's loop from inside his shirt. "This is one of the newer x-rays." He pulled the black film from the file. "And here's one dated from the 1950s. Good, we'll have something for comparison." He held both films up to the light and studied them side-by-side.

"Well?" Robert asked impatiently.

"Keep your boxers on," Noah muttered, keeping his eyes on the x-rays. "They look identical." He returned the older x-ray to the file and turned his eye and jeweler's loop on the newest. "Interesting."

"Can you be a bit more specific?" Robert whispered into the boy's ear.

"There's some sort of mechanical hodgepodge inside. I can make out cogs and wheels and . . . it's like the inside of a watch."

"Is it authentic?"

Noah smiled at the x-ray. "I think I've seen enough," he said, sliding the x-ray back into the folder with its mate. "We've got what we need."

"So that is the Abdication Egg in the display case?" Robert asked, looking Noah in the eye.

"It looks like the Abdication Egg to me," was all Noah would respond.

Gatenyan took the folder from him. "I trust your report will be complete as well as truthful."

"You can count on that, Dr. Gatenyan," Robert said, trying to understand Noah's strange look. "This will put an end to all those unfortunate rumors once and for all."

Gatenyan grunted his satisfaction. Robert motioned Noah to the door.

"I'll have to show you out," Gatenyan said, rising. We'll be on our way, Doctor

They followed him out of the office and down the hall in silence. Noah fought to keep pace with the two men while keeping a tight grip on Robert's arm. He wanted to yell so bad it hurt, but Robert's even demeanor calmed him. Once in the reception area, both retrieved their respective cases.

Robert turned to Gatenyan and extended his hand once more. "Thank you again, Doctor. I know dealing with the press can be a little tedious, but I can promise you some tourist friendly publicity for your trouble."

Gatenyan smiled thinly. "That would certainly be appreciated," he said nodding to Noah. "We find ourselves more and more dependent on admission fees."

Noah started to speak, but Robert spun him around and hustled him toward the door. For once he offered little resistance.

As they hit the frigid, outside air, Noah took in a deep, almost gasping breath. "I'd say we're still in the money," he managed.

"The egg is a fake, then?" Robert didn't sound surprised.

"The newer x-ray is," Noah responded. "It was just a copy of the old one."

"How could you tell?"

"They didn't even try very hard," Noah said with a laugh. "Even the most expert photographer can't return a subject who has left and come back into exactly the same angle and perspective for a second take. It's impossible. When I said the two x-rays were identical, I meant exactly identical down to the orientation, perspective and angle of the wood grain the egg was sitting on.

Robert continued down the steps to the icy mall. Noah chased after him, lugging his heavy suitcase. He swung it forward, striking Robert on the butt. "Don't pull this silent crap with me, Bobby Tate. Before you start actually believing I'm just your flunkey little assistant, let me remind you differently."

Robert stopped and rolled his eyes heavenward. "I'm just trying to plan our next move." He grabbed the suitcase from Noah. "Which I can do a whole lot easier in silence."

"Eat shit and die!" Noah said, hands on hips.

"To answer your question, yes, we're still in the money." Robert looked at Noah evenly. "Though how much is another question."

Noah's brow furrowed. "What do you mean by that? The finder's fee is a million dollars."

"If we find the egg," Robert reminded him. "That's a big if. Still, if worse comes to worse, we still have a story to sell if Madelyn is game."

"Story, shmory!" Noah retorted. "We're finding that damn egg."

"Greedy little thing aren't you?" Robert turned and continued across the mall.

"Ambitious is a better word." Noah followed. "Now what's our next move?"

Robert looked about, studying the expansive square. "There's something I've always wanted to do here."

"Really?" Noah tried to follow Robert's line of vision. "In Russia?"

"No, here . . . in the Kremlin."

"Bobby, it's too cold," Noah whined, bobbing up and down to try and keep warm.

Robert pulled Noah to him and sheltered the younger man in the embrace of his overcoat. "Indulge me," Robert said.

Noah looked up at him, confused. "What are you . . ."

Robert pulled Noah's face to his. Their lips melded. Noah's wide eyes, relaxed and closed, and his arms slipped about Robert's waist inside the warm overcoat. Finally their lips parted.

"Wow," Noah said, momentarily panting.

"I agree." Robert tightened his grip about Noah.

"You surprised me," Noah said, resting his head under Robert's chin. "What was that for?"

Robert released him and stepped back, giving the Kremlin complex a last once over. "That kid," he said, "was one for the good ol' Red, White, & Blue!" He grabbed up Noah's suitcase and headed for the gate.

"Long may she wave!" Noah shouted, chasing after Robert.

Chapter 21

Noah sipped at the dark brew that was supposed to be coffee. He suppressed a now persistent yawn and tried to shake the sleep from his eyes.

"That's done," Robert said. "The letter of credit is in and I completed all the paperwork." He stared at Noah who stood, eyes closed and slightly swaying. "Noah!" His voice jolted the boy back awake.

"All right, all right." Noah shook the spilt coffee off his hand. "I heard you already."

Robert gave him a dubious look. "What did I say then?"

Noah glared up at him. "Look. I've been on a plane for two days . . ."

"Hardly," he interrupted.

"I haven't gotten a wink of beauty sleep."

"I've been with you the whole time and I feel pretty rested." Robert looked at him without understanding.

Noah mocked his words. "Big frigging deal. So you can sleep on a plane. Next time I'm sitting as far away from you as I can. You snore like a Harley-Davidson."

"Oh, please!"

"And I wanted to snuggle some after—"

"Can we just find our seats inside please?" Robert had listened to Noah's bitching all the way from Moscow. He had hoped the less grueling climate in Switzerland would have softened the younger man's progressively deteriorating mood.

"All right, I've had enough of this sludge." Noah dropped the remainder of his coffee into a trash receptacle.

"I thought you said you loved to travel," Robert said, taking his arm.

"I do, in principle." Noah allowed himself to be led into the vaulting baroquesque salon where the auction was to take place. "I just expected more than one rest stop every fifteen hours." His expression softened. "I was hoping for a little more quality time." He slipped an arm about Robert's waist. "With you."

"All we've done is spend time together."

"You know what I mean!" Noah punched Robert playfully in the stomach.

Robert pulled Noah to him. "You sure are gripier than usual . . . and that's saying something."

"I'm hornier than usual," Noah said. He bobbed his eyebrows at Robert.

"Business first."

"Business?" Noah looked like he might take a swing at Robert. "There's that word again. Is that all you ever . . ."

"One million dollars, Noah."

Noah sighed heavily. "Goddammit!" He studied the gold gilt work that made the large, eighteenth century room seem like a wedding cake turned inside out. "Who owns this castle, anyway?" He dropped into one of the folding chairs next to Robert.

"One of the Rothschilds, I think," Robert answered. "It's leased out for various corporate and commercial ventures.

Noah felt himself perking up. "Do we know any of these other people?"

Robert scanned the small crowd of twenty-five or so people. "I'll venture to say most all of these are agents or representatives of the actual buyers. Probably everything for sale here is stolen merchandise."

"Do tell." Noah looked over the crowd.

"This is by invitation only, so one could probably make a few guesses who some of the real buyers might be," Robert said.

"A who's who of the rich but not necessarily of the famous?"

"Precisely." Robert's eyebrows went up suddenly. "Motherfu . . ."

"What?" Noah tried to trace who he was looking at. "Who do you see? Do you recognize someone?"

"Be still," Robert said sharply. "I don't . . ." he tried to duck his head. "Damn! Too late, we've been spotted."

Noah punched him in the arm. "Bobby, if you don't tell me what's going on, I . . . I don't know what I'm going to do but . . ." He felt a presence looming over him and looked up.

"Robert Robert," said the cultured, British voice. "Can it really be you? The man was medium height, solid built and slightly graying at the temples. He extended a manicured hand.

"Colonel Dobrynyn." Robert stood and accepted the hand shake. "It's been a while."

"My dear, Robert." The man's broad smile did not affect the piercing lupine eyes. "I thought you had returned to the private sector . . . some news agency or another. What brings you to this spot on the globe?"

Robert returned the smile. "I'm flattered that you've kept track of me, Colonel. But I'm surprised to see you here as well. I thought your previous employer was no longer in business . . . or that surely someone had killed you by now. At the very least, I heard you had . . . retired."

Dobrynyn waved a hand. "Nonsense, Robert. Surely you don't believe everything you read in those papers you work for."

The two men studied each other for a moment.

"So, Robert, what are you doing here?" Dobrynyn's voice had a slight edge.

"I'm not at liberty to say, Colonel," Robert said with the same edge. "You understand."

Dobrynyn's demeanor changed with chameleon-like ease. "We must get together for a drink when all this is over with." His laugh was lilting. "And who is this charming young man?" He leaned over Noah.

Robert moved closer to Noah. "I'm sorry, Colonel. May I introduce my assistant, Noah Taylor?" He looked down at the boy with an expression full of warning. "Noah, may I introduce Colonel Anatole Dobrynyn of the former Soviet KGB."

Noah swallowed and forced a smile. "Colonel Dobrynyn. What a pleasure."

"Young Mr. Taylor." The Colonel bowed low over Noah's extended hand. "Why is it all youthful American men look like models?"

Noah smiled up at him. "Are all Russian men so . . . flirtatious?"

"It's Colonel Dobrynyn's business to be a smooth operator," Robert interrupted. "He oversaw Eastern and Western European counterintelligence for many years up until the Evil Empire's collapse." He noted Dobrynyn's jaw tighten. "His charm was both respected and feared throughout all of NATO."

"And I hope," Dobrynyn began, his eyes narrowing to a viperish slant, "this is still so today."

"I'm sure it is." Robert could not hide his hatred for this man. "I can think of several friends who would dearly love to look you up again."

"The Cold War is over, dear boy." Colonel Dobrynyn chuckled heartily. "You and I can be friends now."

"Friends?" Robert's eyes narrowed at the Russian. "You and I will never be friends and you know it."

"But Robert, old friend." Dobrynyn smiled, baring his teeth. "That was another time . . . another place. We were adversaries then."

"That we were," Robert said without emotion. "People died."

"We both lost comrades, Robert," Dobrynyn said, "but that is past. We must forgive each other."

Robert tensed. "I can forgive you everything Colonel," he said through clenched teeth, "everything, but one."

Dobrynyn stared into Robert's piercing eyes. "One . . . yes, I remember." He shrugged as if to emphasize his lack of empathy. "It was a pity. But you should have known better—better than to get involved with a fellow operative."

Noah had been watching the two men in silence, but the rising tension in Robert's body, and his clenched fists alarmed Noah into action. "So, Colonel." Noah gestured to the room. "What are you bidding on today?" He stepped lightly on Robert's foot to emphasize the need for detente. "I can't imagine what a Russian intelligence offender would find interesting in a fine arts auction."

Robert took the hint and returned to his seat beside Noah. Noah adjusted his position so that the Colonel could more easily appreciate the cut of his Armani slacks. "Are we to believe there is microfilm stashed in the Rubens," Noah continued. "Or nuclear secrets hidden in the diamonds of the Cartier sapphire set?

The steel in the Colonel's face morphed as quickly as it had arisen. "I'm afraid my only role here is purely for observation. Anytime artifacts of Russian art or heritage are put up for sale, my government likes to make sure it is nothing stolen or smuggled out of the country illegally."

"Ah, then it's the collection of icons that interests you," Noah said.

"Perhaps." Dobrynyn bared his teeth to approximate a smile.

"Will you be bidding on them as well?" Noah studied the Colonel's face.

"I see the proceedings are about to begin." Dobrynyn turned away and nodded to the flurry of activity about the small podium at the front of the room. "Perhaps we can continue our discussion later." He bowed once more at Noah. "Good to see you, too, Robert."

"The same, Colonel." Once again, Robert shook the Colonel's hand. He watched silently as Dobrynyn moved quickly to a seat near the front.

Noah whispered loudly. "What do we do now?"

"Don't let the Colonel fool you." Robert put his arm about the back of Noah's chair. "He's here to bid on the egg, just like the rest."

"For the Russian government?"

"Undoubtedly." Robert tried to shush the boy. An unknown Renoir portrait study was being set up on carved wooden easel. "Watch the auction."

Noah fidgeted in his seat. "How much did Marya say we could bid on the egg?"

"She didn't. We are to top any other bid, period." He shushed Noah again.

Noah watched the bidding for a moment as it past two million Euros. "Why doesn't the Colonel merely claim the egg as stolen property?"

Robert's eyes rolled upwards. "Because the Russians already claim to have recovered it," he whispered. "They'd look like fools to make a fuss here. Now keep quiet and watch the auction."

The Renoir was being carried off and the Cartier sapphire set was brought out draped about the neck of a featureless bust. Noah's interest was captured for a moment and he eyed the spectacular piece of jewelry with great interest. The bidding was not very exciting and Noah grew quickly bored. It was a good piece of jewelry, but hardly art.

"Do you think they'll display the egg for the auction?" Noah asked, once again breaking Robert's concentration.

Robert sighed. "Don't be ridiculous. Only a few people even know the object is for sale. As you said, it's stolen." He looked about to make sure their conversation wasn't being monitored. "I doubt even Colonel Dobrynyn knows what is really for sale behind all the hype about the icons."

"You believe him then?" Noah scanned the people about them as well, recapturing his fantasy of cloak and dagger. "That crap about observing?"

"No, I don't," Robert replied. "You can bet he's authorized to bid a little on the off chance that he could acquire the icons at a discount and return them to Russia."

Noah searched out the Colonel for one more look.

"Quiet now!" Robert straightened.

The sapphire necklace was being carried off and a small rectangle of gold was set up on the easel.

"An icon." Noah caught his breath.

"Please be still and keep quiet!" Robert focused his attention on the dais. "Here's where we earn our keep."

Noah sat up excitedly. Even from a distance he could tell the icon was a very good one.

The auctioneer announced the opening bid as a million Euros. Noah tried to do the math in his head to convert to dollars. The bidding jumped another quarter million before he even got started.

Noah looked over at Robert who sat silently concentrating on the bidding. "Aren't you going to bid?" He asked.

"No sense wasting time until the field of bidders is narrowed down." Robert frowned. "Now keep quiet and watch."

Noah shrugged. The bidding continued in increments of a half million Euros and narrowed quickly to two bidders near the front. One was a black haired man in a dark lawyerish suit. Noah quickly pegged him as a shill for some wealthy collector. The other bidder was a mousey woman, henna-rinsed hair pulled into a tight bun at the back of her head, and wearing a brown three-piece, wool suit that almost made Noah groan. He thought he saw the woman glancing back at the Colonel who sat two seats to the left on the row behind. Noah watched them closely. Sure enough, the woman would look back, acknowledge a nod from the Colonel, and then bid.

"Colonel Dobrynyn is bidding through that frumpy woman on the first row," Noah said excitedly. He started to point.

"Keep quiet?" Robert commanded. He pulled Noah's hand down.

"But . . ."

"I know." Robert kept his eyes glued on the auction. "I've been watching them too."

"But what are they—"

Robert's hand covered Noah's mouth. "I think it's obvious that Dobrynyn is not just bidding on an icon."

Noah pulled Robert's hand away. "Then he does know about the egg after all."

"Obviously."

The bidding had stopped at a six million five bid by the Colonel's shill. Robert pulled a numbered paddle out of his jacket and held it up for the auctioneer to see.

"I have seven million Euros in the rear," the auctioneer droned. "Do I hear seven-fifty?"

True to form the frumpy woman looked to the Colonel who was now staring back at Robert and Noah. Robert ignored him and kept his eyes on the auctioneer, still holding his paddle high.

Dobrynyn quickly nodded to the woman who once again raised the bid.

"I have seven-fifty. . ." the auctioneer began.

"Nine!" Robert called out.

Noah's finger nails dug into Robert's thigh. He was almost bouncing with excitement.

The Colonel nodded once more to the woman who silently raised her paddle in obedience.

"Nine-fifty is bid." The auctioneer looked to the back of the room questioningly.

Robert gave his paddle a wave.

"I have ten million Euros at the rear." The auctioneer smiled and let the crescendo of whispers settle in the room. He looked at the woman on the front row. "Do I have a bid for ten-five?"

The woman looked back at Robert and then at the Colonel.

"I have a bid of ten million Euros," the auctioneer called out calmly. "Do I hear ten million five hundred thousand?"

Colonel Dobrynyn eyes narrowed in Robert's direction.

"Going once," the auctioneer called out.

Dobrynyn gave the frumpy woman a terse nod. She quickly raised her paddle.

"Going . . ." The auctioneer caught himself. "I now have a bid of eleven million." He raised his eyes at Robert. "Would the gentleman like to bid eleven-five?"

Robert nodded without hesitation.

"Eleven million five hundred thousand Euros." said the auctioneer, puffing with pleasure. He gestured with his gavel to the Colonel, now bypassing the woman altogether. The Colonel was visibly reddened and a bead of sweat traced a trail down the side of his face. He nodded.

"I have twelve million," the auctioneer said without waiting for the woman's paddle to rise.

"Thirteen million." Robert's voice echoed through the sudden silence.

"Thirteen million Euros!" The auctioneer almost laughed. He looked at the Colonel expectantly.

Dobrynyn's face was as chiseled stone. "Thirteen-five," he almost growled.

"Fourteen million," Robert said evenly.

The auctioneer stood silently, watching the two men along with everyone else in the room.

"Fourteen-five." Dobrynyn glared.

"Fifteen million." Robert glared back.

The Colonel ground his teeth and took a deep breath. "Fifteen million five hundred thousand Euros." He smiled as another swell of excitement rippled through the room.

Noah forced himself to breath. "Let me, Robert, please?" He pulled at Robert's arm, whispering. "I won't ask you for another thing. Please. Let me bid!"

Robert rolled his eyes. "All right," he said quietly.

Noah suppressed the urge to shout. He straightened and faced the auctioneer. "Twenty million Euros," he called out triumphantly.

Robert raised an eyebrow. "Whatever happened to Sixteen?"

"You jumped a bid," Noah said, determined.

Everyone was looking at Noah now, especially the Colonel. Noah caught himself biting his lip.

"Going once!" The auctioneer voice shook Noah's momentary paralysis. "Going twice!"

Noah refused to meet the Colonel's gaze. He turned to Robert. "Is he going to bid again?"

Robert pursed his lips. "I think you overshot his limit." He studied the Colonel. "He doesn't look very happy about it either."

"Sold!" The auctioneer slammed his gavel down. "Twenty million Euros to paddle number seventeen."

The room exploded. Only Robert's hand on his arm prevented Noah from standing to acknowledge the applause. Instead, Noah tried to maintain an air of aloof disinterest. As the applause began to abate, Noah once again became aware of Dobrynyn, standing in an alcove off to the side. He hadn't even noticed the sudden exit of the Russian entourage that left several empty seats at the front.

Dobrynyn stood staring at Noah and Robert. His face had regained its composure.

"Robert . . ." Noah started.

"I know." Robert squeezed his arm. "Be still and smile at the crowd."

Noah obeyed with little exuberance. Another painting was brought to the platform and a new round of bidding started up.

"We'll wait until all the bidding is over," Robert said into Noah's ear. "Just relax."

Noah bit his lip again. "I'm worried about the Colonel."

"Let me worry about him." Robert sniffed. "He always was a sore loser."

Noah squirmed. "How many corpses lying at the bottom of the Volga have said that?"

"You've just been on a multi-million dollar spending spree." Robert chuckled softly. "Try to enjoy it a little more."

Noah brightened. "This is true. I wonder if I should wear it as a pin or as a choker on a black velvet band."

"What?" Robert looked at him.

Noah sighed. "Gorgeous, but has the sense of humor of an android on Prozac."

Robert ignored him. Dobrynyn had disappeared from the alcove along with his entourage. Robert turned his attention to the more immediate problem of finding a way to get their pricey purchase safely out of the castle to Marya and her people on the outside. He glanced down at the messenger bag wedged between his seat and Noah's. "What do you keep in that bag that's important?" He asked.

"What?" Noah pulled his eyes away from the auction.

"The bag," Robert repeated with a nod.

Noah grabbed up his messenger bag and clutched it tightly in his lap. "What about my bag?"

"Don't be so defensive." Robert looked about them.

"This bag has all my necessities in it," Noah said. He inventoried the bag's contents with his eyes. "I'm not getting on another plane without my necessities."

"Calm down." Robert suppressed a sigh as the auctioneer's gavel came down on the final sale. "Just make sure you have room in that thing for our purchase."

Noah's eyes widened. "You mean . . . ?"

Robert shushed him. "Just do what I tell you."

Noah dug into his bag and pulled out several bags of chips, nuts, and candies. "Where's the nearest trash can."

Robert smirked. "Necessities?"

"You know," Noah said, weighing the bag in his hand. "There's still enough in here to make a pretty good dent in the side of your head."

Robert sniffed. "Trash can in the back."

Noah studied the various goodies in his hand and tried to determine if he really needed to get rid of them.

Robert tried not to smile as he watched the boy. "I know it's a difficult choice," he said softly into Noah's ear. "A jewel encrusted, golden bit of vintage Faberge art worth at current exchange rates about twenty-five million dollars, or a bag of peanut butter cups." His breath tickled Noah's ear.

"Well," Noah said with a coy smile. "Since you put it that way." He got up quickly and headed for the trash receptacle at the rear door.

Robert followed the small group of winning bids to a long table set up behind the auction platform. He turned in his numbered paddle and signed the various forms pushed in front of him by the young blonde seated behind the table. She caught his eye with a smile and nodded toward the alcove where Robert had last seen Colonel Dobrynyn. Now, one of the ubiquitous, uniformed security guards stood there waiting.

Robert sensed Noah's return and glanced back over his shoulder at the younger man. "We need to see that guard in the alcove."

"But that's where . . ."

"Noah," he interrupted. "Just stay with me on this, please." He started for the alcove.

"You need to work on your communication skills." Noah glared at the back of Robert's neck while struggling to keep pace with him.

"And you need to work on your trust," Robert countered without missing a beat.

Noah smiled. "Touché." He switched the lightweight messenger bag to his other hand so he could stand as close to Robert's side as possible.

Without a word the guard turned and headed down the cavernous hallway beyond the alcove. Robert took Noah's arm to steer him and the bag in pursuit of the guard who had taken up a position beside a pair of double oak doors midway down.

Robert could sense Noah's mounting excitement. He feared the boy might burst. "Just hold it all in a few minutes longer," he counseled, giving Noah's arm a light squeeze.

Noah bit his lip and grinned up at Robert.

The guard opened the doors as they approached. Robert lead Noah into the cozy drawing room and the door shut behind them.

"Doctor Tate." A round, red-faced little man approached them extending his hand. "You have made an excellent purchase for your client." He spoke like an Oxford professor.

Robert accepted the hand shake. "I can only hope that my client agrees with you."

"Are you the broker?" Noah asked.

"One and the same," the man said with an ingenuous smile. "Siegfried Schloss, at your service."

Robert cut his eyes at Noah. "This is my assistant, Noah Taylor."

"A great pleasure, young man." Schloss made an elegant bow.

Robert surveyed the room. "I would like to examine our purchase now, if that could be arranged." He looked down at Schloss. "In private, if you don't mind."

Schloss' silly grin never wavered. "Of course, Dr. Tate. I'm sure we can accommodate you." He gestured for them to follow.

They were lead to a round, oak library table separated from the rest of the room by a tall, folding oriental screen with mother-of-pearl inlay. A small black travel case, barely a foot square, sat in the middle of the table.

Schloss flipped open the lid. "Just let me know when you have finished your inspection and I will arrange your security escort from the building." He took their leave with a bow and waddled back to the gilt desk at the door.

Robert and Noah looked at each other. With a shrug, Robert reached into the case and extracted the gleaming, gold icon. "Very nice," was all he could say.

"To hell with the icon," Noah whispered. His hands shook with excitement as he slid the box closer. "What about . . ." He caught his breath.

Robert slipped the icon back into the box and studied its other contents. "I'm not an expert by any means," he said, lifting the fist sized object from its velvety perch. "But this looks like the real thing to me."

Noah wanted to hold the egg so much it hurt, but he didn't trust his trembling hands. "It's beyond exquisite." He stroked the enameled, gold object in Robert's hand, cooing as if it were a nursing infant. "Turn it over," he commanded excitedly.

Robert obeyed, deferring to the cub reporter's expertise.

Noah pulled his jeweler's loop from inside his shirt and fumbled it open with a giggle. "God, I can't stop shaking." He gave Robert a helpless look.

Robert smiled down at him. "Just breathe deeply," he said.

Noah poured over the egg, studying each stone, the texture of the enameling, and finally the tell-tale monogram stamped almost invisibly into a band of gold about the odd-shaped keyhole at the base. He straightened with a sigh. "We're rich!"

"I take it, that means I'm holding the real Abdication Egg?"

Noah raised an eyebrow. "If that's not the Real McCoy, I'll make an omelet out of it."

"Everything's food with you," Robert grumbled. "Pull out your sweater." He pointed to the garment tucked through the handle on Noah's messenger bag.

"What are you going to do with it?" Noah pulled the pastel, mauve sweater out. "It's my best cashmere."

"Good." Robert took the sweater and wrapped it carefully about the egg. "Maybe then you'll be careful and not lose this." He stuffed the roll of cashmere and its jeweled contents into Noah's bag.

"What's wrong with the box?" Noah asked weakly.

"Robert flipped the lid of the black case closed. "That's the first place the wrong people will be tempted to look." He grabbed up the box by its handle. "Ready?"

Noah swallowed hard. "I can't believe we actually did this," he stammered.

"Ready?" Robert repeated.

"I can't believe we're actually going to be paid all that money!" Noah swayed slightly.

Robert gave the boy's arm a squeeze. "Ready?" He asked firmly.

Noah took a deep breath and looked up into Robert's confident eyes. "Sorry." He shook himself. "Ready."

"That's my boy," Robert said. "We just need to keep our focus a little while longer." He tried to pry Noah's hand off the side of the messenger bag. "Don't clutch that bag so close," he said. "Carry it as you normally would."

"You've got to be kidding," Noah responded, almost giggling again.

Robert put an arm around his young protégé's shoulder. "Thirty minutes ago you were nodding off in exhaustion," he said.

"Thirty minutes ago I was poor." Noah said with a wink.

"We don't have the money yet." Robert gave him a squeeze.

Noah smiled up at him. "Maybe you don't," he said, giving the bag a pat. "But, I've got plenty."

"Come on, Ms. Rockefeller." Robert led Noah out from behind the screen. "Everything seems to be in order, Mr. Schloss."

The fat little man struggled up out of his chair behind the desk. "Excellent, Dr. Tate."

"If you could arrange that escort for us, we'd like to be on our way."

Schloss's eyes went to the black case Robert was carrying. "Donner will see you safely out," he said, and punched a button on his telephone.

There was a spitting sound and then a heavy thud rocked the door. Schloss's eyes widened in alarm.

Instinctively, Robert grabbed Noah by the arm and literally dragged him to the back of the room before he could protest. They disappeared behind the oriental screen just as the doors splintered open with a loud crack.

Noah froze. Robert struggled to open a narrow door in the paneling behind the table to a chorus of German shouts and the spitting sound, again followed by another thud. Robert jerked the narrow door open almost pulling it off its hinges. Noah started to speak, but Robert pulled him close to him. He pressed his lips hard to Noah's in a hasty kiss, and then shoved the boy through the door.

"Run, dammit!" He said in a frantic whisper. "Run and don't look back!" He slammed the door behind Noah, but not before the younger man heard the spitting sound that sent a bullet whizzing past his ear into the plaster wall beyond.

"Bobby!" was all he managed as darkness engulfed him.

Chapter 22

Robert felt the bullet singe the ends of the hair above his left ear before he heard the spitting sound of the silencer. He slammed the narrow door shut in front of him.

"It's nice to see you're not a stupid man, Dr. Tate."

Robert froze, unable to recognize the voice. "May I turn around?" He asked politely.

"Slowly, Doctor."

Robert could detect an oddly familiar trace of Northern European accent but was unable to place it. He turned slowly to face the gunman . . . or gunmen, and nodded to the distinguished older man who stood between the set of silenced luger pistols.

"I commend you, Dr. Tate, for not making us chase after you." The dapper gentleman doffed his hat. "Someone could have been badly hurt."

Robert forced a smile. "You have me at a disadvantage," he replied. "I was expecting the Russians."

The man's eyes sparked. "Well, Doctor, that would depend on what you mean by *the Russians*," He gestured to one of the gunmen. "Get the case."

The tall, lanky one lowered his augmented pistol and quickly jerked the black case out of Robert's hand.

"Put it on the table," commanded the older man. He had stepped to the side of the table and stood, one hand stroking his close-cropped beard. "Won't you join me, Doctor?"

Robert raised an eyebrow to the other gunman who gave the tip of his silencer a slight wave in the direction of the table. Dutifully, Robert left his post at the door and walked slowly to the other side of the table. He prayed silently that, for once, Noah had done what he had asked. The tall gunman unsnapped the case clasps.

"I don't believe I know you," Robert said to the older man. He was desperate to stall things a little longer. "I'd like to know who's robbing me."

The older man sniffed with amused disdain. "Robbing you?" He lifted the lid of the case. "I am Prince Alexander Romanov. You are working for me, and this is my family's property."

Robert mentally kicked himself. Now he recognized the accent as the same he had heard in Marya's voice. "If I'm working for you, why were you shooting at me?" Robert tried to hold the man's eyes. "Why hold me at gunpoint?"

The lid to the black case slammed shut. "Where is it?" The Prince's face darkened ominously as he turned to Robert. "Where is it?" His voice boomed.

Robert feigned an innocent smile. "Where is what?"

The sound of automatic weapons firing echoed from the outside. Robert thought of Noah and swallowed hard.

"I don't have time for your stupidity!" Prince Alexander snarled at Robert. "I'll ask you only one more time." He gave a curt nod to the gunman behind Robert.

Robert felt the cold metal of a silencer press against his temple.

Prince Alexander leaned across the table. "Where is the egg?"

Noah stumbled down the narrow stairwell, clutching his now heavy, messenger bag close. He tried to wipe the tears from his eyes to see better, but he was unable to control the outpouring. He tripped at the landing and tried to steady himself against the stone wall. His heart thundered in his chest, making it difficult to hear if anyone was pursuing him, or worse, if there were more gunshots fired in the room above. Robert's name formed once again on his lips but he was unable to make a sound.

Noah's attention shifted to the object in the bag. "Marya!" He thought. If he could only get to Marya and her people. They were his only possible source of help.

With renewed energy, Noah tackled the last winding flight of steps to the bottom landing. He pressed an ear against the oaken door and held his breath, listening. Hearing nothing, he opened it a crack and peered out into a mudroom, bright with sunlight streaming in from the beveled glass panels of a pair of French doors.

"Yes," Noah managed to say as his avenue of escape presented itself. He gave one last look up the stairs, praying desperately to see Robert's smug face peak around the stairwell at him. After a second, he pushed the door open and stepped out onto the slate floor of the mudroom. Beyond the French doors was a small parterre garden surrounded by a hedgerow of yew that almost completely blocked the view into the surrounding expanse of lawn.

"Where's the damn parking lot," Noah muttered under his breath. He tried to identify some landmark that would give him a bearing.

Noah jerked his head around sharply at the sound of shouting coming from behind. He couldn't tell if it was coming from the stairwell he had just left, or if it originated somewhere in the house beyond the mudroom. Not waiting to find out, Noah pushed open the French door and exited into the cold afternoon air. It was another six steps down into the garden, and his calves screamed with each step. He almost stumbled the last couple of steps as a heel wrenched off the bottom of one of his boots.

Once on the grass path below, he reached down and pulled off his Gucci boots and tossed them into the nearby hedgerow. "Damn it to hell," he said as his two favorite shoes disappeared into the hedge. "Damn it, damn it, damn it!" He patted the precious contents of his messenger bag. "It's you and me, baby." Free from the constraints of his expensive leather dress shoes, he ran the length of the snaking grass path to an opening in the hedgerow.

There was more shouting now. It seemed to come from every direction, inside the house and from the ground beyond. Noah peaked out of the hedge opening. He froze at the unmistakable sound of Russian dominating the shouts to his right.

"Colonel Dobrynyn!" Noah pulled back from view. He ran back up the path to the house, pulled open the glass door, and reentered the mudroom. He stood, reviewing his options. The door to the stairwell was definitely out. The other door into the house seemed his best course. It had a diamond shaped glass pane set high in the center to let in the light.

Noah stood on tiptoe, his nose barely clearing the bottom frame of the glass. His eyes traveled the length of the corridor beyond, coming to rest on a squat, blonde man at the rear. The blonde man held an Uzi at the ready and stared back at Noah, wide-eyed. The man started for Noah, and then stopped to shout at someone beyond Noah's line of vision.

Noah spun on his toes and dove for the French doors. He bounded off the porch onto the lawn only to hear the shouts in Russian closing in on the small, protected garden. He opened his mouth instinctively to scream, but luckily no sound issued forth. Instead, he hugged his messenger bag and dove into the hedgerow just as the French doors behind him burst open. Noah forced his way through the yews that snagged at his pants and shirt, scratching his arms and legs. He fell hard onto the ground as automatic gunfire sent a spray of bullets into the hedge above his head. There was more gunfire from another direction but no bullets were sent his way.

Noah raised his head up and squinted through the hedge to see the Russians firing at his pursuer. The glass doors were shattered as the man with the Uzi fell back through them, dead. Noah recognized Colonel Dobrynyn as he led his four men up the path to the house. They fired more shots through the doors before disappearing into the house.

Noah lay panting inside the yew hedge. "Thank you, God," he said over and over, hugging his bag in one hand and squeezing the oddly shaped cross given to him by the husband of the Anastasia claimant. After exhausting his few remaining tears, he sat up, still staring gratefully at the gold-plated cross in his hand. He tried to think of some prayer from his childhood appropriate to his current situation. Unable to come up with anything better, he continued his litany of *thank you, God* and fingered the unusual piece of jewelry for comfort.

"You're a pretty good luck piece." Noah turned the small cross over in his hand. It was certainly not the usual Russian Orthodox design, and he vowed he would research it further if he escaped in one piece. Finally, he tucked it back into his shirt and tried to clear his head. "Okay, Noah," he said to himself. "We can do this."

He crawled to the outer edge of the hedgerow and looked out. Recognizing nothing about the grounds, he looked up at the house itself. A turret on the far corner told his that the front of the house lay at that end. "The parking lot!" Noah sat up on his knees excitedly, oblivious to the tattered pockets of his slacks. "Oh, please let me find that set of car keys!" He pulled open the messenger bag and dug beneath its priceless contents. He pulled out the wad of cashmere that contained the source of all his present troubles and sat it carefully on the ground.

Further rummaging in the bag failed to turn up the set of keys. "Damn!" Noah threw the bag down and started to unroll the cashmere sweater. The wayward set of keys appeared, snagged onto the hem of the sweater. Noah ripped them off the sweater and stuffed them in the pocket of his tattered pants. He looked down at the bulge in his sweater and pulled the cashmere cover away. A ray of sunlight streaming in through the hedge prismed as the jeweled contents came into view. Noah caught his breath and picked up the egg, momentarily forgetting about the keys. He turned it over gingerly, marveling at the craftsmanship. Each gemstone had been exactingly set. The rippling, opalescence of the enameling was perfectly symmetrical, interrupted only by the small keyhole at the bottom.

Noah stared at the keyhole, suddenly drawn to its unique shape. "Oh, my God!" Noah clasped the cross at his breast.

"Where is it, Dr. Tate?"

Robert stared blankly. Prince Alexander's eyes made it clear that the gunman holding the silencer against Robert's temple would pull the trigger.

"Where is the egg?"

Robert inhaled deeply. "I have no idea what you're talking about. I have no idea who you are, and if you belong to the family I'm working for, where is Marya?

Prince Alexander's annoyance was palpable. "You are a very tedious man, Dr. Tate."

"Quite the contrary." Robert smiled despite the cold metal pressing at his temple. "I'm very easy to work with. It's very simple." He measured his words carefully. "I have the item in question . . . though it's certainly not in my immediate possession. The only person I will turn it over to is Marya . . . per prior agreement."

The Prince started to speak, but Robert interrupted. "If indeed you are working with her, then there is no problem. Bring her in and I'll complete the terms of our contract."

Prince Alexander looked at him thoughtfully. "Of course, you're right, Doctor," he said reassuringly. "But there is the problem. My daughter will be unable to join us. She was . . . shot by Russian agents last evening. Surely she told you who I was."

Robert studied the Prince's body language carefully. "I'm sorry to hear that about Marya," he said, despite his instinct that the Prince was lying. "Now here's the other problem. Marya was very secretive about her family, so I know very little."

The Prince considered this. "And why is that a problem?"

"Very simply," Robert said. 'I will need more concrete evidence that you are the authorized representative of my client. It's a necessary formality, I'm sure you'll understand."

"I want the egg now, Doctor." Prince Alexander's demeanor changed in an instant. "Not later. Your life depends on your accepting me for who I say I am." His smile was feral. "Surely professional formalities are not worth your life."

Robert strained his eyes to see the silencer at his temple. "I see your point."

The Prince's agitation was replaced with a smug smile. "Stop stalling, Dr. Tate."

Robert started to speak, but the narrow door behind him burst open. The first shot dropped the gunman holding the silencer to Robert's head. Robert leapt across the table, driving his head into the Prince's solar plexus as the next shot dropped the other gunman. The Prince tumbled to the floor. In one deft move, Robert pulled the winded Prince up off the floor and held him like a shield.

"Nicely done, Robert."

Robert spun his dazed human shield in the direction of the all too familiar voice. "Colonel Dobrynyn." Robert met the Colonel's steely gaze. "I never thought I would be thanking you for saving my life."

"Let's not thank me too soon, my old friend." Dobrynyn gave his men a signal and they moved to secure the room. "And who is the gentleman you're holding onto so tightly?"

Robert relaxed his grip on the Prince who was struggling to regain his composure. "Well, to be frank, Colonel, before now I thought he was one of your people." Robert lied to the Russian out of habit.

The Colonel raised his pistol into view and pointed it directly at the Prince. "Who are you?"

"Alexander Spinsk," The Prince answered convincingly.

Dobrynyn smiled coldly. "And why were you trying to kill my good friend here?"

"I'm afraid Dr. Tate has misinterpreted my motives," Alexander responded. "I was merely trying to frighten some information out of him."

Robert nodded to the broker's body by the desk beyond the screen. "I'd say you were pretty good at frightening people." He ignored the Prince's snarl.

Dobrynyn chuckled. "And where is your young . . . companion, Robert?"

"Oh, you mean Noah?" Robert continued to ignore the Prince. "I'd say he's well off the premises by now." He could almost feel Prince Alexander bristle at this.

Dobrynyn reached for the black box on the table and flipped it open. "Very nice," he said, lifting the icon from its nest of velvet. "But there appears to be something missing." He raised an eyebrow at Robert.

Robert looked at the Colonel without expression.

"Find the young man who was with Tate," Dobrynyn ordered into a small radio. He returned his attention to Robert. "I don't suppose you will volunteer the boy's whereabouts?"

Robert smiled and shrugged. "Try the American Embassy."

Dobrynyn's face darkened. "Very amusing, Robert." He turned his pistol toward Robert. "But now, it would appear, you have finally outlived your usefulness."

Robert faced the unwavering gun barrel with a sigh. "Not again," he whispered to no one in particular.

Chapter 23

Noah sprinted across the grassy expanse away from the hedgerow of yews. The weight of the messenger bag he carried finally became too much for its shoulder strap. Luckily he had an arm supporting the bottom of the bag when it snapped, and his progress was slowed only long enough to shift the bag's weight to the front where he clutched it like a football. He hugged the side of the building as he ran. An occasional shrub along the way provided him some sort of cover as he made his way to the front of the castle. He was panting heavily as he rounded the corner and spotted the circular parking area below several terraces from the front entrance.

Noah stayed in the protection of the foundation shrubberies and scanned the front of the castle down to the parking lot for any sign of movement. He listened for the sound of sirens or any other signal that the horror he was fleeing was actually real. The farther he got from his brush with death, the greater grew his anxiety about Robert. He inched along the front wall, oblivious to the condition of his clothing. He tried to remember if he had heard any further gunshots from inside the castle, but his head was awhirl.

Through a line of fir trees dividing the almost empty parking lot, Noah spotted the small black Audi Robert had rented at the airport. He squeezed the spare set of keys tighter in his hand and fought back the wave of confused emotions and accompanying tears. His only thought now was finding Marya and rescuing Robert. Abandoning caution, he sprinted down the terraces toward the parking lot.

The house behind him seemed to erupt with shouting. Noah heard a scream that threatened to paralyze his legs, until he realized the scream had come from his own lips. There was no stopping the flood of tears that came with the terror of having been discovered. He saw the small explosion in the gravel ahead of him before he heard the gunshot. He ducked his head down and instinctively began to zigzag across the drive toward the island of fir trees. He could hear the footfalls on the steps of the castle behind him.

"No!" Noah almost shouted, refusing to cave in to the overwhelming sense of futility that threatened to overcome him.

Once he had cleared the fir trees which offered him some sort of cover from the sporadic gunfire, he made a beeline for the Audi. The sharp edges of the coarse white gravel lining the drive tore through the soles of his socks, cutting the bottoms of his feet. Ignoring the pain, Noah refused to let it slow his pace. He rounded the back of the Audi in a final burst of speed. Frantically, he struggled to get the key in the car door. He counted four men bearing down on the other side of the parking lot beyond the line of fir trees. When they realized he had reached the car, they began firing off their Uzi's in earnest.

Noah dropped to the driveway for cover behind the car door. He cursed the sharp gravel beneath his knees along with his shaking hands and groaned with relief when he finally engaged the door lock. A hand grabbed him from behind and Noah almost shouted in panic. He turned around sharply to free himself and heard a voice shush him.

"Marya!" Noah croaked. He froze at the sight of the weapon in Marya's hand.

"Just stay down!" Marya moved up beside Noah, crouching beside the car. She signaled to the dense foliage at the perimeter of the parking lot.

Noah's pursuers continued firing in the air above the Audi and shouting.

Noah peered through the car windows. "They're almost here," he said in a whisper.

Again Marya pulled Noah down and bobbed her head up for a peek. The men were walking across the drive, Uzi's at the ready. She signaled again and the surrounding shrubbery erupted in spitting gunfire. The four men tried to retreat back to the safety of the trees, but they were quickly cut down in a flurry of bullets.Noah sat back onto the gravel limply. A small group of men in black jumpsuits surrounded the side of the car.

"Where's Robert?" Marya shook Noah's shoulders for attention.

Noah fought to stop the tears to no avail. He struggled to speak. "Still inside," he said, stammering. "He might be shot." His tears burst their dam.

Marya held Noah's arms tightly. "Where's the egg?"

Noah blinked, trying to repress tears. "The egg?" He couldn't believe his ears. "Who the hell cares about the egg? I'm worried about Bobby."

Marya closed her eyes and took a deep breath. "Of course. I'm sorry." She pulled Noah to his feet. "Where is he?"

Noah looked back at the Castle. "We were in a study on the second floor." He willed his thoughts to focus. "It's just down a hall next to the ballroom where the auction was held."

Marya nodded. "Now, what about the egg?"

Noah stared at her.

"This is important, Noah. Did you get possession of the egg?"

Noah was unable to hide his disgust. "Yes, we got your precious egg." He felt the weight in the tote bag he was still clutching tightly to his side. "Bobby has it." The lie made him turn away from Marya. "We had just authenticated it when some men broke in firing guns. Bobby pushed me out of the room into a side stairwell before they saw." Noah wanted to be sure Marya and her people had a good reason to try and rescue Robert. "The egg is still up there as far as I know." He straightened suddenly. "The Russians!"

"What do you mean?" Marya's eyes narrowed.

"Bobby knew them . . . a Colonel Dobrynyn. He was KGB . . . or FSB." Noah's words were racing. "Or at least he used to be."

Marya interrupted to slow him down. "I know this Colonel. What about him?"

"When I got out of the Castle, I was spotted and I tried to hide in some bushes. Colonel Dobrynyn came running up with about four men and shot the guy who was shooting at me!" Noah paused just to catch his breath. "The Colonel didn't see me, though. They went in the Castle where I came out."

"More complications." Marya spoke quickly in Russian to her men while Noah leaned back against the car.

"All right, Noah." Marya checked the ammunition clip in her Uzi. "Show me where that study is."

"You mean . . ." Noah stared back at the Castle in disbelief. "You mean you want me to go back?"

Marya put an arm around Noah's shoulder. "Do you want us to find Robert?"

Noah moaned, "Dammit, dammit, dammit!"

"We need to move, Noah."

"Okay, okay!" Noah looked down at his swollen feet. "Got another pair of shoes?"

"You've always been too rash, Dobrynyn," Robert said coolly. He ignored the pistol aimed at his head and turned calmly to Prince Alexander. "I guess it's something about the Soviet mentality, Your Highness. Looks like you win the first bidding round."

"Highness?" Dobrynyn's gun lowered slightly.

"Oh, I'm sorry," Robert said ingenuously. "You haven't really been introduced. Your Highness, this is Colonel Anatole Dobrynyn, formerly of the Soviet KGB, now . . . I'm not really sure . . . FSB? Colonel Dobrynyn, I have the honor to introduce His Imperial Highness, Prince Alexander Romanov."

Dobrynyn smiled cannily at the two men. "Now this is a red letter day." He eyed the well-dressed man next to Robert with heightened interest. "Nicely played, Robert. You have my attention."

Robert smiled back coldly. "You were always predictable."

Dobrynyn failed to react to the insult. "So," he said, continuing to study the Prince, "You are the pathetic pretender."

Prince Alexander raised his chin, but maintained an aloof silence.

"Prince Alexander Nikolaevich Romanov." Dobrynyn said each name with relish. "We had almost forgotten your insignificant existence."

Prince Alexander waved a dismissive hand. "I could say the same thing about you Anatole Dobrynyn," he said in perfect Russian, pointedly ignoring the Colonel's title.

Dobrynyn chuckled softly. "You were a mistake, Romanov," he said, continuing in English. "I've never understood why your grandfather was ever allowed to survive."

"Very simple, Colonel." The Prince lifted a haughty eyebrow. "Your illustrious leaders were bankrupt and needed the ransom money."

"Ah, money." Dobrynyn nodded. "The root of all evil."

"Or at least," responded the Prince. "The only language evil listens to." He turned triumphantly to Robert. "I see, Dr. Tate, that you have decided to confirm my identity which I also assume means you are now willing to recognize me as your employer in this venture."

Robert shook his head. "Sorry to have to disappoint you, Prince, but I sort of stopped working for you when you started shooting at me."

"That egg is mine!" Prince Alexander flushed with anger. "It is my family's property."

Dobrynyn interrupted. "That egg is the property of the Russian people . . . stolen property . . . and I intend to recover it."

Prince Alexander started to argue.

"Gentlemen, gentlemen." Robert stepped between the two. "I believe you're both wrong."

The two Russians went silent.

"For all intents and practical purposes, the Abdication Egg is my property," Robert continued. "It is in my possession, and you know what they say." He smiled at the two men. "Possession is nine-tenths of the law."

"Then you are a thief!" Prince Alexander's face contorted in a snarl. "You forget that I paid twenty million Euros for that egg."

"That's not exactly true," said a female voice from the front of the room.

Robert and the two Russians turned, startled.

Marya stood inside the door. She held an Uzi in her left hand at waist level, and her right hand pointed a heavy black pistol directly at Colonel Dobrynyn's head. His guards at both exits had already been disarmed and one of Marya's men had moved quickly to disarm the Colonel.

"The Family paid for that egg, not you," Marya said, lowering her pistol.

"Marya, my dear." Prince Alexander held open his arms.

"Father." Marya nodded to him coolly. "What are you doing here?"

"The same thing as you are, my dear." The Prince lowered his arms. "I'm here for the egg."

"That is my responsibility, not yours," Marya said.

"Bobby?" The weak voice called from the doorway. "Bobby?"

Robert smiled at the sound of Noah's voice. "In here, Noah," he called out.

Noah stepped tentatively into the room and looked about. He almost jumped in the air at the sight of Robert unharmed. "Bobby!" He shouted and ran to him.

Robert caught Noah in his arms and looked down at the weeping, bedraggled boy. "My God, Noah," He said, thankfully noting the messenger bag still in Noah's possession. "Where are your shoes?'

Noah stopped crying long enough to slam a fist against his chest.

"Ouch!" Robert squeezed Noah tightly in his arms. "What I meant to say was, it's good to see you're okay too."

Noah smiled up at him through his tears. He thrust a hand into his messenger bag for a tissue. He felt the solid object wrapped in the sweater and cursed himself for drawing attention to the bag. "You're such a caring person," Noah said, recovering. Luckily a wad of clean tissues lay at the bottom and he was able to retrieve one without much difficulty. "And who says I was worried about you. I'm upset about my Gucci's."

"Don't I get a hug?" Marya asked, holstering her pistol.

"Marya!" Robert released a reluctant Noah from his embrace. "I must say, you're a sight for sore eyes, especially under the circumstances."

Marya pulled him away from Noah and gave him a peck on the cheek. "I see you've met my father."

"I certainly have." Robert pulled out of her embrace. "Colonel Dobrynyn here came in just in time to stop dear old dad from killing me."

"Colonel Dobrynyn?" Marya turned her seductive gaze to the Russian.

Dobrynyn bowed slightly. "I don't believe I've had the pleasure."

"We're wasting time." Prince Alexander slammed a fist on the library table. "The egg! Where is the egg?"

"Patience, Father," Marya said with undisguised contempt. "I'm in charge here. Don't order me about."

Prince Alexander's jaw clenched. He nodded to her with a tight smile. "My apologies, daughter. Old habits are hard to break."

Marya pointedly ignored him. She returned to Robert. "I have to apologize for my father, Robert. He does not represent the wishes of my family." Her eyes cut back to the Prince. "He hasn't for some time."

"Well, gee it's been fun." Noah pushed in between Robert and Marya. "But I'd really like to get back to our hotel where a hot bath is waiting for me." He put a hand on his hip. "So let's conclude our business and you can get back to reliving old times with the family."

Robert put his arm back around Noah's shoulder. "Noah has a point, Marya," he said. "I'd like to finish this before something else goes wrong."

Marya gestured in the air. "Whatever you say, Robert. You do have the egg then?"

"I do." Robert let his eyes wander about the room. "It's close by."

Marya smiled. "Very well, then." She pulled out her cell phone and punched in some numbers. "I'll approve the transfer now." She spoke quickly into the phone in German.

Noah looked up at Robert.

Robert was pleased to see a sparkle back in the boy's eyes. "Okay?" he asked.

Noah nodded up at him excitedly. "Okay."

"It's done, Robert." Marya held out the cell phone for him. "I'm sure you would like to confirm the transfer."

Robert took the phone. "It will only take a moment." He dialed and waited for a replay.

Noah took the opportunity to satisfy his curiosity. "So, Marya," he said, "that's some family tree you have."

Marya smiled and shrugged. "I have a certain amount of pride in that."

"I should say so," Noah continued. "Let's see. Your great-grandfather, the Tsesarevich Alexei, was the son of the last Tsar of Russia . . . your grandfather is a prince . . . your father is a prince . . . that would make you . . ."

"Of little consequence to the monarchy, I'm afraid," Marya replied. "I have a younger brother, and Russian succession only flows through the male line."

"How sexist." Noah frowned.

"A very institutionalized form." Marya laughed.

Noah looked at Marya, then at her father. "Why all the hoopla over an over-sized piece of jewelry? True, the Abdication Egg is an exquisite piece, but let's face it, the thing is one of many from the period."

Marya's eyes locked on her father's. "Every egg is unique," she said. "This one more so than any other."

Noah was not satisfied. "Yes, but…"

"The transfer is confirmed," Robert said, inter-rupting. He handed the cell phone back to Marya.

Marya deposited the small phone into one of the many Velcro pockets scattered over her black jumpsuit. "I trust that everything is satisfactory then?"

"Completely." Robert smiled at Noah. "It's time you unburden yourself, Mr. Taylor."

Noah eyed him excitedly. "We've got the money?"

"Safely deposited," Robert assured him.

Noah leaned in to whisper in his ear. "The entire million?"

"All of it," Robert whispered back with a chuckle.

Noah reached into his messenger bag and pulled out his rolled up sweater. He went to the library table and carefully set down the wad of cashmere. Every eye followed him as he slowly unwrapped the package to reveal the fist-size, gold egg. "The Abdication Egg," he announced triumphantly. He smiled at Colonel Dobrynyn. "The original one."

Marya reached out and lifted the egg from its cashmere nest. "Exquisite," she said, lifting it up to the light.

"Yes it is," Noah agreed. "But I hardly think it was worth all this murder and mayhem."

"It's not the egg, itself, that is so important," Marya said, cradling the egg in her hands. "Rather, what it contains."

"But it's empty," Noah persisted. "Robert and I saw the x-rays."

"x-rays can be deceiving." Marya smiled at the egg. "It's an ingenious design, quite ahead of its time." She turned the egg over in her hand. "A thin layer of enameled gold covering a very stable, but extremely powerful form of malleable explosive resembling pewter."

"The Germans had such an explosive in 1915," Robert said with mounting interest.

Marya raised an eyebrow. "Yes, our agents stole the process from them shortly after it was formulated."

"So it's a very expensive bomb." Noah's frustration grew. "What is the big deal?"

"Yes," Robert said. "Today's explosives technology is far beyond 1915. Something else is special about this egg."

Marya nodded. "Not for you to worry about. "It's family business." She reached to return the egg to the safety of its black carrying case.

"Don't be so secretive, my dear." Prince Alexander grabbed her hand.

"How dare . . ." Marya froze. She looked at her men, now pointing their weapons at her.

"I'll take that." Prince Alexander slipped the egg from Marya's grasp.

Marya gave her men a murderous look. "You'll all die for this!"

One of the men took her weapons before she could act on the threat.

"Don't be so dramatic, daughter," Prince Alexander said. He fondled the jeweled egg with much relish. "As I've said before, the old loyalties are gone. Only money matters in this day and age." He stroked Marya's cheek. "Isn't it time you grow up."

She spat at him. "You'd betray your own family. Grandfather will not forgive you for this."

"I have little need for my father's forgiveness." Prince Alexander laughed and held up the egg. "I have all I need right here."

"Okay," Noah said loudly. "I guess our business is finished here." He pulled at Robert's arm.

"What?" Robert cocked an eyebrow at Noah.

"We'll just be going now," Noah continued. "You all get on with your little family squabble."

"No one's going anywhere right now, Mr. Taylor," Prince Alexander said. He sat the egg on the library table. "Besides, I'm sure you would all like to know what makes the egg so valuable to our family."

Robert caught Colonel Dobrynyn's eye. "You have our undivided attention."

This seemed to please the Prince. "This small bit of jeweler's art holds one of the greatest secrets of all history," he said, patting the gold egg.

"Somewhat over dramatic yourself," commented the Colonel.

"Quite the contrary Colonel." Prince Alexander gave him a condescending smile. "I am being the soul of understatement. Tell me, Dobrynyn. Do you know why the life of the Tsesarevich and the Grand Duchess Anastasia were spared by the Bolsheviks in 1918?

Colonel Dobrynyn shrugged. "They were saved as a bargaining tool. That is all."

"Ah yes!" Prince Alexander was obviously enjoying the moment. "But a bargaining tool for what?"

Dobrynyn sniffed with disdain. "Money. They were good for very little else. The Revolution needed money because your incompetent great-grandfather had left the country bankrupt."

Prince Alexander laughed. "Only the Revolution was left bankrupt, Colonel, not Mother Russia." He picked up the egg again. "The Tsar-Martyr Nicholas II, my father's namesake, systematically emptied the Treasury, transferring funds into numbered Swiss accounts over a period of several years. We estimate those accounts today to be worth close to fifty billion Euros." He watched the group's reaction and smiled.

"Stolen money!" Dobrynyn almost shouted. "That money belongs to the Russian people."

Marya cut him off. "That money belongs to the Tsar!" She faced her father. "After the Tsar's assassination, it belonged to his son, the rightful heir. And now it belongs to his son . . . my grandfather."

Prince Alexander gave a slight wave of his hand. "I beg to differ with you daughter. Those funds belong to whoever holds the account numbers."

"Those numbers," Robert interrupted. "You're saying a list of those accounts is contained inside the Abdication Egg?"

The Prince nodded. "Precisely, Dr. Tate. Written on the thinnest rice paper. Invisible to x-ray examination."

"That money is for the Family!" Marya's face was red with anger. "You have no right to it."

"I have every right to it!" Prince Alexander turned to Dobrynyn. "My father's great plan for this money is to use it to return the monarchy to Russia. Can you imagine anything more preposterous?"

Dobrynyn nodded in agreement. "A ridiculous idea."

Prince Alexander continued. "A sum as great as this will make our family the most powerful private economic force in the European . . . in the world market." He looked at his fuming daughter. "The rest of our family will thank me for preventing the misuse and squandering of this money on the pipe dream of an old man, completely out of touch with reality."

"You don't have the list yet, traitor," Marya said with vehemence. "Only Grandfather has a key."

Prince Alexander pursed his lips. "That was true. I thought I might have gotten my hands on a key from your Great Aunt's estate, but that man she married . . ." He waved a dismissive hand. "He was little help."

"You killed him!" Noah said without thinking.

Robert looked down at him. "Noah, what are you talking about?"

"Those men," Noah said more calmly. "The ones that killed poor old Mr. Gilroy." He pointed to the Prince. "They must have been his hired killers."

Prince Alexander stared at Noah in surprise. "Very good, young man."

Noah looked up at Robert. "I shouldn't have said that, huh?"

"It doesn't help our situation." Robert squeezed Noah's arm. "Don't sweat it."

"At any rate," continued Prince Alexander, obviously annoyed at the interruption. "I do have a key." He extracted a pencil-length bar of metal from his coat pocket. The end was intricately notched on both sides. "Such are the benefits of embracing modern technology. I had the key reproduced from computer enhanced, x-ray copies of the egg's mechanism."

"That's impossible," Marya said, shaking her head. "Much of the keyhole apparatus was lead shielded."

"Hardly an impediment to the techniques of modern imaging, my dear."

"Don't be a fool," Marya replied. "If just one notch on that key is off even a millimeter, and fails to engage, the egg will be destroyed . . . and so will you."

Prince Alexander held the egg fixed on the library tabletop. "The key will work, daughter," he said, and slipped the thin metal bar effortlessly into the egg. "I will live and so will you." He smiled up at Noah, Robert and the Colonel. "A pity I can't say the same for the rest of you."

"Don't, Father!" Marya cried out as the Prince turned the key.

Prince Alexander laughed at their reaction, but only for a moment. The egg seemed to vibrate for a second beneath his fingers as the precision clockwork mechanism within the lock whirred into action. Its coiled wire spring released the years of pent up energy, causing a small flint to strike its ignition plate. The slight clicking sound was audible in the ensuing silence. In an instant, Robert pulled Noah to the floor. Prince Alexander jiggled the key, still expecting the egg to open. The guard beside him snapped to and moved to keep Noah and Robert in his gun sight.

For a split second, the clicking stopped. Prince Alexander smiled with satisfaction and started to speak. He was silenced by the ear-splitting detonation as the egg he held exploded into a thousand sharp shards of metal and corborundum. His hands disintegrated and the flash of the explosion tore way his face.

Noah and Robert were shielded from the blast by the body of the guard who had moved around to hold them at gunpoint. The guard was not so lucky as splinters of precious shrapnel penetrated his back and internal organs. Colonel Dobrynyn and the other guard suffered a similar fate, as they were slammed back into the wall from the force of the blast and schrapnel.

Marya lay on the floor across from Robert and Noah. She had followed Robert's example and dropped to the floor, somewhat protected by the Colonel's body. Her arms and face were cut and bleeding, but she was able to sit up and wipe the blood and falling plaster from her eyes.

Robert pulled Noah to a seated position. "Are you all right?"

Noah tried to smile. "Looks like he managed to get it open after all."

"Marya?" Robert coughed as the dust settled about them.

"I'm alive," Marya managed. She crawled over to the body of her father. "He's dead," she said flatly. A momentary shadow of pain clouded her face which she quickly shook off. "Good riddance!"

Robert helped Noah to his feet. "We need to get out of here," he said with some urgency.

Chapter 24

His skin was still tingling from the warmth of his bath. Noah ran his hands down the silky surface of the new Versace silk shirt that covered the scrapes and scratches of his recent ordeal. He heard the light knock at the door, but chose to ignore it for the moment. Instead, he stood and slipped into the sleek, equally new pair of black Gucci ankle boots.

The knock came again, more insistent.

"Coming!" Noah called out with a yawn. He paused on the way to the door, struck by the fact that he couldn't remember the last time he had slept.

An even louder knock rattled the bedroom door.

Noah sighed. "All right!" He opened the door. "Don't be so impatient."

"I've been standing out here for ten minutes," Robert said as he brushed past Noah into the large suite of walnut and damask.

"You're just in time." Noah turned slowly in front of Robert. "Well? What do you think?"

"Amazing!" Robert rolled his eyes. "How in God's name did you get into those pants?"

"Because they fit!" Noah said, turning away from Robert sharply. He left Robert to try and tame his glistening curls with a little more gel before the Venetian mirror perched above the dresser. "Well, that's the best I can do under the circumstances," he said, waiting in vain for the appropriate compliment from Robert.

Robert stood watching with an impatient look.

"You have no social grace at all," Noah complained, waving a dismissive hand at him.

"What did I do now?" Robert straightened his tie behind Noah in the mirror.

Noah turned to finish the job for him. "You were supposed to tell me how hot I look."

Robert raised an eyebrow at the younger man.

Noah gave him a little push. "I'm about to have my first royal introduction," he said with a pout. "And to a living piece of history at that. Noah turned back to the mirror for a few final adjustments. "A boy could use a little confidence booster about now."

Robert shrugged and sighed. "We'll meet the Tsesarevich, pray that he agrees to pay us the rest of our fees, and then get the hell back to Boston." He pulled Noah into his arms. "You look just fine."

"Fine?"

"You look hot!" Robert touched his forehead to Noah's.

"Finally!" Noah smiled up at him. "What's a guy got to do to get a simple compliment from you?"

"Someone as beautiful as you shouldn't be so needy."

Noah sniffed. "Great. A two-handed compliment now. I don't know whether to kiss you or give you a good knee to the groin."

Robert backed up instinctively. "Can we go down and get this over with now?"

"Come on." Noah took Robert's hand and looped it through his arm. "Now try to behave like a proper escort," he chided.

Robert grimaced and escorted Noah out into the expanse of hallway and down to the grand staircase.

"I feel like Cinderella," Noah said, almost skipping down the stairs.

Robert's long legs had no trouble keeping pace. "Well, don't look now, little boy, but the clock is ticking very close to midnight."

"You're such a pessimist." Noah came to a complete stop at the bottom of the stairs. "We did our part. We delivered the egg into Marya's hands. It's not our fault she couldn't hold on to it."

Robert smiled down at him. "Nice try, Cinderella, but I don't recall ever actually getting it into her hands."

"She picked it up and she can't deny it. Anyway, her hands, her father's hands," Noah shrugged, "it's all the same family."

Robert laughed. "You don't have to sell me."

"Here she comes." Noah nodded toward the opening door across the marbled foyer.

Marya breezed across the shiny tile like an ice skater. She had traded her combat fatigues for a striking pajama suit of garnet red velvet.

"Remember, Bobby, baby," Noah said under his breath, noting Robert's sudden interest. "She's the enemy . . . and not your type."

Robert ignored him. "Marya, you look lovely."

Noah shot him a glare. "You'll pay for that," he muttered under his breath.

Marya inserted herself between the two. "Robert," she said, taking each of them by the arm. "You're sweet as well as handsome."

"Marya," Noah interjected before Robert could answer. "You do look wonderful. And after all those cuts and scratches." He batted his eyes. "You must tell me who handles your makeup. It's absolutely magical."

Marya let go of Noah's arm. "Of course I will, dear," she said with a tight smile. She pulled Robert toward the drawing room. "They're very exclusive, but I'm sure they'll have something, even for your freckles."

Noah's near growl finally got through to Robert that things were not as friendly as they seemed. He resisted Marya's pull and reached out for Noah's hand, pulling him over to his other side.

"My friends," Robert said. "You are lucky to be alive today after all the excitement this morning."

Marya nestled against his arm. "We had our hands on the egg, if only for a short while, Robert."

Noah sniffed. "I'm glad to see you're clear on that point, Princess." His arm went possessively about Robert's waist. "Bobby was worried whether or not we were going to be paid," he paused, "in full."

Robert started to speak again, but Marya interrupted. "Who's Bobby?"

"It's the English diminutive for Robert, dear," Noah said. "I'm so sorry. Bobby . . . I mean Robert and I have been together so long, I sometimes forget to curb the familiarity . . . the intimacy when we're around strangers . . . outsiders like yourself."

"Intimacy?" Robert began.

"Don't be silly," Marya said, meeting Noah's cold gaze across Robert's chest. "Dear little *Nemo*, I think we've all become very close these last five days."

"We only just met two weeks ago," Robert tried to whisper in Noah's ear.

Noah ignored him. "*Noah*, honey."

"What, dear?" Marya pushed open the half of a double pocket door wide enough for Robert and her to squeeze through.

"My name, *Marlo*, dear!" Noah thrust open the other door.

"Who's *Marlo*?" Robert shook his head.

Marya left the two of them at the door and glided over the faded oriental carpet to the massive fireplace across the drawing room. A single overstuffed chair faced the blazing fire with its back to door. A uniformed male nurse stood nearby, watching them warily.

Marya fell to her knees beside the chair and put her hand on the coat sleeve resting on the chair arm. "Grandfather," she spoke softly. "Are you feeling a little better?"

A gnarled hand reached up to stroke Marya's cheek.

Marya smiled. "The agent we hired to recover the egg is here, grandfather," she said gently.

The figure said something unintelligible.

"What'd he say?" Noah whispered up at Robert.

Robert shushed him.

Marya stood and motioned for them to come over.

"Let me do the talking," Robert warned.

Noah started to answer him, but Robert pulled him by the arm over to the fireplace. He stared down at the old man whose own steely gaze was sizing up the visitors. The chair swallowed up his thin, pale frame, and he adjusted the braces enveloping his misshapened legs with equally misshapened hands.

"Grandfather," Marya remained kneeling. "May I introduce Dr. Robert Tate of the American Central

Intelligence Agency, and his assistant, Mr. Noah Taylor?"

"Colleague," Noah stammered.

"I beg your pardon?" Marya looked at him puzzled.

Noah ignored her gaze and smiled at the wizened man in the chair. "I'm Dr. Tate's colleague, not his assistant." He couldn't help staring at the old man's appearance.

Marya ignored Noah as well. "I have the honor to present the Tsesarevich Nicholai Alexandrovich Romanov, my grandfather."

The Tsesarevich smiled back at Noah. "You are disturbed by my appearance, Mr. Taylor."

Noah stammered something and Robert came to his aid. "Forgive my . . . colleague's lack of tact, Your Highness. He has no knowledge of your medical history. You are, for all intents and practical purposes, a remarkable survivor."

The Tsesarevich nodded at this. "I am indeed that. My father survived the Revolution and the assassination of our family. I survived the cold war and the crippling destruction of my joints by hemophilia."

"Hemophilia?" Noah said, recovering.

"An inherited disorder," Robert replied flatly, "in European royals with descent from England's Queen Victoria."

The Tsesarevich waved a dismissive hand. "A small matter compared to the other indignities I have been made to suffer."

Robert nodded.

"I understand you want to be paid." The Tsesarevich assessed them with an icy gaze. "You've already been compensated beyond your expenses. I have also paid twenty million Euros for a property I have not received."

Noah straightened. "Well technically, Your Highness. . ."

Robert cut him off with a look. "What Mr. Taylor was trying to say, is that our agreement was delivery of the egg into the Family's possession. That was certainly done."

The Tsesarevich's eyes narrowed at Robert. Their gaze stayed locked for what seemed an eternity. Finally the Tsesarevich relaxed back in his chair.

"My own son's treachery was the one contingency I failed to provide for in planning this whole affair."

"How could you have known, grandfather?" Marya took his hand. "No one suspected father would stoop to such greed."

"It is my responsibility," the Tsesarevich said with an air of finality. "A life's dream destroyed by the very one who would have benefitted most."

Marya's jaw set. "He didn't share your dream, grandfather . . . our dream."

Noah could no longer contain himself. "What dream? What is this all about anyway?" He slapped Robert's restraining hand away.

"Please forgive him, Your Highness," Robert said in apology. "He's a bit young and overwrought after today's events."

Noah's hands went to his hips. "Stop apologizing for me."

Marya patted the Tsesarevich's hand. "It's gone now, grandfather. I guess there would be no harm in telling them."

"Quite right." The aged prince shifted uncomfortably in his chair. Marya adjusted the pillows wedged in about him. "The situation is impossible now," the Tsesarevich continued weakly. "The opportunity is lost." His head bowed for a moment and he took a deep breath. "The monarchy left Mother Russia with the heir. My father barely escaped Russia with his life, much less any of his possessions."

Robert recalled the intelligence reports he had pulled up on the CIA database. "He and the Grand Duchess were traded to the Germans."

"To solidify a secret, non-aggression pact between that murderer Lenin and the Kaiser." The old prince smiled. "The royalty of Europe were practically all of the same blood line then."

"So that's how your family was saved." Noah stared at the new Tsesarevich, trying to see the resemblances between the fragile relic of antiquity before him, and the delicate fourteen-year-old royal prince he had seen pictures of in the history books.

"My father and his sister were all that was left of the Imperial Family." The Tsesarevich's face darkened. "The rest . . . all executed." A hollow silence engulfed the room.

Noah swallowed. "Anastasia?" The name hung in the air for a moment.

"We still don't know how the two were separated." A deep sadness overcame the Tsesarevich. "But the experience damaged her . . . beyond restoration. We wanted to bring her back into the family after she fought so hard to prove her existence. But after my father officially recognized her, she pulled away from the family completely." His voice failed.

"No one believed her," Marya continued for him. "When word got out about this alleged Anastasia, there were so many fakes being marketed throughout Europe."

"That's understandable," Robert sympathized.

Noah wasn't satisfied. "But surely the fact that she was in possession of a key to the Abdication Egg was proof enough of her claim from the beginning."

The Tsesarevich shook his head.

"She never told anyone," Marya answered for him. "We never knew she had a key . . . or may have had a key until recently opened KGB archives described a gift to the Grand Duchess Anastasia shortly before the abdication. Its description matched the Faberge egg sold to that New Orleans museum." Marya paused to pat her grandfather's hand once more. "Faberge's records included a veiled description of what we recognized as one of the keys. It was the surprise contained in the egg."

Noah took a deep breath. "What do you mean veiled description?"

"The key was oddly shaped," Marya explained. "It resembled a Coptic cross in some ways.

"What's going on?" Robert took hold of Noah's arm. "I know you're up to something."

Noah smiled up at him. "Oh, nothing," he said. "Unless this is what everyone is talking about." He pulled up one of the many chains about his neck and extracted the small trinket from inside his shirt. "Mr. Gilroy gave me this as a memento of my visit with him . . . just before he was killed." He dangled the oddly shaped cross for all to see.

The Tsesarevich gasped and paled alarmingly.

Marya stood and reached out to touch the object. "The key."

"Good God, Noah." Robert took the key in his hand. "You've had this all the time?

Noah nodded. "Mr. Gilroy wasn't interested in keeping it. It wasn't worth anything much, and he liked me. He didn't know it was a key."

"Liked you?" Robert shook his head. He let Marya examine the key. "If only you had given us a little more information about this key, we could have put two and two together while we had the egg in our possession."

"I'm sorry, Robert." Marya closed her eyes in defeat. "You must understand how difficult it is to trust anyone under the circumstances."

The fire crackled in the cavernous fireplace as the dangling key mesmerized the room.

"Well," Noah said, breaking the silence. "Let's suppose for just a moment."

Robert straightened. "What are you talking about now?"

"I'm just opening the discussion up for a little hypothetical give and take." Noah turned to the Tsesarevich. "Suppose I had put two and two together?"

The Tsesarevich shifted once more in his chair.

Marya was quickly beside him. "This serves no useful purpose, Noah."

"I'm just curious," Noah replied.

Robert gave him a look. "Noah . . ."

"I'm just interested in how much the information in that egg is worth?"

The Tsesarevich waved away his granddaughter's comforting pat. "It means the survival of this family," he rasped. "I spent everything we had to acquire the egg."

"What?" Noah gulped.

"The Tsar-Martyr's hope . . . now my grandfather's holy mission," Marya said, "was to use the monies on deposit in Switzerland to fund his plans to reinstate the monarchy in post-communist Russia."

"You can't be serious." Robert almost laughed. "Reinstate the Romanov dynasty?"

"It could be a real possibility," Marya argued. "Other governments have risen and fallen with far less resources than we would have at our disposal if that list of accounts had survived the explosion."

"Well, that's all very interesting," Noah continued. He unhooked the chain from around his neck and handed the key over to Marya. "But what I would like to know is, how much you would pay us if that list were in our possession . . . right now . . . hypothetically?"

There was silence again. Marya looked at her grandfather.

The Tsesarevich studied Noah intently. "Hypothetically, young man, you mean in excess of the one million dollars you have already been paid?"

Noah returned his stare just as intently. "Yes. The million was to recover the egg."

"Noah . . ." Robert began again.

Noah shushed him. "The egg is gone. Now how much to recover the egg's . . . surprise?"

The Tsesarevich trembled slightly. "Do you have the list, Mr. Taylor?"

"We're just speaking hypothetically here," Noah said. "How much?"

"Five million," the prince said firmly.

Noah gasped. "Five million . . ." He fell back against Robert.

"Goddamn it, Noah," Robert whispered in his ear. "Do you have that list?"

Noah poked his shaking fingers into his back pocket and extracted his thin, black leather wallet. He pulled out a folded piece of discolored, painfully thin paper.

Robert took it from him. He stared at it, incredulous. "I'd say that we are in possession of the list, Your Highness."

The Tsesarevich looked as if he might leap out of his chair.

Marya held him back. "How?" She looked up at Robert. "You can't be serious."

"Don't ask me to explain it," Robert said. He turned the priceless piece of paper over in his fingers and smiled at Noah. "I defer to the genius of my colleague, Mr. Taylor."

Noah stood triumphantly, hands on hips. "And it's about time!"

The Tsesarevich had calmed enough to speak. "If that is the list, young man, I will gladly pay your price."

"Oh it's the list, all right." Noah said with great confidence. "I removed it from the egg while I was hiding from Colonel Dobrynyn and his men."

Robert waved the paper at him. "Why didn't you tell me you had a key?"

"I didn't know," Noah said with a shrug. "It only came to me then, when I had both the egg and the key together."

"But why didn't you say anything?"

Noah sighed. "I was a little preoccupied, you know, facing death around every corner, to have a little chat with you."

"I must confirm the list's authenticity," the Tsesarevich said with undisguised annoyance at the delays. "Read me the first set of numbers at the top of the list. I am the only person living who knows what they should be."

Robert dutifully unfolded the well-preserved paper. He read off the first, shorter line of numbers slowly. The Tsesarevich nodded with increasing excitement after each digit.

"It is the list," he stammered, almost gasping. "There is no question. It's authentic!"

Marya mirrored his joy. "Well done, Noah," she said.

Noah blushed with satisfaction. "I couldn't have done it without Bobby's help."

"Bobby," Marya mused. "I like that name."

"It suits him, don't you think?" Noah said.

Robert rolled his eyes. "If you'll confirm the transfer of funds, Your Highness, I'll leave the list in your hands." He folded the paper again. "Noah and I have a plane to catch."

Marya flipped open a laptop computer on the side table. After several clicks of the mouse, she typed in a set of instructions. "They'll need your pin number now, grandfather." She sat the small computer on the Tsesarevich's lap and he completed the transaction.

Marya held the laptop up to Robert. "Would you like to confirm . . . Bobby?"

Robert accessed his banks website and confirmed the deposit. "Excellent," he said. He handed the list over to the Tsesarevich. "A pleasure doing business with you, sir."

The Tsesarevich paid him no attention and clutched the paper to his breast.

"Thank God!" Noah almost moaned. "I was close to trading that paper for a ham sandwich."

Marya took Noah's arm, laughing. "You must have heard my stomach carrying on."

Noah sighed audibly. "I don't think I've eaten for days."

"Hours," Robert said to himself. "Minutes!"

"You must stay for dinner," Marya insisted. "Drinks and *hor d'oeuvre* in the conservatory."

"Let's do it," Noah responded.

Robert interrupted. "We have a plane to catch, Noah."

"Let's not be rude, Bobby." Noah frowned at him. "Marya has been gracious enough to invite us for dinner, and I'm not taking one more step on an empty stomach."

Robert shook his head in defeat. "Of course not."

Marya started for the door, arm in arm with Noah. "Do you like Russian food?"

Noah shrugged. "I'm sure I do," he said without hesitation. 'What are we having?"

"We'll start with a little pirozhki and koulibiaka." Marya smacked her lips.

"Oh," Noah said, obviously in the dark. "I'm not sure what that is."

"Do you really care?" Robert muttered behind them.

"And lamb shashlyk!" Marya added with relish.

"Scrumptious." Noah disappeared through the door laughing with Marya.

"Jesus, God Almighty!" Robert swallowed against what was becoming a chronic rising tide of acid in his stomach. "They aren't human." Reluctantly, he followed after them.

Chapter 25

"I'm not saying you're not a good researcher, Robert." Madelyn clicked her nails on the polished surface of her desk. "Of course you're good. Too good! That's my whole point."

"What about, Noah?" Robert waved dramatically at no one in particular. "This job was his livelyhood."

Madelyn glanced up at Noah, who was standing back at the large picture window overlooking the business district. He gave Madelyn a desperate look, though not for the reasons Robert was expounding on.

"I'm sorry, Robert," Madelyn continued. "But the decision has been made."

Noah grinned and gave her a thumbs-up out of Robert's line of sight.

"What are we supposed to do for a living then?" Robert slumped back in his chair.

"Oh, for Christ's sake, Robert!" Madelyn massaged her aching temples. "Keep doing what you've been doing. You're obviously suited for it. And what are you worried about anyway. The two of you pocketed a fortune."

Robert sat up defensively. "After taxes, there isn't much of it all left."

"He's right, you know," Noah chimed in. He fondled the new Tiffany broach that sparkled on the lapel of his Armani suit. "Six million just doesn't stretch like it used to."

Robert glared at him. "You're not helping."

"And I don't plan to." Noah sat down in the chair beside him. "This is ridiculous. Madelyn is right, and I don't understand why you can't admit it. You have a perfectly good P.I. license, and the money to open your own agency." Noah put a hand to Robert's mouth before he could answer. "Make that our agency. You definitely need a partner."

"I love it!" Madelyn cut Robert off once again. "And occasionally you can slip me a little freelance news article on some of your juicier cases."

"Stop!" Robert pointed a finger at each of them. "You're both living in fantasy land. What cases? What business? We stumbled into one unusual set of circumstances. It was purely accidental. We will probably never come across another such situation." He took Noah's hand. "Listen to me. This was just a fluke. P.I.'s spend their days doing credit checks and staking out cheap motels, watching for cheating spouses. They don't jet around the world foiling international plots like James Bond."

Noah stared at him blankly. "It's me isn't it?"

"What?"

Noah's eyes moistened. "You don't want me for a partner. You really can't stand me can you?" His voice cracked.

"Oh, for God's sake!" Robert threw his hands up.

Madelyn shook a finger at him. "Now, Robert, don't take this out on Noah."

"I'm not—"

"You may be right about run of the mill private eyes," Madelyn continued. "But that's hardly you. You're not some ex-cop with a bad back. You're ex-CIA. You have international intelligence contacts. Hell, Robert! You are James Bond!"

"I'm a history professor!"

Madelyn threw a notepad at him. "Yeah, and Lyndon Johnson was a cattle rancher!"

"I thought you liked me," Noah almost sobbed. "I thought we worked well together."

"Oh, Noah, stop, please." Robert stood up and fled to the window at the back of the room.

Madelyn and Noah exchanged glances.

"Robert," Madelyn began. "The two of you do work well together. You made a small fortune together. What in God's name do you have against that?"

"You're not listening. Either of you!" Robert folded his arms. "This was a shot in the dark. A once in a lifetime occurrence. We have no other cases and no prospects for any."

"Ah, but that's where you're wrong." Madelyn fumbled through a stack of message notes on her desk. "It's here some place . . ."

"What?" Noah brightened. "Another case?"

"Don't be ridiculous," Robert said.

"Ha!" Madelyn waved a small message slip. "The Tate and Taylor Agency's next golden egg."

"Tate and Taylor Agency?" Noah's brow wrinkled. "Tate and Taylor . . . Taylor and Tate . . . We'll straighten all that out later." He turned excitedly to Robert. "We'll have to have card's printed."

Robert turned away in disgust. "Both of you need professional help."

"I'm serious, Robert." Madelyn waved the paper at him. "I did a lot of high powered P.R. for the two of you last night at that State Department dinner for Ambassador What's-His-Name from Mexico."

"Ambassador Rodriquez?" Robert asked, keeping his back to her.

"That's the one." Madelyn handed the paper to Noah. "I talked the two of you up to everyone there."

"Who's Garrett Abhorn?" Noah studied the paper. "That name sounds so familiar."

"Garrett Abhorn?" Robert turned his head. "The billionaire? Silicon Valley type?"

Madelyn smiled. "One and the same. He was very interested in meeting both of you. He's having a little industrial espionage problem."

"What would he need outside help for?" Robert turned back to the window. "These technology industries have their own, very competent security departments."

"Yes, dear," Madelyn said. "But when a foreign government's involved, it can be a little out of their league."

"Oh, this is perfect." Noah jumped up excitedly. "Call him Robert. Right now!"

"No need." Madelyn sat back in her chair. "He wants you both to fly out to his home in San Francisco on Thursday to discuss the particulars."

"Thursday!" Noah paced about Madelyn's chair. "There are so many details to take care of before then. We can set up the office at your house, Robert. You have plenty of room and there's no sense increasing the overhead unnecessarily, early in the game. I'll take care of the stationery design, printing, etcetera." Noah bit his lip in concentration. "We'll need a lawyer to properly register all the paperwork. Oh, remember Donald Gantz. He used to work in Legal. He's opened up his own practice now. I'll bet—"

Robert snatched the paper from Noah's hand. "This is insane." He stared at the name.

"Just think, Robert," Madelyn said, almost purring. "You'll have more time for writing that history stuff you love so much."

"I'll handle the business side," Noah threw in. "I did all the bookkeeping, inventory and ordering at my mom's restaurant all the time I was going to school. You won't have to bother yourself with any of those details."

Robert shook his head. "You can't make a living at this."

"Oh, I hope you don't mind," Madelyn said. "I took the liberty of quoting Mr. Abhorn a hundred thousand dollar retainer against expenses and, of course, your usual five thousand dollar a day fee." She paused for effect. "He didn't even blink an eye."

Noah fell back into his chair with an audible gasp.

Robert continued staring at the paper.

"Well?" Madelyn clicked her nails harder on the desk.

Robert sighed and stared at the floor. Finally, he looked up at Noah. "You can set things up in the study."

"Yes!" Noah pulled at the air.

"With as little disturbance as possible," Robert added. "I don't want the furniture scarred up by fax machines and copiers."

Noah squealed and threw his arms about Robert's neck. "Don't worry. I'll corner the market on lace doilies."

Robert groaned. "A sheet of clear plastic or glass over the tables would do just fine."

"Whatever." Noah tightened his grip about Robert's neck. "We should really do something to properly cement this . . . partnership." He smiled up at Robert seductively.

"I agree," Robert gazed over her head out the window. "We need to do something."

Noah closed his eyes, and leaned his face into Robert's expectantly.

Robert pulled free. "Have your lawyer friend draw up an appropriate partnership agreement." He headed for the door. "We'll meet back at the house later today after I've made our travel arrangements."

Noah slowly settled his heels back to the floor and opened his eyes. He looked back over his shoulder at Madelyn who gave him a sympathetic smile.

"Almost," Noah said with a drawn out sigh.

"Oh yeah, and Noah?" Robert peeked his head back through the door.

"What?"

"Try to pack a little lighter this time."

"Kiss my ass!"

"And Noah?"

Noah crossed his arms over this chest. "What?" He asked, glaring across the room at Robert.

"You're staying the night with me."

"What?" Noah's jaw dropped.

"And this time, I'm cooking . . . something sane . . . something civilized . . ." Robert's voice trailed away in the hallway beyond.

Noah closed his eyes. His arms wrapped himself in a hug. After a minute he turned back to Madelyn. "I think I have a date."

Madelyn raised her eyebrows. "He's a little older than you, isn't he, dear?"

Noah laughed and headed for the door. "I'll make sure he takes his vitamins!" he said on his way out.

"This ought to be interesting," Madelyn said, clicking her nails over the desk surface like a concert pianist.

DOUGLAS KING

is also the author of
The Q Factor and *The High Range.*
He works as a medical investigator
and lives in Beaumont, Texas.

www.ingramcontent.com/pod-product-compliance
Lightning Source LLC
Chambersburg PA
CBHW030025180626
46810CB00001B/218